"Arch, wait!"

He turned, surprised, and saw Mandy hurrying after him. In her hand was a plate filled with an enormous slice of cake. He started back toward her, admiring how elegant she looked in that wine-colored dress.

"Here." She held out the plate. "You saved it from falling. You earned a slice." She was a little out of breath, as if she'd jogged, cake and all, to catch him.

He tried to remember the last time someone had reached out to him like this to show him a kindness. He couldn't. "You're a good person." He blurted it out like an awkward kid. He had no experience with generosity.

"I just made a whole lot of wedding cake." Her smile was fleeting, but kind.

"Well, this will make the walk home a whole lot better."

There was silence while they looked at each other. He needed to let her get back to her sister's wedding. "Nice to meet you, Mandy. Thanks for sticking up for me back there."

"Of course." She took a step back and waved. "Welcome home, Arch."

Dear Reader,

Sometimes the best way to find a story is to ask a simple two-word question. What if? Those two words were how *Home Free* came to be.

When I first thought about the Sierra Legacy series, I planned just two books—the stories of Nora and Wade Hoffman. But then that tricky what-if question popped into my mind. What if one of the older Hoffman brothers didn't flee to Mexico after all? What if he made another choice? And most of all, what if he came home again?

I couldn't resist answering those questions. So now I offer you Arch Hoffman's story. At first I was nervous to write it. How could I make someone who'd done such terrible things into the hero of a romance novel? But as I got to know Arch, I came to love him, and I hope you do, too. He's served his time, paid his dues and is ready to start his life again. But he quickly learns that freedom means a lot more than just walking through the prison gates. It's something he'll fight for every day.

And the woman who steals his heart? She's been trapped in a different kind of prison, with thick, stifling walls of loss, fear and doubt. Meeting Arch changes everything. Love changes everything. It might even have the power to set them both free.

Thank you for giving Arch a chance. I hope you enjoy *Home Free*.

Claire McEwen

PS: If you would like to learn more about organizations that help people adjust to life after prison, please visit the Resources page on my website, clairemcewen.com. I love hearing from readers, so please stop by the Contact page while you're there if you'd like to connect on social media or via email.

CLAIRE McEWEN

Home Free

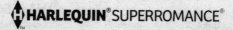

Recycling programs
for this product may
not exist in your area.

ISBN-13: 978-0-373-61010-5

Home Free

Copyright © 2016 by Claire Haiken

Printed in U.S.A.

Claire McEwen lives by the ocean in Northern California with her husband, son and a scruffy, mischievous terrier, whose unique looks and goofy hijinks provided inspiration for an important character in *Return to Marker Ranch*. When not dreaming up new stories, Claire can be found digging in her garden with a lot of enthusiasm but, unfortunately, no green thumb. She loves discovering flea-market treasures, walking on the beach, dancing, traveling and reading, of course! Claire enjoys Facebook, Twitter, Pinterest and Instagram, and likes musing about writing and all things romantic on her blog, *Romance All Around Us*. Please visit her website, clairemcewen.com, for more information.

Books by Claire McEwen

HARLEQUIN SUPERROMANCE

Return to Marker Ranch
Wild Horses
Convincing the Rancher
More Than a Rancher
A Ranch to Keep

Other titles by this author available in ebook format.

For anyone who has to overcome the past so they can reach for the future.

And for my sisters.

CHAPTER ONE

WHEN MANDY ALLEN planned her sister's perfect wedding, she never imagined crying alone in their ranch house kitchen with only the wedding cake for company. But those were definitely tears sliding down her cheeks. And if they didn't stop soon, mascara would stripe her face like a zebra's. Mandy dabbed her eyes with the hem of her apron, appalled by the black smudges. Self-pity never looked good on anyone.

The problem wasn't the cake. *That* was her masterpiece, despite the anxiety that had almost kept her from finishing it. Anxiety that crackled and fizzed like a bad-reception radio set to her own personal self-doubt channel, reminding her that she'd never done this kind of baking before. What if it was a disaster? What if it tasted terrible? What if it looked terrible?

But thankfully, her anxiety was unfounded. The cake *wasn't* terrible. In fact, it was beautiful. The three tiers, cream colored and painted with chocolate icing, delicately detailed scenes of horses, cattle, even the high Sierra peaks that rose behind their ranch.

The problem wasn't the wedding, either. The old barn looked magical decorated with garlands and fairy lights. The guests had just finished Mandy's specially seasoned barbecue with all the fixings. Now they were drinking, dancing, whooping it up.

Nor was the problem seeing her dad for the first time in over a year, with his new wife on his arm, relaxed and happy with his life under the Florida sun.

The problem was that everything around her was changing. Every*one* was changing. Everyone except Mandy. She was as stuck as a truck in a high desert wash. Lost. Mired. And she had no idea how to dig herself out and get moving again.

The chime of the hall clock sliced through thoughts as sticky as bread dough. She had to get the cake to the reception. There'd be plenty of time after the guests had gone home to stuff her head in the pity pot.

She picked up the tiny fondant cowboy boots she'd made, pink for Lori and brown for Wade. Placing the boots on top of the cake, she tilted them so they leaned on each other. Perfect, for the perfect couple.

She grabbed her camera and snapped a few pictures. With luck, photos of this cake would convince other couples to hire her to bake *their* wedding cakes.

And then it hit her. In her stress over the cake, she'd forgotten how big it was. And how heavy. How would she get it to the barn?

Her anxiety switched back on, hissing and popping in waves that rolled right through her stomach. Why had she assembled the cake here? She should have taken it to the reception in separate layers. Why hadn't she thought this through more carefully?

But the cake was finished, looking elegant on Mama's old silver tray, so there was no going back. *Stop worrying. It's just a cake. Don't be scared about carrying a cake.*

She yanked off her apron. Smoothed down the skirt of her bridesmaid dress. Slid the tray to the edge of the table.

Nothing on the cake even jiggled. It was rock solid. She lifted the tray and baby stepped to the screen door, pushing it open with her hip. A few more steps and she was through the door and down the porch stairs. The hard part was done.

Mandy started down the packed-dirt road that led to the barn. No problem. Like walking on a sidewalk. She imagined Lori's face when she saw the cake. Her wedding-day smile would grow even bigger.

The sharp snick of breaking branches froze

Mandy's limbs. It seemed to come from a thicket of scrubby willows about fifty yards ahead of her. *A bear? Not today.* Not now when she was all alone carrying a massive hunk of sugar, a bear's favorite treat. The shrub shook, there was a crackling noise, and Mandy's heart just about stopped when something burst out of the thick tangle.

Not a bear, thank goodness, but a miniature donkey that shook its head and looked around. It was gray and fuzzy and it didn't belong here. It must be another stray. People were always dumping their unwanted animals on her doorstep. Her heart kicked up a beat.

The donkey spotted her, long ears flicking forward. Mandy made her voice as stern as she could. "Shoo!"

It obviously didn't know the meaning of the word, because it broke into a toy-pony gallop, heading straight toward her. It looked so happy, but Mandy's heart shifted into overdrive. "Shoo!"

The donkey sped up. Mandy swiftly stepped back and to the side of the lane, lifting the tray chest-high. It would be okay. The donkey was going to miss her…

But the donkey slammed against her hip as it careened by, spinning Mandy around in a staggering circle. She clutched the tray in desperation as it tilted and teetered.

"Hang on!" A man's voice broke through her grasping panic. She caught a glimpse of him, sprinting from the direction of the house. In a split second he was there, reaching to catch her fall.

"Not me!" she managed. "The *cake*!"

Hands shot out. "Let go! I've got it!"

She opened her fingers and surrendered to fate and gravity, pitching backward, landing hard, butt, shoulders, head, all hitting the dirt before she rolled once. Stomach to the ground, cheek in the dust, she stared one-eyed at the grass by the lane and the bright October sky beyond. *Ouch.*

"Are you all right?"

The urgency in the man's voice had her automatically reassuring him. "I'm okay. Scraped, but okay." Then her mind lurched from survival to reality. The man. The cake. *Oh, God, the cake!* She closed her eyes, afraid to look. Her sister's wedding cake. Smashed in the dirt.

"Your cake is okay, too."

His words were small pieces of a miracle. How was it even possible? Mandy pushed herself up to sitting, every part of her stiff, shaky and stinging.

The dark-haired man was on one knee, as if he was about to propose. And in his arms, perfectly upright, perfectly intact, was her perfect cake.

Mandy stared at him, wondering if she'd fallen right into some kind of fairy tale. Because only in stories did someone this handsome show up out of nowhere and save the day. He even had the wavy black hair of a fairy-tale prince.

Holy cow, she was staring at him like a possum at a flashlight. She scrambled to her feet, brushing at her hands and elbows, trying to ignore all the throbbing and stinging. "Thank you!" Her throat was pebbled with gratitude, tumbling the words out ragged as she leaned over and lifted the tray from his outstretched hands. "I can't believe you saved it!"

"My pleasure." He rose from the dirt. And rose. And rose. There had to be over six feet of him.

"It was a *really* good catch." She sounded like a kid meeting a sports hero, all awestruck. But he was overwhelming. Each piece of him, from his height to the sharp cheekbones that slashed across his angular face, was larger than average. He was hard to take in all at once. And he'd saved her cake.

He looked down at her, eyes shadowed under dark brows. His voice was low pitched, the gentle edge a surprise in such a big man. "That was quite a fall. Are you hurt?"

"I expect so." She knew so, but there was no time to deal with it now. She'd break out the first aid kit once she got the cake to the reception.

"Your arm is bleeding." He fished in his pocket

and pulled out a crumpled napkin. There was a fast-food logo on it. "Why don't you let me hold the cake for a minute?"

She hesitated. "You'll be careful, right?"

"Very." He set the napkin on the edge of the tray. Then he took the cake from her easily, as if it weighed nothing.

Mandy picked up the napkin and pressed it to her elbow, surprised when blood bloomed through it. "I'm a mess."

"You're messy. That's different." His slight smile was kind. "There's dust on your dress, near the hem. Can you brush it off? And you've got some grass in your hair, too."

She threaded fingers through her hair and found the dry blades. "Ugh. This isn't what I had in mind when I planned this wedding."

"You're a wedding planner?"

Mandy bit back a laugh, remembering the stress of the past weeks. "Far from it. It's my sister's wedding day and I wanted everything to be perfect for her. Left on her own, she would have gotten married on a break between ranch chores." The last of the adrenaline from her fall drained away, and Mandy's voice bumped against her throat. "I'm just so grateful you came along."

"You're the first person who's said that to me in a mighty long time."

Something rough in his voice drew her glance,

but he looked away. There was an awkward pause as she tried to figure out the meaning behind his words. She settled for brushing the dust off her dress as best she could. She was a wreck. It didn't help that she'd been awake most of the past forty-eight hours cooking for the wedding.

"I wouldn't have dropped it, except that darn donkey…" She looked around. The animal was nowhere to be seen. "There *was* a donkey…"

"I saw it go by. I think it's over by the house somewhere."

So she wasn't having some kind of stress-induced hallucination. That was good news. "It's just going to have to stay there, then. I have to get this to the reception." She realized suddenly that he wasn't dressed for a wedding. Unless Levi's and a tight black T-shirt were formal wear for him. "You're a guest?"

He hesitated. "Actually, I'm not."

"Oh!" Her brain felt scrambled. Maybe she'd hit her head harder than she realized. "I'm sorry, I assumed… Can I help you with something?"

"To be honest, I didn't know there was a wedding. I came by because someone in town told me my brother might be here. He's your neighbor. Wade Hoffman?"

Mandy's breath caught on the dark lump of dread settling below her sternum. "You're Wade's brother?" Wade had two brothers. Both criminals, both on the run.

"My name's Arch Hoffman. I haven't been back to Benson for a long time."

She knew why he hadn't been around town. If the rumors were true, he'd been hiding out in Mexico with his brother and father to escape criminal charges for theft, drug dealing and God knew what else. Mandy forced her shaking hands to steady. She glanced in the direction of the barn. The music was loud and she was still pretty far away. Would anyone hear her if she screamed for help?

"I guess you've heard of me."

Blast. Her fear must be easy to see. "I have, a bit," she admitted. She stole a peek at him. He didn't *look* like a criminal. But that was how the Hoffman brothers had always worked, wasn't it? A layer of charm smeared over cunning and crime. Like icing piled up to hide a fallen cake. "Your brother is marrying my sister today."

He stopped. "You're kidding. My little brother's getting married? Today?"

"You didn't know?"

"I haven't spoken to my brother in over ten years."

She couldn't think how to answer such weighted words. "Well, I guess we should go find him."

Though she didn't look forward to ruining Wade's wedding day.

"That would be great. And I'd be happy to carry your cake for you."

"Thanks." They walked, Mandy brushing her skirts and trying to rearrange her hair as they went. But as the barn got closer, her worries got bigger. If Arch strolled into the wedding, all Mandy's attempts to make the celebration perfect would be ruined. Upstaged by the inevitable gossip about Arch's exploits and wrongs.

"I've got lousy timing, huh?" His quiet words echoed her thoughts.

She was suddenly too tired to be kind. "You do."

"I won't mess up the party. You can trust me."

Ha. From all she'd heard over the years, Arch Hoffman was about as trustworthy as a bear in the beehives. She stayed silent, but he seemed intent on making conversation.

"So you made this cake yourself? These pictures on the sides and everything?"

She heard the note of forced cheer in his voice and felt selfish, all of a sudden, for worrying about the wedding. He was estranged from his family. This couldn't be an easy moment for him.

"Yes."

"And you're really gonna let my little brother

chop this up? It's a work of art. Seems like you should put it in some kind of cake museum."

It was just flattery, but it warmed her anyway. "I don't think they have those. I did take photos, though."

"I sure hope so. Are you a baker?"

"I have a small business. Just here on the ranch, using our kitchen. I make pies, muffins, cupcakes, things like that. This is my first wedding cake."

He tilted his head slightly, as if trying to admire it from the side. "I guarantee that once folks see it, it won't be your last."

"That's what I hope." Mandy felt the words release into the air like fluttering doves. She'd never said it aloud before. How much she wanted to expand her business. Or go to school. Or apprentice somewhere. To pursue her dreams. But just knowing the words were out had her heart stuttering. Anxiety never stayed away for long.

They were almost to the barn, approaching from the side. Mandy could hear the hum of guests talking and laughing. The DJ was playing that old song "Achy Breaky Heart." Probably half the crowd was doing the classic line dance.

She wasn't great at speaking her mind, but if there ever was a time to get over that, it was now. She forced herself to look right at Arch, the heat rising from her cheek in waves so thick it almost clouded her vision. "I don't think you should come in."

"You sure about that? Because it would make their wedding day truly memorable. Folks around here would be talking about it for a long time to come."

Horrified, she almost protested but then saw how his smile tipped down at the corners. "You're being sarcastic."

"I may not have spent a minute of my life in good company, but I know enough not to crash my brother's wedding."

He was saying exactly what she wanted to hear, but it hurt her heart. What must it be like to know you weren't welcome at your own brother's reception? Of course, he'd brought it on himself, but there was something in her that could never stand to leave a fellow creature out in the cold. Which was why she had way too many strays on this ranch, she reminded herself. And she'd be a fool to make Arch Hoffman one of them. "Thank you for helping me carry the cake." She reached for the tray and took its weight carefully. "What will you do?"

For the first time since he'd shown up like a miracle and caught the cake, he looked uncertain. "I'll figure something out."

She knew the stories. She knew he'd committed crimes and raised hell when he lived around here. But he'd helped her beyond measure today. And now he needed help. "Look, Wade and Lori are leaving for their honeymoon right after the reception. They'll be gone for a few weeks. If you need to speak with your brother, now's the time."

Arch looked over her head toward the barn door. "I can't walk in there."

"No, you can't." She paused, willing her tired brain to think. "Can you wait awhile? Maybe forty-five minutes? Let them cut the cake and have another dance or two. Then I'll send Wade to talk to you."

"You don't have to do that." But the relief in his eyes said the opposite.

"Of course I do," she assured him. "It's the right thing."

"And you're someone who does the right thing."

His words had all the old guilt and regret knotting in her stomach. Tears pricked. Her mom should be here today, seeing Lori marry. Maybe if Mandy had done the right thing all those years ago, that would be possible.

"Whoa." Arch's hands took hold of the opposite side of the tray, steadying it. "I said the wrong thing. Damn, I'm sorry, I…" He broke off.

"No, it's okay." *Damn* was right. When would she learn to control the feelings that lived just under her skin?

"Hey, here's a thought. You deliver this cake

and I'll go look for that mysterious donkey of yours before it causes any more trouble."

The donkey. She'd forgotten about it. Her worries over the cake and this magnetic man had wiped that responsibility from her memory. "I'd so appreciate that. If you find him, he can go in with the goat. There's a small paddock behind the other barn, further down this lane."

"Right." He squared his shoulders. A task was probably just what he needed right now to get his mind off his troubles. "Hope that goat is ready for a new roommate."

"She'll have to make do. She was dropped off here just last week."

His grin softened all the angles of his face. "You must have a reputation for being a softie."

Mandy couldn't help but smile back. "I think you're right."

"Why so many strays?"

"It's getting worse with the drought. Ranches are downsizing. People are losing jobs. I never thought I'd be running an animal shelter." She felt her smile fade. "It breaks my heart. Especially when a dog shows up. They seem so lost and confused when they're abandoned."

"The world could use more people like you. I can see that already."

Her skin warmed again. She wasn't used to

being noticed. "Thanks. I'd better head into the barn. See you soon?"

"As soon as I find that donkey." Arch walked away with a lanky stride that covered ground with zero effort. The guy was a giant. And in his faded jeans and that T-shirt, he was gravity for the eyes. Handsome didn't begin to describe him. But he was also *Arch Hoffman.*

And he'd just turned back to her. And said something.

"What?" She blinked. He'd caught her staring. At his backside.

"You sure you're okay? After that fall?"

"Yes." A squeaky syllable was all she could manage. She'd been *ogling* him.

"So head in there and show off that cake. It's something to be proud of."

Surprise, gratitude, relief. He could have mentioned her staring at him. Instead he'd given her a compliment. He was nice. Arch Hoffman, the car-stealing, drug-dealing, bad-boy legend of Benson, California, was kind of nice. "Thanks, Arch," Mandy called softly.

She turned toward the entrance to the barn, stepping carefully through the wide double doors with the oohs and aahs of appreciation rising in gratifying waves around her. She shoved all of her worries about Arch Hoffman's arrival to the side of her mind. He'd just have to wait. This was her sister's moment, and Wade's moment. A moment of sheer happiness, meant to be savored like the perfect wedding cake she held in her hands.

CHAPTER TWO

THERE WAS NO sign of the renegade donkey. Arch scanned the dry lawn in front of the ranch house that looked just like it should. Historic, its wood siding painted white and perfectly maintained. The cushioned rocking chairs on the front porch looking so comfortable he wanted to sink into one and sleep. For months.

Freedom was the best thing to ever happen to him, and the most exhausting. Crazy how much the world could change in a decade. Or maybe it was him that had changed, ten years stuck in the prison time warp, now out and wandering lost between who he'd been and who he hoped to become.

Which had led him here. To this hometown he didn't want to come home to. To this low place, begging help from a brother who hated him. And now on this fool's errand, to retrieve a miniature donkey who clearly didn't want to be found.

But no way was he giving up. Because catching that cake had meant something more than just a lucky save. It was one of the few times in his life that he'd done something besides try to save his own skin. And the look of gratitude in that pretty woman's eyes had warmed his chest and thawed something there. If she could look at him that way, maybe he finally had a chance at being a better man than he'd been before. He'd do a lot to get her to look at him like that again.

Arch rounded the house and spotted a rope draped over a railing near the back door. Coiling it, he looked around. It was quiet here behind the house. A small patch of grass ran into an orchard off to his right. There were a few apples still hanging from the trees, and he picked one. Donkey bait.

To his left was a stand of pines. He walked toward them, suddenly needing their wholesome scent. He closed his eyes to better hear the hiss of wind though their branches. The sound ran soothing hands over his skin. He'd imagined this in prison. Funny how something he'd never appreciated when he lived around here became something he longed for once he was locked in a cell.

A huff of breath broke his reverie. Arch opened his eyes, homing in on where the sound came from.

The donkey's knee-high nose peeked out from behind one of the pines. It was probably terrified. Maybe only just abandoned here. That would explain why it charged past that woman in such a panic.

That woman. It wasn't right to call someone so beautiful such everyday words. But he hadn't asked her name. He guessed she had to be one of the Allens. They'd owned this ranch, Lone Mountain Ranch, forever. He'd grown up just down the road, but he didn't recall ever meeting her. She was clearly several years younger than him. Probably still a kid when he'd left.

She was all grown up now, but she was tiny. With her slight frame, her golden curls, her wide blue eyes the color of the sky over the mountains, all she'd need was a pair of wings to be Peter Pan's fairy pal. *Tinker Bell.* That suited her.

He inched a step closer to the donkey. "C'mon, little dude." Arch kept his voice quiet, just above a breath. "Let's get you back home."

The tiny animal huffed out a breath and disappeared behind the tree. Arch knelt, like he would with a dog, and held out the apple. The donkey peered around the pine again, its internal war of curiosity and caution apparent in its flicking ears. Finally one long ear tipped forward. Then the other. Curiosity and the promise of a treat won out. The donkey minced up on dainty hooves, blowing and snuffing at Arch's knuckles, and reached for the apple.

One slow, careful motion and Arch had the

rope around its neck. While the donkey crunched the apple, Arch tied one end of the rope like a collar. Not ideal, but the little guy had no halter on.

Then Arch brought his free hand up to pet the soft fur of the animal's neck. After a few moments, he felt the donkey's muscles relax. It swallowed the apple and eyed a distant grass tuft longingly. Arch rose, leading it to the grass for a nibble. He could see its ribs when it moved. Rage rose up, pumping his blood faster, worrying in its power. *Keep it in perspective.* Yes, someone had been cruel to this helpless animal. That didn't mean it was Arch's job to find him and beat the shit out of him. No matter how much he'd like to.

Not his job. He had one focus, and he needed to keep it. To find work. Something he could believe in. Something he could lose himself in so he didn't get lost again.

"C'mon, now." Arch tugged on the rope, but the donkey planted its sturdy legs and stood its ground, devouring the grass like it was the last food he'd ever see. "I'm sure Tinker Bell has better stuff than that." The donkey flicked a suspicious glance his way and kept on grazing.

Arch hated to pull any harder on the rope around its neck. The donkey wasn't much bigger than a dog, so he knelt and scooped it up instead. It struggled, catching him on the thigh with a sharp hoof, but Arch managed to stagger with it over to the apple tree. He set it down, grabbed a couple more apples off the branch and waved one in front of the donkey's nose.

"C'mon, Shrimp. I've got to get back to the barn." Shrimp seemed like a good name for the little guy. Didn't shrimps just float around and eat? Biting a piece off the apple, Arch held it out as a lure to get the donkey walking. It worked like magic. Shrimp trotted willingly at his side, as long as Arch provided a bite of apple every so often.

Arch tried to keep his distance from the reception, sticking close to the pines that bordered the ranch. He spotted a more modern-looking barn down the lane. Shrimp's new digs should be behind it.

Music and laughter from the party floated through the warm afternoon air. A couple walked out of the reception, cake plates and champagne glasses in hand. They toasted each other with a clink of their glasses. Arch pulled Shrimp behind a pine to stay out of view, surprised by the envy hollowing his chest. What would it be like to be those people? Invited to nice parties like this, dressed in good clothes, confident that you were a decent person who knew how to behave?

He breathed in, relaxing the jealous ache until it was dull and heavy. Easier to live with. Regret wouldn't get him anywhere. Envy didn't help, either. He was who he was, and he'd done what he'd done. He had to accept that and go forward, grateful for a second chance. But the sense that he wouldn't make it, that the world was written in a language he'd never learn to speak, hung in the air around him. It was a relief to spot the goat pen, to lead Shrimp inside, to remove the rope and leave the tiny donkey munching on a big pile of oat hay.

It was good to accomplish a solid, everyday task. A nice breather before he set out to do the impossible—convince his brother to let him stay awhile on their family ranch.

The goat and donkey seemed to be getting along fine. Arch took a breath that came out shaky on the exhalation. It was time to face his past. He started back toward the wedding and saw Wade almost immediately. He was standing next to a woman Arch recognized after a moment's study. His sister, Nora. Of course she'd be here, too, and she hated him even more than Wade did.

His siblings waited alongside the wooden barn, out of view of the guests. Tinker Bell stood with them, her hands hidden in her skirts, fingers nervously rustling the fabric. No one spoke as he approached.

Silence was awkward, but it gave him a moment to take them both in. Wade had been a boy when Arch had last seen him. Now he was tall and strong in a black suit and cowboy boots, his dark hair cut close to his head. His face was a tangle of grim lines that didn't belong at his wedding celebration.

Nora's arms were folded across her chest like body armor. Her eyes were gray shadows, watchful. She moved closer to Wade. She'd been fiercely protective of their little brother, standing up to Arch time and again to keep him from dragging Wade along on whatever deal he had going. She was clearly still ready to protect him, even with Wade grown and married. "What the hell are you doing here, Arch?"

The venom in her voice stopped him in his tracks. "Asking for help."

She shook her head. "Oh, no, we are *not* sheltering you. I don't know why you left Mexico, but you need to get on back there. And with no help from us."

"I'm not coming from Mexico." Words started and stopped in Arch's head. He hadn't planned this out well. He should have had some kind of speech prepared.

"I don't care where you've been. You shouldn't be here." Her words cracked like gunfire across the yards between them.

Finally Wade stirred. "Let's listen to him, Nora. It can't hurt to listen."

It was disconcerting, hearing Wade's voice so

deep and sure. Arch cleared his throat. Fortunately, ten years in prison had schooled him in keeping feelings at bay. This was his chance, and he needed to get it right. "I never went to Mexico. I got as far as San Diego with Dad and Blake. I left them there."

His sister and brother stared at him in stunned silence. Tinker Bell seemed to come out of whatever trance she'd been in and stepped back a few feet. "I should go. I'm intruding."

He didn't want her to go. She was like a beam of light he could focus on in this dark moment. "Stay? Please?"

Three sets of eyes widened at his odd request.

"Only if you want to…" Arch added. "If you're willing to."

She studied him, and then nodded slightly. Her gaze jumped to Nora.

"It's okay, Mandy," Nora said. "We're family— though you may be regretting that fact right now."

"No regrets." Her simple answer was a tiny oasis in this complicated moment.

Mandy. Arch held on to the name, tucked it away into his mind to think about later. "Thanks," he told her. And used all that gold—of her hair, of her radiant skin—as the courage he needed to keep talking. "When I left here with Dad and Blake, I was already sick of them. It was terrible, the things we did. I knew by then that my whole life had become one big mistake. Down in San Diego, they robbed a guy at gunpoint. A decent guy—just your average working man. He had a wife and his little kid with him."

Arch cleared his throat, balled his shaking hands into fists. Saw the encouraging look on Mandy's face and inhaled it like the oxygen that seemed to have disappeared from the air around him. "I saw myself clearly, in the fear in their eyes. That man, brought down in front of his family. The terror on his wife's face. She pulled her little boy into her stomach and just held him so close…" He had to stop again. Being in their presence, seeing the disgust in his brother's and sister's eyes, and the horror and sorrow on Mandy's face, cracked all the walls he'd built to hold back the guilt.

He pushed himself on. "In that moment, everything changed. I couldn't stand what I saw. What I'd become. I left Dad and Blake that night. Never said goodbye. Just went to a bar, had one last beer, then walked to the ocean to touch the water. To breathe in that fresh air one last time. Then I found a police station and turned myself in."

The icy edge had thawed from Nora's gaze. Her jaw, so set, relaxed a fraction. "We didn't know. Why didn't you write?"

His laugh was a bitter syllable. "And say what? You hated me. For good reason. I'd spent every day making your life miserable. You were better off rid of me."

He saw the memories cloud Nora's eyes. He wished he could do something, work hard enough, beg hard enough, to erase them for her. Their dad's hand crashing down across her face. Him, the numb bastard he'd been, doing nothing. Daddy's little henchman. Shame shoved the bile to the back of his throat.

"And now?" Wade stepped in front of Nora, sheltering her with his body, as if he could keep those memories from overwhelming her. "What's happening with you now?"

Arch heard the real question. *Did you escape?* "I'm out. Legally. I did my time, almost ten years of it, and got released a couple months ago. I tried to get work down in Southern California, but no one wants to hire someone who answers 'yes' to the felony question on their job application."

"So you're here for money?" Wade slid a hand into his suit jacket. "I've got cash. You can take it and go."

Arch closed his eyes against the shame. It filled his veins, pushing on his skin, making it feel too tight. "It's not money. My parole officer helped me get assistance from the government. I receive a check each month."

He watched them all look down and away. He

got it. It was hard to look *himself* in the mirror when he thought about it.

"Look, being out in the world, after so long in prison, it's overwhelming. Ten years when you're not allowed to make choices and suddenly *everything* is a choice. What to eat, what to wear, what to do. Everything moves fast out in the world, and it's all random. No schedule. Not like in jail."

He paused, looking at Mandy and Wade, willing them to understand. If they did, maybe they'd sway Nora. "I'm desperate. That's why I came home. I want to lie low on the Marker Ranch for a week or two. Get my bearings. Try to figure out what to do next. I had no idea you two had moved back to Benson. I thought the ranch was still abandoned. But I asked someone when I got to town today, and they told me Wade was running it now. And they sent me here to Lone Mountain, to find you."

"Marker Ranch is Wade's livelihood." A shrill note careened across Nora's voice. "I don't think you staying here is a good idea."

"Nora." Wade put a hand on her arm. "He's our brother. And he's served his time. Paid his dues."

"To the law, maybe. Not to us!"

Her fury was justified, but her words still bruised. "I swear to you that I'm clean. No drugs, no deals. All I want is to live a regular life. I don't know how to do that, but I want, more than anything, to learn.

And if there's a way to apologize enough, to make amends to you and Wade, I want to do that, too."

Doubt was thick in the air all around them. Arch waited. He'd learned to pray a little in prison, so he prayed now. He *needed* to be in the mountains, to breathe this clean air, to get grounded. "I have a parole officer. I check in by phone each week. He'll have the local sheriff check on me, too."

Nora and Wade exchanged a long, what-the-hell-should-we-do kind of look. Arch studied the mountains beyond them, the granite peaks rising to meet the afternoon sky and the fall-burnished aspen gilding the lower slopes. Trying to give them a moment of privacy. Trying to find the peace he'd felt earlier when he'd listened to the pines and caught Shrimp.

They must have reached some kind of understanding, because Wade cleared his throat and turned to face him squarely. "The house on Marker Ranch is empty. Nora lives with her husband, Todd, on his property now. And I live here with my fiancée..." He paused and a smile lifted all the tension off his face. "I mean, my *wife*, Lori. Mandy's sister. So there's plenty of room for you to stay there."

"But if there are any problems, you'll have to go," Nora added.

Relief, so sweet it choked him up again, shook

his voice. "I understand. There won't be any problems."

"The thing is," Wade continued, "I'm leaving on my honeymoon. Tonight. And Nora's leaving tomorrow to do some work up near the Oregon border for a few weeks. So you'll be on your own."

Nora turned to Wade. "Todd will be around. He was going to take care of Marker Ranch anyway. He can keep an eye on Arch."

It was humiliating to be spoken about in the third person. As someone who needed to be watched. But how could he blame them? They didn't know him beyond their memories, and those memories sucked.

Mandy broke the awkward pause. "I'll be here, next door, if he needs anything."

She was so sweet. Somehow, when he'd caught that cake, he'd caught an ally along with it.

Wade shook his head. "We can't ask that of you." Distrust weighted every staccato syllable. It made sense. For all his little brother knew, he was a rapist, too.

"It's not asking anything. We're neighbors. I'm happy to help out." The sharp note in Mandy's voice surprised him. She might be sweet, but she was tough.

Nora looked surprised, too. She studied Mandy for a moment. "Are you sure?"

Mandy nodded. "He saved the wedding cake, you know. I almost dropped it. And I think he caught a stray donkey for me, as well."

Nora's stern expression softened at Mandy's words. "You and your strays. Looks like you found another one today."

Arch saw Mandy flush a little. "I'm just grateful she did," he threw in, to cover her discomfort. "And I did find the donkey. It's safe with the goat."

"Thanks," Mandy said, and the warmth in her eyes was a tonic.

It seemed to soothe Wade, too, because that worry was gone from his eyes. "I still have a few horses and my cattle grazing on the ranch. I'll expect you to look after them. That way Todd won't have to. And there are a lot of repairs to do. We'll leave you a list."

"I can fix stuff," Arch told him. "I took machine shop, woodworking, metalwork—pretty much every class they offered while I was locked up. Otherwise I would have gone crazy. I even worked with livestock the last few years. The prison had a program. But not a full-scale cattle operation."

Wade gave a wan smile. "Well, we're not that yet. We've got a small herd and big plans."

"Then I know I can do it." He turned to Nora. "I'll listen to your husband. I'll get his advice if I have any questions. And I can ask…" He paused, strangely aware that it was the first time he was going to say her name. "Mandy. It will help to know I can turn to both of them with any concerns."

He glanced at Mandy, noting the faint flush on her cheeks. There was some kind of connection between them. Or maybe not. After ten years locked away from women, he had no idea. But damn, she was beautiful. And her name had been honey on his tongue.

Nora's brows drew in, schoolteacher serious. "We're giving you the chance. It's up to you to take it and run with it."

"Thanks, truly." Arch wished he could give her more reassurance. But nothing he could say would help. All he could do was *not* screw this up.

He turned to Wade, swallowing to clear the catch in his throat that just wouldn't go away. "I'm sorry to interrupt your wedding. I had no idea you were getting married when I came here today. Congratulations." He stepped back, giving them all space. "I don't want you to miss any more of your party. I'll just head on over to the ranch."

Wade nodded. "The house isn't great, but it's livable. Nora and I fixed it up a little when we stayed there."

Arch couldn't help but smile at that. "Trust me, after prison it will be a palace."

"I'll come see you later tonight to make sure you're settled," Nora said.

"We leave a key on the beam above the kitchen door," Wade added. "Just go on in and make yourself at home."

Home. Marker Ranch had never been a safe haven. Funny that it felt like one now. "Thanks," Arch muttered through the tightness in his throat. Maybe it was too much, but he had to say it. "I know sorry doesn't fix anything, but I wish I'd been different. Been a better brother. Been an honest man. Prison gave me a lot of time to regret the way I was."

Wade smiled faintly and reached out, bumping Arch's shoulder with his knuckles. "Just don't screw this up too badly."

"I won't." Arch glanced at Mandy. "Thanks for helping me out today."

"You're welcome." Her voice was everything gentle and warm. "Thanks for rescuing the cake."

Arch nodded and stepped back, wanting to free them up to finish out the wedding. He watched as the three of them turned back to the reception. Nora took Wade's hand in hers and put an arm around Mandy. They were a unit. Family. Friends.

Loneliness wrapped its cold hands around his insides.

But friendship and family had to be earned. Especially after you'd thrown it all away.

Arch turned to go, grateful that he had a place he *could* go. His feet ached from all the walking he'd done today, and it was still a couple of miles between Marker Ranch and this one, but he welcomed the pain. Each step on the dirt road was a reminder. He was free. He could walk fast, or slow, or he could run if he wanted, for the first time in a decade.

His heart lightened at the thought. He was free. His fifty-third day of freedom, and even when it had brought him this low—broke, unwanted and crawling home for help—he still cherished it beyond anything. He veered left at the driveway that would take him off Mandy's ranch.

"Arch!"

He turned, surprised, and saw Mandy hurrying after him. In her hand was a paper plate piled high with an enormous slice of cake. He started back toward her, admiring how elegant she looked in that wine-colored dress.

"You saved it. You earned a slice." She was a little out of breath, like she'd jogged, cake and all, to catch him.

Arch tried to remember the last time someone had reached out to show him a kindness like this—he couldn't. The plate was heavy in his hand, she'd put so much cake on it. "You're a good person." He blurted it out like an awkward kid. He had no experience with generosity.

"I just made a whole lot of cake." Her smile was fleeting but kind.

"Well, this will make the walk home a whole lot better."

There was silence while they looked at each other. Total strangers who'd done each other a good deed today, and maybe found a small seed of friendship. He needed to let her get back to her sister's wedding. "Nice to meet you, Mandy. Thanks for sticking up for me back there."

"Of course." She took a step back and waved. "Welcome home, Arch."

It was more of a welcome than he'd ever, in his most wishful dreams, hoped to get. He watched her walk lightly back up the drive, her full skirt swaying right down to the tops of her pretty brown cowboy boots. She was much more than a fairy like Tinker Bell. She was a guardian angel. A vision from heaven.

He looked down at the plate she'd brought him. White cake, chocolate cake, a few different kinds of icing. The first mouthful was a revelation of sugar and cream. He closed his eyes and tried to absorb the flavors. To savor such a fine taste. She might have heaped his plate, but her kindness today was sweeter than any cake. And he would never, ever get enough of sweetness like that.

CHAPTER THREE

THE SKY WAS glowing sunset pink when Mandy stepped out of the barn to shake the crumbs off the last tablecloth. The wedding was over. Lori and Wade had been sent on their honeymoon in style, with *just married* scrawled across the rear window of Wade's pickup and cans clanking along behind the bumper. Every last guest had been thanked and waved off. The food had been hauled back to the house and the dishes, too.

Mandy tossed the cloth onto the heap in the back of her truck and went inside to find her father. He was folding the rental tables and leaning them in neat stacks along the barn wall.

"I can ask one of the hands to finish those tomorrow, Daddy."

Her dad tipped another table on its side. "I may not be ranching anymore, but I'm still able. Tracy's got me going to the gym."

His new wife bustled up, a round figure in bright clothing and dyed-red hair. When Mandy found out her dad was in love, she'd pictured someone more like her willowy, dreamy mom.

Tracy couldn't be more opposite. She reminded Mandy of a plump parrot. Even her voice was chirpy. "Let's finish up, honey. We should get on the road to Reno."

Mandy snuffed a flicker of resentment. They'd only flown in yesterday. She'd hoped for more time with her father. But Tracy was clearly in charge of their relationship.

"I guess you're right." Her dad's voice echoed a little of Mandy's gloom as he set the table on the stack. "I think I'm just having trouble accepting that one of my babies is married."

"It's wonderful," Tracy cooed. "They're happy. Just like we are."

Mandy reached for a box of flower arrangements, walking them out to the truck to hide the emotion rolling over her. What was wrong with her? Her mom had died over a decade ago. Her dad had raised Mandy and Lori on his own and battled depression, as well. He deserved to be happy. She should be happy for him.

Her father and Tracy followed her out to the truck. "Today has made me want a party of our own, honey." Tracy clung to her husband's elbow. "Maybe we could have a reception? Since ours was only a courthouse wedding?" Her bright eyes flitted to Mandy. "You'd come celebrate with us, right?"

Florida. Mandy had never been. Flamingos,

alligators and palm trees. That was how she imagined it. It all sounded good—except the alligators. "Of course."

Her dad's hand reached out to cover Mandy's in familiar comfort. "And what about you? Anyone special in your life?"

Mandy had been ducking this question all day from well-meaning friends and relatives. "You know me, Daddy. I prefer quiet life here on the ranch. And no one's come knocking on my door."

His frown weighed on her. "You're young. You should get out more."

"I go out sometimes. But I'm busy. I have my chickens, my strays, the ranch and my baking business. There just aren't enough hours in the day."

Her dad squeezed her hand and let go. "Well, if you're happy, then I am. But it's not just about finding someone special. You should be following your dreams. Especially now that Lori is married. She and Wade will combine the ranches and run them just fine as one. But that's not your dream, honey. It never was. You should find out what you really want to do."

Her cheeks went hot. Did he really see her as that lost? "I *am* doing what I want to do."

"That's great." He regarded her thoughtfully for a moment. "You know, if you want to open up a bakery in town, Benson sure could use one.

Maybe I could help out with the initial costs. Or help you get a loan."

Money, planning, decision making. It all loomed in a thick and impenetrable wall. Just like it did every time Mandy thought about opening a real bakery. Anxiety threaded through her, pulling tension, making knots. "Thank you." She gave him a big hug, relishing his warm strength. "I'll think about it."

The weatherworn lines of her father's face creased into a smile as he looked down at her. "You just say the word and I'll do whatever I can."

All the ways she'd missed him since he started his new life in Florida ached in her heart. She inhaled his familiar scent—pure comfort—and stepped back, looking around the barn before she started bawling like the little girl she felt like. "It's hard to believe it, but I think we really are done here."

"You did an incredible job." Tracy fluttered her fingers toward the barn. "Everything looked gorgeous, and that cake was just out of this world. If you open a bakery, you'll have people lined up for miles."

Mandy laughed at that. "I don't think we have enough people in the town of Benson to make a line much farther than the door, but thank you."

Her dad glanced at his watch and Mandy's heart dipped. "You have to get going, don't you?"

"We do. Our flight is so early, we booked a hotel near the airport for tonight. I wish we could stay longer, but Tracy has to get back to the shop."

"How's that going?" Mandy had been so busy the past few days, she hadn't even thought to ask.

"Oh, it's amazing." Tracy's face lit under all her layers of makeup. "Busy. We get so many tourists on Sanibel Island, and they all want a piece of ocean decor to take home with them."

"Sounds perfect." It was hard to imagine her father, the tough rancher, selling seagull statues and shell-shaped ashtrays. More evidence that Mandy's world had changed completely.

"You're sure you'll be okay running the ranch solo for a few weeks?"

Her father would stay to help her if she asked. And Mandy really wanted to ask. Not just ask, *beg*. But she couldn't. He'd moved to Florida to get away from the ranch and the stress and the pain of losing his first wife. She couldn't ask him to take all that on again, even for just three weeks.

"I'll be just fine, Daddy. With Lori gone, it's my one and only chance to boss the ranch hands around. It will be fun."

His smile was what she needed. She didn't want to be a burden to him anymore.

"If you say so, sweetie. But call me if you need anything, okay?"

"Will do, Daddy. Now let's get you guys on the road before it gets too dark out there."

Mandy walked them to their car, cherishing her father's goodbye hugs, enduring Tracy's lipstick kisses. She watched them bounce away down the drive in their tiny rental car, turn onto the main road and disappear. The high mountain peaks behind the ranch shone in the last light of the sun, the gold cast making them seem even more ethereal, more unreachable. Jim, the ranch manager, had finished up the feeding a while ago, and the ranch seemed especially quiet. It was just her and the whisper of evening wind in the pines.

She'd done it. She'd given Lori a lovely wedding. But without the adrenaline of party guests and tasks, the last remaining energy in her body evaporated. The two hours of sleep she'd had in the past twenty-four hours fizzed out. She stumbled to the truck, almost too tired to miss Lori or her dad. Almost too tired to feel the loneliness of the empty ranch and the mountain night. Almost too tired to feed the stray cats and Lori's dog. Definitely too tired to think about the way life had moved one step farther today, leaving her here alone on the empty ranch.

DURING ALMOST A decade in prison, Arch had
never once thought he'd come home to Marker
Ranch. But here he was, standing in the gravel
driveway in front of the saggy farmhouse, apprehension thickening the air and memories creep-
ing across his skin.

There was the old wicker chair, still on the
porch, where his dad used to sit in the evenings.
He'd nurse the bottle of JD in his hands and deliver slurred lectures to Arch and his brother
Blake, schooling them in the finer points of running a con, stealing a car, manufacturing meth.

Most parents taught their kids right from wrong.
What kind of father groomed his sons to be criminals? Anger simmered and Arch exhaled, trying
to let it go. It was old poison. And he couldn't pass
on all the blame. His dad might have offered him
a toxic brew, but he'd chosen to drink it down.

"It's weird coming back, isn't it?"

Arch jumped straight out of his thought and
turned to see Nora walking toward him. "You
startled me. I didn't see you pull up."

"Sorry. I parked by the barn. I wanted to take
a look at the cattle." She walked past him and
plopped down on the porch steps. She looked a
lot more like the sister he remembered, with her
party dress replaced by faded jeans and a dark
blue sweatshirt.

She pointed to the duffel bag on the ground

next to him. The sum total of all his possessions. He'd stashed it in the bushes outside Mandy's ranch today, to avoid looking like the vagrant he really was. "Have you gone inside yet?"

He shook his head. "I took my time walking over. Then I went to see the horses and cattle. You and Wade have done a lot with this place."

"The ranch, yes. This house, not so much," Nora said. "Wade's bedroom is the nicest. Lori made him fix it up when they were first together. The rest of it is still pretty shabby."

"I was just standing here remembering it all. Growing up with Dad. How he'd sit on the porch and bully. He was a mean drunk."

"And he was almost always drunk." Nora glared at their dad's old chair with narrowed eyes. "I should've burned that thing when Wade and I first moved back."

"Maybe we can do it together."

The glance she shot him was skeptical. "Were you telling the truth earlier? That you left him and Blake?"

"You think I made it all up?" He pulled his wallet out of his back pocket and handed her his parole officer's card. "Steve's a good guy. You can call him if you want. He'd actually really like to talk with a family member."

She took the card, and he watched her eyes flick quickly over the words. "Can I keep this?"

He nodded. "You can trust me on this one thing, if nothing else—I haven't heard a word from Dad or Blake since I walked away. I figure they're in Mexico, if they're even still alive."

"And now that you're out, are you going to contact them?"

"No!" The thought had a foul taste. "I'm not going near them. And I'm not making their kinds of choices."

"I want to believe you," Nora said quietly. "But I don't know you."

"I get it. You know me as a bully. Someone who made your life miserable. I tried to pull you down with me. To get you to deal drugs at school."

She nodded. "I'm not gonna lie, Arch. You were mean. You scared me."

It was hard to speak through the mass of remorse rising in his throat. "It's not an excuse, but I thought that was how a man was meant to be. Showing how tough I was and how little I cared. But now I know I was just weak." He studied the fall of her long hair, half covering her face as she looked out over the driveway. "You were the strong one, Nora. You kept your head above it all. How did you do it? How did you stay out of Dad's grip?"

She didn't look at him. "I just knew I hated

how he was. How you and Blake were. I didn't want anything to do with any of it."

"I wish I'd seen it like you did. After Mom ran off, I turned to Dad. I didn't question that he was teaching me to hate, or guiding me to break the law. I became his puppet."

"I'm glad you broke away from him." Her voice was barely audible—like she felt all the emotion, too. She picked at the paint peeling off the step with a fingernail. "Ever since you showed up today, I've been trying to remember something good between us. Something that would make me feel okay about you coming home. And I actually remembered something."

"You did?" He couldn't think of anything he'd ever done that didn't fill him with guilt.

"Remember how Dad would steal cattle on occasion?"

"I used to help him do it." One more regret on his long list.

"Well, I remembered one time when Dad grabbed a couple of cows with young calves. He wanted to just shoot the little ones, because they were a hassle. I was really upset, and you stood up to him. You told him he shouldn't do it. And then you helped me make a separate pen for them, way off in the corner of the ranch where Dad wouldn't see them."

There it was, one memory lit up in gold, while

the rest were shrouded in gray gloom. "I remember that. I went out and got bottles so we could feed them."

She finally looked at him and he could see her wistful smile, even in the deepening dusk. "And you and I fed them together, until they were bigger. And then one night, you borrowed a trailer and we drove three hours to take them back to the ranch they'd come from. You cut the wires and put them back in the pasture. And we mended the fence back up again and went home."

"I remember," he said, staring at her in wonder. "But I'd totally forgotten."

"It's nice to know there was something good between us."

"I wish we had more memories like that. Believe me, I've gone over and over every wrong move I made. Everything I wish I'd done differently. I don't know how many apologies to give, but they're there if you want them."

She was silent. Because what could apologies do to unravel all the hurt he'd caused? The weight of it was a boulder on his back.

Finally she spoke. "I don't know if there's much of a future between you and me. Maybe we can find some more memories like those calves, but there are some things I'm not sure can be repaired. I want you to know, though, that I think you were brave to turn yourself in. I realize it couldn't have been an easy decision."

"It was the only choice I had if I ever wanted to be free." It was almost fully dark now. He pointed to the sky. "The first stars. One of the things I missed most in jail."

"Ten years of no stars." She looked up, too. "It's hard to imagine."

"Don't try. It's depressing. Life went on for everyone else. You and Wade did well for yourselves."

Warmth and pride softened her tone. "I can't believe he's off on his honeymoon."

"You raised him well," Arch said. "You kept him on the right path."

"I'm proud of him. He was a soldier, you know. He fought in Afghanistan."

Arch whistled low. "I didn't know. And what about you?"

"I'm a plant biologist. I consult on ranches, trying to help them use less water in the drought. And I work with my husband, Todd. We're creating a sanctuary for wild horses."

"You married a cowboy?"

She laughed. "I married an ex-activist who used to try to fix the world. Now he fixes engines and saves wild horses on the side."

"He sounds complicated. He treats you well?"

The words felt clumsy on his tongue. He wasn't used to being brotherly.

The smile that broke across her face told him what he needed to know. "He's a good guy. *Really* good. You'll meet him tomorrow when he stops by."

"I'm looking forward to it." He was lying. Todd obviously had a strong sense of justice. Which meant he'd probably want to kick Arch's ass for the way he'd treated Nora when they were young. But Arch would just have to take it if Todd resorted to violence. *No fighting* was high up there on the list of rules he had to follow now that he was on parole.

Nora stood, pulling her keys out of her pocket. "Speaking of Todd, I need to get home."

Arch nodded. "Thanks for coming by."

She pulled a folded index card out from the back pocket of her jeans. "Here's Todd's number. Call him with any questions. And please take care of this place. Wade's worked so hard on it."

"I will." Arch walked her to the barn, listening as Nora gave him instructions on how to use their account at the feed store. And then they were at her truck. She stuck out an awkward hand and he shook it once.

"Okay, then," she said. "Good luck." She climbed in behind the steering wheel, shut the door, gave a wave through the window and pulled a U-turn toward the driveway. Arch watched her go, leaning against the barn since his legs seemed to have gone boneless with relief.

Talking with Nora had been awkward. But it had gone better than he had any right to hope for.

He stayed there a few minutes, listening to the silence left in the wake of her truck. Silence laced with a touch of hope.

Autumn evenings lost their warmth quickly here in the mountains. After watching a few more stars emerge, Arch walked back to the house, grabbed his duffel bag and let himself in the kitchen door.

Inside he stopped, taking in the neatly scrubbed countertops, the faded linoleum. He moved on into the living room, recognizing the familiar furniture, the scarred, paneled walls, everything even older and more run-down than he remembered it. It was clean, though, which it had never been when they were young. Clean, but still a gut job.

A clock ticked in the hall. Other than that there was just thick, musty silence. For ten years he'd lived and slept with the sounds of hundreds of men clinging to him like dirt that he couldn't wash off. He'd craved silence during nights surrounded by their moans and snores. But now the quiet closed over him and all the emptiness was almost overwhelming.

He was being an idiot. Quiet was just that. Quiet. He should be happy to finally have a chance to experience it. He'd get used to it—and to everything else about life after jail.

He didn't feel ready to go upstairs, but exhaustion was hitting. He'd hitchhiked the past couple of days up from Los Angeles, sleeping rough. He needed a shower and bed.

He grabbed his duffel and climbed the rickety wooden stairs to face the past lurking in his childhood bedroom. The sagging mattress and the iron bed frame just as he'd left them. Beyond the bed, the window opened out over the porch roof. He'd climbed out of it just about every night when he was a kid, so ready to grow up fast and raise hell.

His bag landed on the bed with a hollow thump. He wished he could talk to the kid he'd been. Grip him by the belt and pull him back inside. Give him a good shaking and a glimpse into what his future would hold. Scare him straight.

Arch shook his head to clear the regret making his vision swim. No wishing could undo what had been done. No wishing could give him back the ten years he'd spent surviving behind bars. All he could do was leave that trouble-hungry boy in the past. All he could do was take what he'd learned and use it to finally become a man.

CHAPTER FOUR

WHEN MANDY TOLD Lori that she'd run their ranch, what she'd really meant was that Jim, the ranch manager, and Ethan, his second in command, would run the ranch. Her plan was to nod, smile and agree with whatever they said.

But instead, here she was, just twelve hours after Lori's wedding, locked in her truck and surrounded by hulking cattle. Jim had thrown out his back last night and the doctor told him to stay home for a while. And Ethan's mom had taken a fall and broken her hip, so he was on his way to the airport. He'd likely be gone for weeks.

Mandy smacked the steering wheel with the palm of her hand, cursing her employees and their personal crises. Robert's wife had gone into labor this morning—almost a month early. Juan and Ely had both called in sick with a horrible stomach flu. And Terry, due to some kind of scheduling mix-up, was on vacation for the next few weeks.

All of their reasons for not being here this morning were completely legitimate, but they still meant that Mandy was alone in this truck, trying to calm the shaking in her legs and the slamming of her heart.

She was terrified of cattle. Terrified of any large animal. Heck, even the miniature donkey made her nervous.

She cracked her window to get some fresh air. No cattle approached. That was hopeful. Maybe if she rolled the window down all the way, then sat on it, then stood on it, she could climb over the roof of the cab to the truck bed. Her feet wouldn't even touch the ground. She could toss the hay from there and never have to go near any cattle.

All it would take was a few simple steps. Unclip seat belt. Roll glass down. Put hands on window frame. Mandy leaned her head out, then her torso, getting ready to turn around so she could sit on the sill. A black steer just a couple of yards away raised its head and tilted huge ears in her direction. Mandy froze. Held her breath. Started to lower herself back into the cab. But the steer was curious and quick. It stuck its enormous nose in her face. Something slimy plastered her cheek.

"No!" Mandy fell back into the cab, scrambling to roll up the window, almost catching the steer's nose in the process.

Skin cells recoiled from the slime on her face. She grabbed a bandanna off the passenger seat and scrubbed, trying to keep on breathing. *Calm down. Calm down. Calm down.*

The familiar self-disgust set in. What was wrong with her? She was born and raised on a ranch. This shouldn't be a big deal.

But it was. It had been for years. Ever since the day her mom died. Tears stung and Mandy swiped at them. When would all the fear stop?

A flicker of motion across the black backs of the cattle caught her eye. Dark hair under a brown cowboy hat. Long legs in faded jeans. Shoulders wide under his padded canvas jacket. *Arch Hoffman.*

He was standing on the rail of the fence, waving with both arms to get her attention. She rolled down the window. "Hey," she called, knowing that it didn't matter what she said. There was no way she was getting out of this situation without looking like an idiot.

"What's going on?" He shouted the words, but it was still hard to hear him over the indignant mooing. The steers wanted breakfast, and they were confused and frustrated. *Well, boys, welcome to the club.* She'd been confused and frustrated for years now.

"Not much," she called back in a lame attempt at nonchalance. "What's up with you?"

She could see the confusion on Arch's face even from this distance. He probably hadn't been expecting small talk. "Um, not much. You need a little help there?"

She forced a breezy voice. "I'm okay...just need to get out of this truck and get feeding."

"Oh." He paused for a moment, as if trying to come up with the right words. "It's just that...you fell into the cab."

How long had he been there, watching her make a fool of herself? "Oh, ya know, just lost my balance for a minute." It was almost impossible to sound casual while yelling over the ruckus of forty upset steers.

Arch jumped off the fence and Mandy lost sight of him. She had a tiny moment to hope that he'd decided she was fine and was gone on his way. Then she saw him swing up on the back of a big black gelding and guide it along the fence to the gate. Leaning gracefully from the saddle, he let himself into the pasture, closing the gate behind him.

Mandy reached for the door handle, but her hand was shaking so hard she couldn't grasp it. She wanted to get out and face Arch while tossing hay out of the truck like a pro. But fear had its cold claws sunk in deep.

With a wave of his rope, Arch cleared the steers easily from his path. He took their place at her truck window, looking down at her from his relaxed perch in the saddle. "Do you want me to feed them?"

His voice was a balm of gentle concern that almost brought out the tears fizzing hot beneath her eyes. She felt her cheeks heat, too, and knew her usually pale skin had gone scarlet. She couldn't answer. But she nodded.

"Okay," he said. "Just sit tight."

She watched him in the side mirror as he guided his horse alongside the vehicle and leaned over, grabbing a few flakes of the hay she'd stacked there. He threw them to his right and several of the steers trotted toward the pile. Quickly he grabbed more hay and tossed it out behind the truck, creating another feeding area. Soon the pasture was littered with piles of hay surrounded by happy cattle. Mandy buried her face in her hands. He made it look so simple.

"All fed," Arch called and brought his horse around to stand by her window again. "Are you okay to drive?"

"Yeah, sure." Her voice scraped over the words.

"I'll open the gate. Why don't you bring the truck outside the pasture and park it?"

Mandy nodded and turned on the engine in mindless obedience, glad he was in charge, because her brain was blank in the aftermath of panic.

Arch opened the gate and she bumped through

it over the rough ground. She parked and watched Arch shut the gate in her rearview mirror. He rode so well. Slinging an easy leg over the horse's back, he dismounted and led his horse toward her.

Dread tipped her stomach. He'd want an explanation. But what could she possibly say without sounding totally crazy?

She stared straight ahead, but he didn't go away. She heard his footsteps crunching on the dry earth and then he was at her window, looking down at her with a mystified expression. "Mandy, are you all right? You're so pale... Are you sick?"

She could only hold his gaze for a moment. There was too much mortifying worry in his eyes. "Not sick." She ran her fingertips over the steering wheel in nervous zigzags, tracing the cord that wrapped the vinyl.

"Then?" he prompted.

She couldn't spit out the humiliating truth. If she stared at the steering wheel hard enough, maybe it would keep her tears at bay.

Arch brought his hand to her arm, and she jumped at the touch. "Are you frightened?"

The truth, said out loud, was jarring. She yanked her arm away from his fingers. "No!" It was a shrill bleat of a lie, but she went with it. "I didn't get a lot of sleep last night—too wound up after the wedding. When I got out of the truck to feed, I felt dizzy. That's when you saw me fall back."

His eyes were set deep beneath strong black brows. The skin around them creased with wear. Not smile lines. Hard-lived lines. When he searched her face, she knew he could see way too much. So she kept babbling. "I was just wondering if I should drive back out and feed them over the fence when you showed up. You saved me a lot of trouble and time."

"But—"

"I've still got a lot of chores to do," she interrupted. "I'm so glad you came along."

"Mandy..." he tried again.

But she flashed him a plastic smile, desperate for space between them. "Boy, do I owe you! Yesterday you saved the cake, and today you salvaged my chore schedule."

He was still intent on her, as if he could see right through her crazy. "What about the dizziness? Will you be okay?"

"I'm fine. I'll just drink some water," she assured him. "And try to get more sleep." Lying didn't come naturally. A low ache was seeping through her skull. She put the truck in gear.

"Wait," he said. "I came by to say thank you. For sticking up for me yesterday. For the cake, too."

"Hey, it was no problem!" Since when did she

talk like someone's hearty uncle? "But really nice of you to come by and say so. You must be really busy. So I'll let you get on with it. Thanks, Arch!" Mandy gave a vigorous wave, and he got the message and stepped back, that mystified look still on his face. She pressed the truck's accelerator a little too hard and it jolted her forward, adding insult to awkwardness.

Mandy steered the pickup haphazardly away from the pasture. Adrenaline coursed as if she'd just barely escaped with her survival. It was embarrassing enough being afraid of everything. It would be worse if people found out. Especially Arch Hoffman. He'd spent ten years in jail and lived a life of crime before that. He'd probably never been frightened of anything in his life. Plus, he just looked so capable. Of anything.

Mandy parked by the barn and buried the heat of her face in her hands. What was wrong with her? When would she get over her fears? And why had she lied about them, again?

The answer was obvious. She was a coward. A coward with a bunch more livestock to feed. She'd have to run along the fence like a maniac, tossing hay over at different places as fast as she could. It was risky. The cattle might push each other against the barbed wire trying to get the hay.

Later today she'd call around and see if she

could find temporary workers to help out on the ranch. For now, she'd just have to survive. She knew one thing for sure—there was no way she was going into a pasture with those scary, slobbery creatures again.

ARCH WATCHED MANDY'S truck swerve away in a cloud of dust. He'd thought they'd made a connection yesterday. That maybe they'd started some kind of friendship. He'd lain awake like a fool last night, reliving that moment when she'd brought him the cake. When she'd made him feel like he mattered.

As soon as he got done with his morning chores, he'd resolved to go find her, to thank her, to let her know what her kindness had meant. He'd ridden through the gate that separated their properties with high hopes. Of what he wasn't sure. Maybe just more of what it felt like to be near her. Because she'd seen him as a real person, not just an ex-convict. Maybe because she was beautiful, and he wanted to see that beauty again.

But when he'd found her, none of that had been there. Except her beauty, of course. That wasn't even dimmed by her pale skin, her worried eyes or the traces of dirt on her cheek. But the warmth, the sense that she cared, were all gone. Instead she'd almost run him over, trying to get away as fast as possible. Something had changed for her completely. But what?

It hit him like a blow to the sternum. She'd gone back to the wedding reception yesterday and talked with Nora and Wade about the bad he'd done. About what a heartless brother he'd been. *That* was what had changed. He couldn't blame her for trying to avoid him. If he heard those stories, he'd hate that guy, too.

Anger rose, at himself, at his choices. Anger was his lifelong companion, the cartoon devil on his shoulder. In prison, there'd been a chaplain, Pastor Doug, who'd become Arch's mentor and friend. Doug called anger the go-to emotion, because it was the first to show up. The pastor's words rose from memory and settled him. *Stop. Identify the feelings.* All *of them.*

Arch took a deep breath and tried to make space in his mind. There was anger, always. But there was more. Frustration that his past was coloring every moment of the present. Disappointment that Mandy wasn't looking at him the way she had yesterday. Shame that he wasn't worthy of anyone's regard. Fear that he never would be.

Losing the glimmer of hope she'd offered him felt big. Truth was, he'd been hanging on to it like a lifeline. But trying to get that hope from Mandy, or from anyone, was a big mistake. The only hope that mattered was the feeling deep inside him.

That small, stubborn belief that he could be a better person.

He had to remake his life on his own. And standing around here feeling sorry for himself wasn't going to get him far.

Arch swung onto the big gelding. Funny, he didn't even know the horse's name. He'd seemed strong and calm. The best choice for a big guy like Arch. And they'd gotten along well so far.

He'd found a path that connected the two ranches via a big well at the top of both properties. He'd take that way home now. And along the way he'd try to put Mandy out of his thoughts.

Fall in the eastern Sierra brought cold mornings, even on sunny days. His breath was visible where the peaks cast their shadows. Arch focused on gratitude, for the chilly air in his lungs and the feel of the big horse under him. If there was a definition of freedom, it had to be this. Riding alone in the quiet of the autumn mountains. Granite boulders scattered everywhere, turning landscape into moonscape. Sagebrush clinging to the dry soil.

Arch leaned down and broke off a sprig, inhaling its earthy, rich scent. And something inside him broke open, his gratitude expanding in a warm, soaring feeling that lifted his shoulders and lightened his heart. The deepest relief. The purest joy. Elation. Because he was here in this beauty. He was home. He was free. And that miracle mattered, more than anything.

THE TRAIL WOUND lower into the deep valley that sheltered Marker Ranch. When the terrain leveled, Arch let the gelding break into a lope, loving the speed and the horse's smooth gait. Eventually the trail became dirt road. They passed recently painted outbuildings. Mended fences. Arch slowed the horse to a walk near the newly repaired barn.

A dark blue pickup was parked alongside it. A man was leaning on the tailgate, waiting. The horse's pace quickened, as if he recognized the visitor.

"You found trouble," the man called.

Arch stopped the horse a few paces away. "Pardon me?"

The man stepped forward and rubbed the horse's nose, and Arch caught a glimpse of a lean face under the brim of a worn brown felt hat. "Trouble. That's this horse's name."

Arch couldn't contain his laugh. "I always was good at finding trouble. Guess not much has changed. You must be Todd."

"I sure am." Todd ran a hand over Trouble's neck and stepped back to take the big horse in. "He's looking good."

"He's great to ride. I don't know much about

any of the horses. I just picked him because he's big."

"You picked well. He used to be wild, you know. Found him sweltering in a government corral about sixty miles south of here. He was angry as hell, so no one would adopt him. But with some time and patience, he came around."

Arch swung his leg over Trouble's back, his legs just a little wobbly when he hit the ground. His brother-in-law stuck his hand out and Arch took it, gratified by the firm grip. "Thanks for stopping by," he said. "Good to meet you."

Todd just nodded, assessing him the same as he'd done to the horse. Calm and observant. Then his glance went to Arch's arm, where Trouble was trying to nibble at his sleeve. "Trouble likes you. So that's a good sign."

"He's a good horse," Arch said. "You did a fine job with him."

"I gentled him, but your brother Wade trained him," Todd said. "Trouble's the second mustang he's trained."

His little brother trained wild horses. Arch was getting random pieces of the puzzle. If he put them together, maybe he could learn all he'd missed. "Well, I'll have to compliment him, then."

Todd gave the horse a gentle pat on the neck,

but his voice was firm. "He's put a lot of work into his horses. And into fixing up this ranch."

"I know," Arch told him.

"No, you *don't* know, actually." Todd stood up straighter. He wasn't a huge guy. Tall, for sure, but still a couple of inches shorter than Arch, and lanky and lean. "You don't know the work your brother and sister put in to clean this place up. It took months. It made them a little crazy. They've lived with snide comments and dirty looks because of the things *you* did. Things they had no part in."

Todd didn't need bulk and muscle. The guy was a ninja with words, cutting and slashing right to the point, leaving wounds salted with pure truth. The pain of it made Arch gruff. "You're right. I was born and raised a complete asshole. When I got old enough, I continued that family tradition all on my own."

"You've got no excuse?" Todd crossed his arms, waiting.

"Nope. I did stuff that is inexcusable. Look, Todd, I don't have a list of reasons. I was who I was. The guy my dad taught me to be. I hate that guy, but I *was* that guy. In some ways I'll never be rid of him." The pain of it coiled in his guts.

"So what's changed? Why should we trust you now?"

"I don't have a good answer for that. One day I realized I didn't want to be that guy anymore, so I turned myself in. Now I'm ready to be someone new. I'm not sure who that is, but I know he'll be a better man than the first version." He tried to think of a more eloquent way to put it. But all he found inside was raw regret. "That's all I got."

Todd looked at him thoughtfully. "I knew I'd like you," he said.

"What?" If Todd had started speaking a foreign language, Arch wouldn't have been more surprised.

"When Nora came back into the reception yesterday and told me you were back and that you'd turned yourself in, I knew I'd like you. I'm glad you don't have excuses. If you did, you'd just be avoiding responsibility."

Arch stared at his brother-in-law in shock. They were okay? Just like that? "I promised Nora and Wade they'd have nothing to regret by taking me in. I mean to keep that promise."

"I think you do," Todd said. "And I think you will. But if you don't, I'll have to kick you out. Got it?"

"Got it." He'd never met anyone as straightforward as this. It was refreshing.

Todd ran a hand down Trouble's neck. "He doesn't seem too warm, and he's definitely not tired. Let's take a ride through the ranch. If you have any questions, maybe I can answer them."

Arch nodded. "Sure. I have a lot of questions."

"I'll just go grab a horse, then." Todd stepped into the tack room just inside the barn door and came back out with a halter and rope in hand.

"You need any help?" Arch called.

"Nah. I got it. I helped train them all, so it's like visiting relatives." Todd shot Arch a grin. "Only maybe not quite so complicated as that. Be right back." He jogged down the lane that led to the pasture.

Arch led Trouble over to a trough by the barn wall so the gelding could grab a drink. Leaning on the big horse's flank, he tried to take in his day so far. A roller coaster. He'd lost his connection with Mandy but gained a new one with Todd. Mandy had lost faith, but Todd might actually believe in him.

Pastor Doug had reminded him over and over again that freedom wasn't some magical cure for everything. That it would be up and down, sometimes smooth and sometimes rough. That some people would accept him and some would turn their backs. It was only his first full day home, but Arch was seeing the truth of the pastor's words.

He thought of Mandy driving away from him as fast as she could, and something in his chest ached. He knew he was lucky to have met Doug and to have learned so much from him. But sometimes he wished that his teacher wasn't right quite so often.

CHAPTER FIVE

ARCH SIFTED THROUGH Wade's collection of screws and bolts, all neatly labeled, none the size he needed. One of the gates was falling to pieces, and Todd had put the repair job at the top of Arch's to-do list when they toured the ranch together yesterday. Arch picked up a half-inch bolt and studied it. Maybe he could make it work. But it was hard to focus, because he was still worried about Mandy.

His disappointment from yesterday had faded, and intuition had replaced emotion. Intuition deep down, telling him something was wrong. That it wasn't just him she'd been fleeing in her truck yesterday. And with her on the ranch alone, it was easy to imagine what that something might be. Maybe a ranch hand was giving her trouble now that her sister and Wade were away. Or maybe she was ill and didn't want to see a doctor for some reason.

But she'd made it clear that she didn't want *his* help. So who should he tell? Todd was the obvious person. Arch set the bolt back in its compartment. He'd go to town. Stop by Todd's repair shop and share his concerns about Mandy. Then he could get the right-size bolts from the hardware store, too.

Arch folded his list, shoved it in the pocket of his jeans and headed for the house. After a quick wash and a change of shirt, he grabbed the keys to Wade's old pickup. And stopped, staring at them lying so innocent in his hand. He had no license. Getting out of jail meant starting from scratch.

His heart rate picked up a few extra beats. He shouldn't be driving. He'd be breaking the law. Violating parole.

He went to the old rotary phone in the hallway and picked up the receiver. But there was no dial tone. Of course. No one had been living here lately. It made sense they'd turn off the service to save money.

He jangled the keys in his palm. Mandy might be in trouble. The buzz of worry drowned out his concerns. The road to town went through open country. Then he'd just have to make it a few blocks in town to Todd's shop. It would be fine. It had to be.

In the truck, a few jarring stalls in first gear reminded Arch that he hadn't driven in ten years. He took a couple of laps, steering the old Chevy around the barn and down the lane to the lower pastures before he three-point turned in jerky motions and headed toward the road.

Driving through open country was easy, but Todd's repair shop was near downtown Benson, and each landmark Arch passed was an uncomfortable reminder of old mistakes.

First there was the bridge just outside town, where he and his adolescent buddies had smoked and made trouble. They'd throw nails in the road to pop tires, stupid stuff like that.

Then he passed the liquor store, where his underage bulk and bullying had made Mr. Howell so nervous, he'd sold him alcohol without an ID.

Almost to Todd's shop, Arch caught a glimpse of the back lot behind the outdoor store. The place he'd beat the crap out of Will Barkley for just looking at Arch's girlfriend Kit. Then left him bleeding in the dust.

Shame stole his senses. He pulled over. He lived with a dormant monster inside him. A punk-kid monster who'd thought nothing of hurting another person.

And Kit. He hadn't thrown any punches at her, but he'd inflicted pain. The kind that came from walking away from a five-year relationship without even a goodbye. He'd told himself it was for her own good. If she didn't know where he was, the police couldn't pin anything on her. But the truth was, he could have called, or left a note. He'd been too much of a coward to face her sadness.

He looked around the deserted street, as if he might see Kit walking right by. But what was he thinking? She'd been fiery, determined to get the hell out of Benson and see the world. No way was she still around town. Which was good, because he didn't know how he'd face her. One more relationship he'd destroyed. One more mess that *I'm sorry* could never clean up.

Arch swiped damp palms down his jeans. He had to stay in the present. Mandy might need help. That was the reality, what he needed to focus on. He put the truck back into gear and pulled carefully away from the curb. He could find a few hundred bad deeds to regret in this town. But that would have to wait for another day.

Todd's shop appeared on his left. Arch avoided the gravel parking lot, pulling the truck to the curb instead. He'd have to face local folks sometime, but he'd rather not do it trying to remember how to park between other cars.

A man in a straw cowboy hat was slouching on a bench just outside the shop. He stood when he saw Arch crossing the street. And Arch's blood curdled. Connor Purcell.

Arch's hands coiled automatically. He willed them to straighten. They weren't kids anymore, and fists wouldn't help here.

Connor shifted to block the entrance to Todd's shop. His Ken-doll looks were puffy around the edges now, but he had the same mean glint in his baby blues. "What the hell? Arch Hoffman?" He pulled a phone out of his pocket. "I guess I need to call the sheriff so he can finally arrest you."

Arch stopped where he was. If he got too close, he might throw a punch, just for old times' sake. Connor was the son of a rich rancher, and when they were kids he'd made it a point to taunt Arch at every turn, mocking his old clothes, his too-long hair, his poverty. He'd kept the insults coming until freshman year of high school, when Arch had grown about a foot and started working out. And broke Connor's nose.

"Didn't expect to run into you at a repair shop, Connor." Arch kept his voice casual. "Didn't realize you even used machines—don't you worry that they'll get your pretty hands dirty?"

Connor stared at him blankly. He'd never been one for complex thoughts. If there wasn't a straightforward insult coming at him, he got a little stuck. Arch smiled at the thought, which evidently unnerved Connor further, because he muttered, "I'm calling the sheriff," and pawed at his phone.

"Go ahead," Arch offered mildly. "Have him come over. I'd like to meet him."

Connor flopped back onto the bench with the

phone to his ear, calling his bluff. Well, Arch had to make himself known to the sheriff sometime this week, so in a way Connor was helping him with that errand. Though he was glad he'd parked Wade's truck across the street. He'd been an idiot to drive. But... Mandy. That same urgency gripped him. He stepped into the shop. "Todd, you here?" he called. "It's Arch. Arch Hoffman."

He heard the grinding of wheels across cement, as if Todd had been somewhere under the big tractor Arch could see in the back of the building. And then his brother-in-law emerged from the gloom of his shop, wiping his hands on a rag he pulled from his back pocket.

"Arch." His friendly expression changed to concern when he saw Connor's scowling face behind him. "Is there a problem here?"

"Connor's upset about me being here in town. So he's calling the sheriff." Arch kept it matter-of-fact.

"Oh!" Todd looked at Connor, who was apparently on hold. "Arch is my brother-in-law. He's welcome here."

Connor shook his head. "You don't know him. He's nothing but trouble. He's been hiding from the law down in Mexico. If he's here, justice can finally be done."

Arch smiled a little. He couldn't help it. The

universe must have a hell of a sense of humor to make Connor Purcell his Benson welcoming committee. "Hey, it's okay," he assured Todd, who was looking pretty uncomfortable. "When I first decided to come back here, I was afraid I'd get run right out of town. So this is good. You know what they say about facing your fears head-on."

Todd's lean face creased into smile lines. "You're not worried?"

"I'm pretty sure my parole officer already gave the sheriff a heads-up that I'm here." Arch glanced at Connor, who was spouting indignant words into his phone. "Look, can I talk to you about something? Privately?"

"Sure." Todd led him across the parking lot, stopping out of Connor's earshot.

Arch explained about Mandy's behavior the day before. How it had been bothering him ever since. "In jail I learned to trust my gut when I felt like there was a problem. And something definitely wasn't right with Mandy yesterday."

Todd looked at him carefully. "Huh. Seems like she'd have called me if she needed anything. But if you're worried like you say…" He trailed off. Shook his head. "I can't go out there. Not now. I've got Connor breathing down my neck to get this tractor going again. The job's taking longer than I thought it would, and he's decided to stay put until I finish." He glared at the rancher. "I guess he feels like I'd slack off without his imposing presence."

Arch couldn't help but chuckle. "Yeah, he's always been real helpful like that. He spent junior high gluing my locker shut and pouring soda on me at lunch."

"I imagine you gave him a run for his money eventually," Todd said.

"Well." Arch grinned at the memory. "The tires on the fancy truck his daddy bought him for his sixteenth birthday had the strangest habit of going flat every Thursday like clockwork." He shook his head in mock wonder. "It was the damnedest thing."

Todd laughed and clapped him on the back. "I would have liked to see that." Then he sobered. "Look, I'm gonna need you to go out there and check on Mandy. Can you do it? I doubt I'll be out of here until feeding time tonight. My horses will get a late supper as it is."

Arch recalled Mandy's fake smiles and hasty retreat. "I don't know if I can help. She doesn't seem to like me very much."

"Mandy?" Todd shook his head. "Nah. She's the sweetest person I've ever met. I'm sure it's nothing personal."

"When I stopped by yesterday, she couldn't get

away from me fast enough. I don't want to make her uncomfortable."

"Maybe you just make her a little nervous," Todd said. "You're a big guy, fresh out of prison, and let's just say your reputation precedes you. As our friend the sheriff's speedy arrival demonstrates." He pointed to the patrol car pulling into the parking lot, lights flashing. "C'mon. Let's get this over with."

Todd walked toward the car and Arch fell into step next to him. "Just tell Mandy I sent you," Todd went on. "And that you're there to make sure she's all right."

"Will do." Arch tried to ignore how much he wanted to see Mandy again. He didn't expect her to smile at him like she had the day they met. But at least he'd find out if she was okay. It would be good to ease this worry that plagued him.

They were near the sheriff's car now, and Arch swallowed hard. Those flashing lights set every cell in his body on edge.

"Deputy." Todd shook hands with the man who stepped out of the car. "Thanks for coming by. Though I think you've been called out here for nothing. One of my customers was just a little concerned to see that my brother-in-law is back in town."

The man looked straight at Arch, and Arch's

stomach turned. Patrick Norris. Connor's best bud and partner in crime in high school. Now deputized.

"Well, look who's crawled back to town." The deputy's voice was rich with menacing glee. He glanced at Connor, who was approaching eagerly. "He's been giving you trouble?"

"No, he hasn't." Todd spoke before Connor could get a word in. "Connor got upset the moment Arch set foot on my property. But Arch has as much right to be here as any of us."

Deputy Norris stuck out his chest enough to strain the buttons on his uniform. Arch could see the bully's gleam in his eye. The deputy was loving this moment of power, and it was clear he was going to make the most of it. "With all due respect, Todd, you weren't around back when Arch and his family wreaked havoc in this town. So I'll ask you to step away while I deal with him."

"With all due respect, Deputy, I won't see a man illegally detained for crimes he's already served his time for." Todd stepped forward, a little in front of Arch.

The deputy's pale little eyes shot back and forth between Todd and Arch. And to where Connor was standing a few feet farther back. "Where are you staying?" he asked.

"Out at Marker Ranch."

"Humph. We'll need to search it, then. Make sure you aren't setting up any more drug labs out there."

"You're welcome to. Just come with a warrant." Arch forced his voice to stay even. Searches were a part of parole, and he had to remember that the occasional property search was a hell of a lot better than prison. But the thought of Patrick Norris doing the searching made him uneasy.

"How'd you get here? To Benson?" The deputy pulled a little notebook and pencil from his pocket and wrote something on it.

"I caught rides from Los Angeles."

"How'd you get to town today?"

There it was. His first mistake on parole. Possibly his only one, because Norris was looking for a reason to lock him up, and Arch had given him one by driving here. Cold sweat trickled down his back. He could lie like a coward. Or tell the truth and lose his freedom for sure.

"He rode the bike I loaned him," Todd offered suddenly. "It's parked around the back of the shop."

"Humph." The deputy eyed Arch. "Is that true, Hoffman?"

Arch stilled his features to mask the gratitude he felt for his brother-in-law. "Yup. That's how I'll travel, until I get my license back. My parole officer should have called your office already to fill you in on all that."

"Parole officer, huh?" The deputy's eyes went thoughtful in a way that chilled Arch's bones. "I didn't talk to him. But I know we have to be extra careful when we have an ex-convict around." He pulled the handcuffs off his belt. "Considering that you're a parolee, I'm sure you'll understand why I need to put these on you while I give the office a call."

"No, I don't understand at all." Arch eyed the cuffs with loathing. "I'm not causing any problems. Go call your office and see what my parole officer had to say. I'll stay right here."

"I'll vouch for him," Todd said.

But Deputy Norris had devolved into Patrick Norris, and Patrick couldn't resist the chance to show his power. He shook his head. "I can't be too careful. Arch knows the drill. Parolees are second-class citizens. Plus, you've spent plenty of time in cuffs, right, Arch? So it's no big deal." He waddled closer to Arch. "Turn around," he ordered.

Hot bile convulsed up Arch's throat and he was sure he'd be sick all over Patrick's shiny brown shoes. Somehow he held it in.

"This is *not* okay." Todd started forward. "It can't be legal."

"Just leave it." Arch shoved the words out over

the nasty taste in his mouth. The last thing he wanted was for his brother-in-law to get himself in trouble defending him. Todd had already lied to cover Arch's mistake with the truck, and even that wouldn't go over well with Nora. "Let Patrick get his rocks off. The sooner he has his fun, the sooner we can all get on with our day."

He put his hands behind his back and offered them to Patrick. "Try not to get too excited, Patty. I'm assuming you and Connor usually reserve these kinds of games for your private time together."

Connor came at him with fist raised, but Todd caught his arm before he made contact. "What… you need him cuffed so you can get up the guts to hit him? Back off, Connor."

Connor brought his hand down reluctantly, settling for spitting on the ground near Arch's feet instead.

The cuffs wrapped hard talons around Arch's wrists.

Todd pulled his phone out of his pocket and held it up. "I'm going to take a video of whatever the hell you two clowns try next. So just keep in mind that whatever happens here may go viral."

Patrick gave Todd a look of fury, and Arch braced himself for what was sure to be a rough pat down. Anxiety and shame warred. The claustrophobic cuffs felt like they were snapped around his lungs as well as his wrists.

Patrick bent down to start his search at Arch's ankles. Todd leaned right over his shoulder with his phone camera and started narrating. "Deputy Patrick Norris has cuffed an innocent man simply because he is on parole," he intoned in a solemn voice. It sounded ridiculous, as Todd clearly meant it to be, and Arch's stress was replaced by an overwhelming urge to laugh. Norris ran his hands up Arch's legs and patted around, while Todd continued his narration. "Deputy Norris is now feeling the innocent man's crotch."

The breath Arch had been holding came out in a hoot of laughter, and Patrick dropped his hands and stood up, running his hands over the pockets of Arch's jeans. "Empty your pockets!" he barked.

"The deputy is asking the man to empty his pockets," Todd said.

"And I can't," Arch added. "Because I've been handcuffed." His eyes met Todd's and the two men burst out laughing.

Patrick shoved his hands into Arch's pockets and brought out Arch's car keys, holding them up triumphantly. "Ha! Explain these!"

"Deputy Norris has found a set of keys," Todd proclaimed, his laughter breaking through his words. He brought his phone close to the deputy's hand. "I am zooming in on his discovery."

"Back off!" Patrick yelled, his voice sounding like the teenager Arch remembered.

"They're my brother's house keys," Arch answered. Which was the partial truth.

The deputy set them on the ground and gave Arch a few more pats on his torso, Todd closely documenting each touch. "Satisfied with your little movie?" Patrick sneered when he'd finished. "Just what we need, a hippie activist in our town."

"Sorry, Deputy." Todd looked as if he was enjoying this entire exchange mightily. "But you're stuck with me. We'll just have to find a way to get along. Peace and rainbows and all that."

Patrick shook his head and stomped over to the patrol car to call his office.

Arch stared at Todd in admiration. "What the hell, bro? I'd high-five you if I could."

"This sucks." Todd nodded toward Arch's trapped hands. "But I'm saving this video. We'll laugh about it for years to come."

"You've been in these types of situations before," Arch said.

"I was an environmental activist for a long time." Todd dropped his voice low, glancing over to make sure neither Connor nor Patrick could hear. "I've been arrested a time or two for protests, things like that."

"And my sister married you?" Arch knew that Nora had an understandable horror of anything unlawful.

"It took some convincing." Todd smiled like a guy who really did believe in peace and rainbows. "She's an amazing person."

Deputy Norris was off his call and scribbling furiously in his notebook. Arch could tell he hadn't gotten the information he'd hoped for. His face was puckered and red like he'd taken a shot of moonshine.

Arch leaned over so Todd could hear his whisper. "Keep that video camera ready. These guys are definitely carrying an old grudge. Maybe they finally figured out who was behind those Thursday flat tires."

Todd gave him a wink and then took a couple of steps closer to Connor, who was lurking near his deputy buddy. "I'm sorry." His voice mimicked polite apology. "But with the sheriff here today, I'm getting really behind schedule. So your tractor won't be ready until tomorrow morning. You'll have to come back and pick it up then."

"But—"

Todd cut him off. "There are only so many minutes in a day, and you've used a bunch of them up with this bullshit."

Connor stalked off to lean on his big pickup, parked near the door of the shop. He folded his arms and waited, obviously intent on seeing the end result of the chaos he'd caused.

Deputy Norris's reluctance to end his big moment was evident in each step he took toward Arch. He clutched the handcuff keys like a toy he didn't want to share. "My boss says he spoke with your parole officer. He knows you did your time. You're clear, for now. He said to tell you that he'll be checking in on you pretty often."

Relief surged through Arch's veins. He'd made a huge mistake driving here today. He wouldn't make it again.

"So unlock the cuffs," Todd urged. Arch tried to convey his gratitude in a glance. He wouldn't beg, but he wanted the metal off him with a longing so deep it ached. They were a symbol of every sadistic creep he'd come across in jail. Creeps just like Patrick Norris. He couldn't count the times he'd been tripped, hands cuffed and unable to catch his fall, by some pissed-off prison guard. This felt way too close to those dark times.

Arch turned, and Patrick unlocked the cuffs. "Better behave yourself, Hoffman, or I'll be slapping these right back on."

"I'm getting this all on video," Todd reminded him.

Arch shoved his freed hands into his pockets, just to keep them under control.

"I think you're out of line, Deputy," Todd said.

"And I mean to speak with the sheriff about what went on here today. Mike Davidson's a good man, and he won't be happy when I tell him how Arch was treated."

The deputy looked uncomfortable, glancing over at his buddy. But Connor looked away, as if he'd had no part in all of this unpleasantness. It was kind of sad to see how the two men hadn't changed. "He always did make you do his dirty work, Patrick." Arch kept his voice quiet, so Connor wouldn't hear. "I'm surprised you're still content to be his lackey after all these years."

"Shut up, Arch," Patrick sneered, a high school kid again.

Arch gave up trying to reach the humanity in him. "If you're finished, Todd and I have things we need to do."

Todd stayed with Arch, watching as the deputy's car and Connor's oversize pickup rolled out of the lot. "Not the greatest homecoming." He clapped a hand to Arch's shoulder. "I apologize that happened at my shop." Disgust dripped from Todd's voice. "It's obvious those two have it in for you."

"Well, not for nothing. I did all I could to give them, and everyone else in this town, a hard time when I lived here. I don't like their vigilante attitude, but I don't blame them for seeing me as a menace."

"But they have to realize that ten years in jail can change things," Todd said.

"A lot of guys are changed for the worse by doing time. And the verdict is still out on me." Arch's voice shook even though he tried to hold it still. "I made my first big mistake, driving down here today. It's my old attitude coming through. Thinking that whatever I want or need is above the law."

"I don't see it that way," Todd said. "You drove here because you were worried about Mandy. To me that's different. Nora has told me plenty of stories about you. But honestly, now that I've met you, it's hard to connect you with that guy."

"Oh, I'm him." Arch felt the bitter taste of it in his mouth. "And he's me. I live with that every day."

"Well, maybe if someone I respected got upset about your return I'd have more understanding. But Connor—what an idiot. Throwing his money around like it will buy him anything. If I didn't want to get his tractor off my property so badly, I'd take it to pieces and leave it for him to put back together. I don't need his business enough to put up with him again."

Unfamiliar emotion washed over Arch's skin. "I wish I'd known you when I was younger," he blurted out. "I could have used a friend like you."

Todd's answering nod was accompanied by a

devil's smile. "You might just change your mind. Because now that I covered for you with that bike story, you *have* to ride out of here on my bike. I'd bet a hundred bucks that Deputy Norris is waiting around the corner to catch you driving that old truck. You *do* know how to ride a bike, don't you?"

Arch winced. "It's been a long time."

"Hang on." Todd walked around the side of his shop. Arch waited. Hating that he needed help like this. That he had to rely on Todd's generosity.

Todd came back wheeling a black mountain bike with a bright blue helmet dangling from the handlebars. "Your new wheels," he told him. "And we have helmet laws in California, so make sure you wear this."

Arch eyed the bike. He'd ridden when he was a kid, but not since he got his first car. And the helmet looked like some kind of weird blue mushroom.

"Yeah, it's not cool." Todd read his thoughts. "But it would be way less cool to be the parolee who gets locked up for not wearing his bike helmet."

Arch took the helmet from Todd's outstretched hand, clapped it on his head and snapped it under the chin. "Ya know...getting out of prison might be even more humbling than being there in the first place."

"Hey, what doesn't kill you makes you stronger, right?" Todd passed him the bike. "Hold this. I'm gonna adjust the seat way up for you. You're like a fricking giant, bro. I'm pretty sure your arm is the size of one of my legs."

"Not much to do in jail besides lift weights," Arch answered, steadying the bike. "And it pays to be big in there. People don't mess with you if they know you can crush them."

Todd had the seat raised in moments. "I think you're set, then. Happy riding. Stay off the gravel or you might pop a tire. There's a spare and some tools in that pouch under the seat if you do. You know how to change a bike tire?"

Arch shook his head. "Nope, but I'll figure it out if it comes to that."

Todd glanced at his watch. "I'd better get back to Connor's tractor. Can't wait to get that thing finished."

"I appreciate you standing up for me, Todd. I really do." Arch paused awkwardly, not sure what to say. "Well, I better get riding. This isn't quite how I imagined my day going, but I'm grateful for the new wheels."

He swung his leg over the bike. Then glanced back at Todd. "You mind heading back to work? I'd rather not have an audience when I fall on my ass."

"Are you kidding? I'm taking a video to send

to Nora." Todd whipped out his phone again and held it up. "Get riding."

Arch pushed off and pedaled, relieved to realize it *was* just like riding a bicycle. He was out of the parking lot and heading down the street in moments, though in a slightly wobbly style. Todd was still filming, and he waved cheerfully when Arch glanced back. Nora would get a good laugh out of it, which was fine, because she definitely deserved a few laughs at his expense. And Arch owed a debt to Todd for standing by him today.

Deputy Norris was parked half a block down, lurking behind the feed store. Arch saluted him as he rode by. Norris's answering salute featured his middle finger.

Arch started pedaling in earnest. It was a clear, crisp day. Fall with an edge of winter. Seasons. Changes. He looked forward to it all after a decade of prison sameness. And now that he couldn't drive, he'd be experiencing those changes up close wherever he went. Which would be scenic, but very chilly when winter arrived. He'd better get a driver's license soon.

He passed the motel on the edge of town. The old grocery, Blue Water Mercantile, was still out here, too. He'd have to pedal back for some food tomorrow. And there was the Dusty Saddle—the old dive bar looked unchanged.

Pedaling alongside the road of his hometown

was humbling and more than a little strange. But once he got in the rhythm, pushing and pulling his boots in the toe clips, it was kind of therapeutic. Just one foot up and one foot down, making slow and steady progress. It wasn't much, just a few yards of ground at a time. But right now, it would have to be enough.

CHAPTER SIX

MANDY PEERED AT the horses through the rails of the corral. There were six of them making an evening meal of the alfalfa she'd dropped over the fence. This was her third time feeding on her own and she still couldn't find the courage to enter the pasture and use the actual hay rack.

She kept hoping she'd find a ranch hand to hire. But none of the neighbors she'd called knew of anyone looking for work. No one had answered the help-wanted ad she'd hung on the feed store bulletin board. So she was on her own. And now she had to catch a horse.

Dakota was limping. Mandy had been watching the mare for several minutes, hoping she was imagining it. But clearly she wasn't. So despite shaking knees and stampeding heart, she had to check Dakota's leg.

The halter and lead rope pressed unfamiliar weight on Mandy's shoulder. Years ago, approaching a horse had been second nature. But now just approaching the fence was an enormous effort.

Mandy forced her feet onto the lowest rail. Then

hefted herself onto the second rail with her body leaning over the top of the fence. Her breath came in short gulps. There seemed to be a lot less air up here.

"Dakota, come here." She'd been aiming for calm and commanding, but her words came out shaky and squeaky.

Dakota lifted her head and fixed her mild eyes on Mandy, chewing a piece of hay contemplatively.

"Come on," Mandy pleaded.

Dakota sighed, put her head down and kept eating. Apparently she was on vacation, just like Lori.

Time for plan B. Mandy reached into her back pocket and pulled out her secret weapon. "Dakota, come get the carrot!"

Six horsey heads whooshed up, ears tilting forward. Six horses rushed toward her, a large speckled gray lunging to ensure it was first in line.

"Yikes!" Mandy dropped the carrot and launched herself backward off the fence. She staggered back, collided with a clump of sagebrush, lost her balance and sat down abruptly, right in the middle of it.

"Ugh." She was sunk butt-down in the prickly shrub. Twigs stabbed into her back and thighs, and her scraped elbow was bleeding again. She stared at the evening sky, tears prickling. It would be dark soon. She *had* to figure this out.

"Mandy, is that you?"

The voice came from behind her. Low and a little rough. Arch Hoffman. *Again.*

"Yes," she said casually. Like she always passed the time sitting in the bushes. She didn't even try to get up. What was the point? He'd seen her collide with a donkey and drop a wedding cake. He'd seen her tip over inside her truck to escape a cow. There was no dignity left for her to salvage.

"It's me. Arch."

She peered through the feathery tips of the sagebrush. He was pushing a mountain bike toward her, which seemed odd. Arch the ex-convict out for a jaunt on a bicycle? The bright blue helmet on his head didn't suit his black T-shirt and ex–bad boy glamour.

He set the bike down on the ground and hurried over. "Do you need a hand?" His silhouette was backlit by the setting sun.

She sighed, wishing this wasn't happening. "Thanks. That would be great."

He reached down and took her hands, easily lifting her out of the bushes. He turned her as if to brush off her back, then jerked away, obviously thinking better of it.

"I've got it." She ran her hands over the seat of her jeans, trying to dislodge the twigs and leaves stuck to her. Her face radiated heat, as if she'd pulled the lid off a cooking pot to peer inside.

Maybe she could distract him from her red face with a little polite chitchat. "You're doing some biking?"

A faint flush stole over his cheekbones. "I drove into town, then realized I shouldn't be driving without a license. So Todd lent me his bike."

"Oh." That explained the cheery blue helmet. It was way more Todd's style than Arch's. "That was nice of him. And it's a pretty evening for a ride."

"Yeah. Tiring, though. I'm not used to biking."

"I can understand that."

There was an awkward pause. Probably because it was time for Mandy to explain why she'd been in the bushes. "I was climbing down from the fence. I lost my balance," she told him, nodding toward the sagebrush. "Thanks for pulling me out. You seem to come by whenever I'm having a clumsy moment."

His grin was white teeth and weak knees. "Happy to oblige. You have a lot of adventures here on the ranch. Cakes flying, mini donkeys."

"It keeps me busy."

There was another silence. She was terrible at this. Tongue-tied in his big presence. His dark hair was tangled almost down to his shoulders. It wasn't fair—he even looked good in helmet head. "Why are you here?" she finally asked.

He cleared his throat, the hand he ran through

his hair making it even more wild. "I was worried about you."

"Oh." She glanced down and noticed a piece of sage caught in the ends of her hair. No wonder the guy was worried. She was a mess.

"When I saw you feeding those cattle yesterday, you seemed upset. And you're out here on this big ranch on your own and I…" He broke off, studying her face. "I was just worried."

"That's kind of you. But I'm fine." She glanced over the fence. Dakota was heading for the water trough, still limping. The poor horse needed help that Mandy couldn't give. She took a deep breath and sent all of her embarrassment out on the exhalation. "Actually, I'm *not* fine."

"What's wrong?" Arch glanced around. "Is someone bothering you? Is it one of the ranch hands?"

"What hands? They're all away. Or hurt. Or ill."

"Every single one? Mandy, why didn't you tell me? Or Todd? We can help you."

She shrugged. "I don't know. If Lori were here, she'd just take care of it all."

"There's nothing wrong with needing some help. I don't know a ton about ranching, but I'll do what I can. What do you need?"

She looked at him, wondering how much to admit. He was intimidating. But he'd also ridden all the way from town on a bike, just to check on her. "Everything. I need help with the whole thing."

He studied her carefully, and she could see understanding clicking into place behind his eyes. "You're frightened." His voice was gentle.

"Yes." The word came tumbling out. She pressed her palms to her cheeks to cool them. "I'm terrified."

"Of what, exactly? Feeding?"

"Everything. The animals. The way they move. How big they are."

"But you have that donkey, and that goat."

"They were abandoned here. I didn't want them."

He looked at the fence in front of them. "Horses?"

She shuddered. "They're the worst."

He was silent, his expression serious, no sign of the laughter or teasing she'd expected. "So why did you agree to take charge of the ranch if you're scared of the animals?"

"I didn't want to worry Lori. She's had so much responsibility for so long. I wanted her to have a break, enjoy her honeymoon and not even think about the ranch."

"You're kind like that."

She flushed. "Or dumb. I figured the ranch hands would do all the work and just check with me on any big decisions. But every one of them is suddenly having some kind of personal issue, so here I am."

"And you and your sister didn't come up with a plan in case this happened?"

"No." What the heck. She might as well confess everything. "She doesn't really know how I feel about livestock."

His eyes widened. "How is that even possible?"

Even after so many years, it was still hard to say out loud. "Our mom died...in a riding accident. Ever since, I get this terrible anxiety every time I'm near the big animals." Mandy pinched her nails into her palms, the sting bringing her mind into the present, away from the image of her mother lying broken on the ground. It was better to keep talking than to see it again.

"Someone needed to do all the things my mom had done—the cooking, the house chores, so I just stepped into that role. And Lori loves ranching, so she was happy to take on all that work."

"But didn't she ever want your help?"

It sounded crazy. It was crazy. But it was her life. "Whenever she asked me to ride or to help out with something, I just told her that I had too much housework. After a while, she stopped asking."

Arch whistled low. "And I thought my family had secrets."

"I think sometimes, in ranching families, it

feels like there isn't a lot of room for weakness. There's just too much to be done to sit around and chat about your feelings."

"Well, that I can relate to," Arch said. "Weakness was scorched out of us at an early age."

There was so much old pain behind his words. She didn't know how to respond, so she pointed to Dakota. "My biggest worry, right now, is that Lori's horse is limping."

He walked to the fence and studied the way Dakota stood, resting on her three good legs. Then he turned to face Mandy. "I can help you. With this, and with everything."

She stared, trying to fathom so much generosity. "How? It's too much of your time. Between the two ranches, you'll spend most of your days doing chores."

The corner of his mouth curled in dark humor. "What else am I going to do? I just got out of jail—I don't exactly have a busy social schedule."

She felt bad for smiling, but it was a little funny. "I can see that. But I don't want to be a burden."

"*I'm* the burden. I'm the guy who had to beg his brother and sister for a place to stay when I know full well they don't want me here."

"That's not true." The bleak tone in his voice saddened her.

"You're kind. But people have good reasons for feeling the way they do about me. I accept that."

She was silent, taking in what he'd said. It was harsh, but he was brave enough to face his past head-on.

"Anyway, you could never be a burden. You're the one who convinced Wade and Nora to let me stay. I owe you. Let me help you."

Mandy hesitated, wanting to say yes. Not wanting to need him. Why had all the strength and resilience in the family gene pool gone to Lori?

Arch seemed determined to convince her. "Let me be useful. It will give me a purpose, and I need that. I'm a little lost right now."

That made two of them. It was so tempting to give in—to turn the chores over to him and go back to her usual routines around the house. She could tend to her stray animals and focus on her baking. But something in her balked. She was so tired of her fear. She hated the way it lurked around every corner of the ranch, threatening to freeze her in her tracks.

"I'd like the help. But I don't want you to do it all for me. I want you to help *me* do the chores."

His dark eyes went wider. "I don't mind just taking them on."

She felt as surprised as he looked. But she'd been scared for too long—she couldn't even help a hurt horse. "I want to work with the animals again. I'm so tired of feeling stuck." There was no relief in the confession. Just an old weariness.

His gaze roved over her face, and the sympathy in his eyes brought a lump to her throat. "I guess I feel the same way." He hesitated. "Maybe we can get each other unstuck."

His words brought the first glimmer of hope Mandy had felt in a long time. Maybe he had his own reasons for helping her, maybe he was just trying to give his life a little focus, but that was okay. He had courage, and she needed to figure out how to get some. "I'd like that," she told him softly. "I'd really like to get unstuck."

"Well, let's get started, then. Deal?" He held out his hand to shake hers. His skin was warm and his grip firm, sheltering her hand from the cool air. They shook once, and then he spotted her scraped elbow.

"Hang on." He shifted his grip and turned her arm. "You're all messed up again."

"Just another scrape." Now that she was paying attention, it throbbed.

"A scrape on a scrape. It's full of dirt. Do you have a first aid kit in the barn?"

"It should be on the shelf by the door." She tugged her arm away. "I'll go get it."

"How about you grab that hose by the trough and clean your elbow? I'll get the kit." He turned to the barn without waiting for her answer. He was bossy, but he was looking out for her. She walked around the fence to the trough and turned on the hose. The icy well water made her gasp, but it sluiced out the dirt.

Arch came back with the white plastic box and Mandy shut off the water. He opened the lid and pulled out first aid supplies with quick, efficient movements. But his touch on her arm was surprisingly gentle. "This is gonna sting." He sprayed her wound with some kind of disinfectant that had her biting her lip, but she kept quiet. She'd shown enough weakness around Arch. At least she could tough *this* out.

He patted the area dry with gauze, then opened a big patch of a bandage and set it on her elbow. "Good as new. Almost." He smoothed the edges with fingertips that sent currents of awareness over her skin. She hadn't been touched by a man in way too long. Could he tell? Apprehension had her glancing at his face. His lips were slightly open in concentration. Black stubble patterned his cheeks. There were permanent lines between his brows, around his eyes. He was older than her, with the face of someone who'd lived hard, and not always well.

"There." He crumpled up the wrapper and gauze, shoving them in his pocket.

She could feel the place he'd touched, still echoing with sensation. She nodded and picked up the halter she'd set down before, fiddling with it to hide her confusion.

Arch packed up the kit. "I'll just go put this away."

She listened to his firm tread on the gravel as he walked back to the barn, glad for a few moments to clear her head. She obviously needed to go on a date, or talk to a guy, or do *something* if Arch Hoffman was getting her all hot and bothered. Mandy leaned on the fence, watching the horses and breathing in the cooling air. It had been so long since she'd gone on a date, she wouldn't even know what to do with herself.

Arch was back, and he leaned on the fence next to her, arms folded on the top rail while hers only made it to the middle. He watched the horses for a moment before he spoke. "Horses are big, you know. A lot of people are scared of animals this large."

"Not people around here." Mandy couldn't think of anyone else who lived on a ranch and didn't ride.

He looked down at her, and she saw an understanding that could come only from someone who'd known their own pain. "Anyone might be scared of animals after losing their mom in a riding accident. I don't think it's anything to be ashamed of."

He was being kind. But it didn't change the fact that she was weak. "All sorts of people have bad things happen to them. And they're okay afterward. So why did *I* fall apart?"

"Maybe because you've got such a big heart."

She looked at him, startled, and saw the flush that went through the stubble on his cheek. As if he hadn't meant to say the words.

"I mean, I *think* you do. I don't know you that well. But I saw how hard you were working on your sister's wedding day. I saw that little donkey you took in even when he scared you. So it seems like you're someone who cares a lot."

She examined herself in this new light he offered. "I hadn't really thought of it that way. I just figured I'm a sucker who can't say no to a stray animal."

"Because you have a big heart."

There was a lump in her throat that kept her from answering. Maybe he was right. But she hated the way her tears were always so near the surface.

Arch straightened up off the fence. "So tell me what you were trying to do with Lori's horse before that sagebrush got in your way."

"I wanted to catch her and see if there's anything stuck in her hoof."

"Got a hoof pick?"

She walked to where she'd left it on a fence post and handed it to him.

"Okay, let's get her. You want me to bring her out? It might be best if you start with a horse that's tied instead of trying to walk into that whole group."

Relief tempered her nerves. "Yes, that would be perfect."

She handed him the halter and opened the gate so he could walk over to the horses. Dakota snuffled his outstretched knuckles and stood quietly while he slipped the halter on. Arch led the mare out of the corral and tied her to a fence post.

Mandy closed the gate and took a tentative step toward them. Logically, she knew that Dakota wasn't huge—just over fifteen hands—average horse height. But thanks to her fear-fueled imagination, each time Mandy took a step closer, the mare seemed to grow another few inches.

"Stand by me." Arch held out his arm in a gesture of welcome. "Right here by her shoulder. I'll hold her head."

The mare's rich coat was glossy in the sunlight. Mandy could imagine how silky it would feel. The aroma of horse enveloped her as she made it to Arch's side and raised a shaking hand.

"You can do it," Arch said.

Dakota shifted her weight, stomped a foot, and Mandy stumbled backward, her retreat automatic.

Arch and Dakota stared at her in human and horsey astonishment.

"Wow," Arch said quietly. "This is really hard for you."

"Yup. Welcome to my world."

"Thank you," he deadpanned. "I'm glad to be here."

He'd gotten her laughing, which was probably his plan. "Now, Dakota, on the other hand, is confused. She was just wiggling around a little, no harm intended."

"Sorry, Dakota," Mandy offered.

"Why don't you stay there and get used to her. I'll check her hoof for you."

Mandy watched as he leaned into Dakota's shoulder and ran a capable hand down her leg to encourage the mare to lift her foot.

"Good call," he said. "She's got a big old rock in here."

Curiosity had Mandy taking a cautious step forward. Arch straightened a little so she could see the rock wedged between the horse's metal shoe and the frog—the soft inner part of the hoof. "Poor thing," she breathed as Arch carefully applied the pick to the edge of the rock, levering it out.

"It's good no one is riding her right now." He used the pick to point out the dark spot on the hoof where the rock had been. "That stone left a bruise. It should heal on its own as long as she has good rest and you…I mean, *we* keep her hooves clean. We'll check them each time I come." Arch set the mare's foot down gently, straightened up and ran a hand over Dakota's back.

Mandy nodded, feeling foolish. He'd made the whole process look so easy.

"You want to try to touch her again? Just let her sniff your hand?"

She couldn't, *wouldn't* be such a coward this time. Horses moved around. It was nothing to be afraid of. Mandy forced a heavy foot forward, then another. She held out her hand and let Dakota's velvet nose find her knuckles. It wasn't scary. It was soft and sweet.

"I really appreciate you getting that rock out," Mandy said. "My sister would be heartbroken if anything happened to her horse."

"I'm no expert, but I'd say if her limp isn't significantly better in a couple days, you should call the vet, just to be sure."

It felt good to have a plan. Especially uttered in Arch's confident voice. "Thanks."

He untied Dakota and backed her up a few paces, kindly ignoring Mandy's rapid retreat to open the gate and put it in between her and the moving animal. Once he'd removed the mare's halter and sent her ambling back to her dinner, he came through the gate again and helped Mandy latch it. "How's the rest of the feeding going? You want some help?"

She flushed. But couldn't turn down his offer

when just the thought of feeding cattle sent anxiety crackling across her skin. "Yeah. I do."

He fell into step beside her, and they started toward the feed barn. The moment Mandy stepped inside, the barn cats came running. They were too wild to adopt out, content to hunt mice and other creatures that were drawn to the hay stacked here.

"Hey, guys," she said, reaching for the food bowls she kept on a shelf along the wall. Kibble was stored in a metal garbage can just below. Arch helped her pry the tight lid off so she could fill the bowls.

"How many do you have right now?"

"Cats?"

"Strays."

She tried to count. "Probably about fifteen cats in or around the different barns, eight up at the house, the goat and the donkey, three rabbits and a turkey. And one dog, a really nice blue heeler, but someone is coming by to adopt him later tonight. I'm going to try to find homes for the house cats this weekend. I'll put a table up by the grocery store." She reached up to pull the hay hooks off a nail on the wall.

He held out his hand for them, and she hesitated, hating to be the girlie girl who couldn't do her own chores.

"Mandy," he said softly. "I'm about a foot taller

and probably twice your weight. Let me move the bales?"

She handed the hooks over and went to get the wire cutters they'd need. Arch tossed a hay bale into the back of the pickup truck parked at the barn's entrance. He made it look like nothing, like he was tossing a ball at the park. It felt almost unfair, seeing as how she'd pushed and pulled and heaved at each bale this morning.

And the way his muscles bunched in his arms and slid under the thin fabric of his T-shirt was unfair, too. Because she was pretty sure that no man had ever looked that good. He lifted his arm to wipe some hay off his face, and she caught a glimpse of a tattoo around the upper part of his bicep. Barbed wire, inked in black. Was it a reminder of his captivity? His roots on the ranch? His dark and prickly life that he was just starting to untangle? Whatever it was to him, it was a good reminder to her, to back off from things that were sharp and forbidding.

He turned and caught her watching him.

Flushing, she grasped for a distraction. "Thanks for helping."

"Of course." He lowered his arm and thankfully his sleeve slid down to hide his tattoo. He studied her, as if thinking something through. "Can I ask you something?"

"Yes."

"Yesterday, in the truck. When you were feeding the cattle. Were you upset at me? Because of who I am? Because of my past?"

His stark words and his automatic assumption that he was unwanted saddened her. "It wasn't you at all. I was upset that I was so scared to feed. And too ashamed to tell you. That's all."

His face seemed to lose a few of its shadows. "I'm glad to hear it." He started, as if realizing how his words might come across. "Not glad that you felt bad. Glad it wasn't *me* making you feel bad."

He'd given her relief today—he was offering his time and his help. She could do the same for him. "Look, I've heard things about you and what you did. And those things make me uncomfortable. But I also know ten years is a long time. There's no way you could come out of all that time in prison unchanged."

"I could be worse."

"But you're not. You're here helping me. Not hanging out with the people you used to. Not drinking or doing anything illegal."

"I did today. I drove. Just jumped in Wade's truck and drove to town, in violation of my parole." He took a step toward her, palms out. "There's something in me. This part of me that thinks I don't have to play by the rules."

"You'll learn," she said.

"I sure hope so." Turning away, he rammed the hooks into another bale of hay. He walked to the truck and threw it in. "How many of these bales do we need?"

"Just one more."

He walked back to get one more bale, but she wasn't going to let what had just passed between them slip away. She couldn't.

"You're being too hard on yourself," she said as she pulled the keys out of her pocket.

He delivered the last of the hay and they got into the truck. "I think there's just something inside me that's broken."

She knew the feeling well. She started the engine and drove them along the dirt lane to the upper pastures where cattle were waiting. She slowed to miss a jackrabbit that bolted out of the dusk in front of them, and glanced at Arch. He was staring out the side window, his mouth drawn into a flat line. She fought the urge to smooth her fingers over his tight jaw. A bad idea. She had to find the words to soothe him instead. "I read somewhere that it takes ninety days to break a habit."

The glance he shot her had all the shades of the growing night in it. "I don't have ninety days. I make another mistake like I did today and I'll get locked up."

"I want to help you." The words were out before she'd had time to think them through. But maybe truth was like that. It just jumped right out of your soul before you could weigh out the pros and cons.

"Why?"

"Why do *you* want to help *me*?" she countered.

His laugh cut through the cab. "Because you've been kind to me from the moment you laid eyes on me. And because maybe I need to help someone."

"Well, maybe I need to help someone, too." She pulled up by the gate, uneasily eyeing the milling cattle on the other side.

He put a hand on the door as if he was ready to get out into the night air. "Just remember, not every stray can be helped."

Something rose in her. A need to fight the darkness that was threatening to pull him back down, after all he'd been through to claw his way out.

"Ha." She cut the engine and set the brake with a vehement shove of her foot. "You don't know me, Arch Hoffman. You think you do, but there's a lot more to me than some girl who's scared of horses and has too many cats. I'll help you get your new life started, just like you're going to help me feed these cattle. So get used to it." She shoved her door open and stepped out into the evening chill.

He came around the front of the truck and stood tall over her, his eyes darker than dusk as they flickered over her face. "I don't know what the hell I did to deserve your belief in me. But I'm grateful for it. More than I can possibly explain."

Each word was a confession of something more. Of his loneliness. Of a man who'd rarely had anyone on his side. She could see it so clearly, even here in the almost dark of the day.

And then he turned away and she heard the clank of the opening tailgate, the snick of the wire cutters releasing the hay. The dry sound as he pulled the bale apart.

The air around her came alive with this connection between them. This strange and unexpected bond that mattered more to her than anything had in a long, long time.

CHAPTER SEVEN

ARCH TOOK A bite of Mandy's blueberry muffin and was transported to another planet. A happy place where nothing mattered but sugary, fluffy bread. He closed his eyes and just went with it. If this was breakfast, then what the hell had he been eating in prison all those years? None of these flavors, or this cloud-soft texture, had existed behind bars.

He opened his eyes when Mandy set a cup of hot coffee in front of him, the rich smell rising like perfume from every exotic place he'd ever read about. "If I could make food like this, I'd never leave my kitchen," he told her.

"I'm glad you like it." She leaned over and added two more muffins to the plate in front of him and he just about wept. "Seems like the least I could do since you got up early to help with my morning chores."

"Well, if this is my reward, you're not getting rid of me. All of your employees will return to work, your sister and my brother will come back from their honeymoon, and I'll still be showing up every morning, begging for muffins. Another stray on the back porch."

Her smile was like sunlight after a rainstorm. He'd crack lame jokes all day just to see it. Maybe he needed to think of a few to tell her during chores. She'd been just as nervous around the animals this morning as she had last night.

Now it was his turn to be nervous. Because after chores she'd announced that now *she* was going to help *him*. He'd followed her into her kitchen worried that her version of help might be preachy lectures.

But miracle of miracles, so far Mandy's form of help wasn't a lecture. It was muffins. A brilliant move. Because the promise of food like this was enough to get anyone to change their life for the better.

Mandy pulled out a notebook, a pen and a big stack of paper from a drawer. Then she sat across from him at the scarred pine table. "Let's make a list," she said.

"About what?" His mouth was half-full of muffin. Undignified. Bad mannered. But he couldn't stop eating.

"You." Mandy tapped her pencil, all business. "I said I'd help you and I meant it."

Uh-oh. He caught the set of her jaw, the narrowed determination in her eyes. She might be a damsel in distress when it came to working with large animals, but Mandy was clearly a force to be reckoned with when she had a stray like him in need of rescuing.

"You like hopeless causes, don't you?" He sipped the coffee and felt it go straight to his early-rising soul.

"Hopeless?" She gave an exasperated eye roll. "Don't you think you're being a little melodramatic?"

He grinned at that. "Maybe."

"You just got out of jail and you're overwhelmed. I get it. Thus, the list." She scribbled a couple of words down on the paper. "It's what I do whenever things feel like too much for me. So…" She tapped her pencil on the notebook. "Driver's license. That's the first thing, right?"

"It would certainly help," he told her.

She picked up the thick stack of paper and handed it across the table. "California driver's handbook. I printed it out for you last night. So you can start studying."

He stared at the huge packet. She'd dropped him off at Marker Ranch last night and then gone home to do this. For him. He cleared his throat. "Thanks," he told her, ruffling the edges of the packet. "This will help a lot."

She nodded briskly. "Now, what about a job? You're busy with Marker Ranch right now, and helping me, but maybe you could find something for just a few hours a week, to build up some references?"

"If I can find someone around here to hire me, absolutely."

"What are you interested in doing?"

"Making money. Getting off welfare."

She kicked him under the table. "Be serious! If you could do any job, what would it be?"

He knew the answer, way down deep. But saying it out loud was difficult. "It's probably a long shot, but does anyone in this town do metalwork?"

Her pencil hovered above the paper. "You mean sheet metal?"

"I mean all kinds of stuff. It could be sheet metal or signs, maybe railings, or gates...or even art." His voice deflated a little on the last word. Funny how the things you wanted the most were the hardest to say.

She looked at him sharply, obviously curious. "There's a guy who does stuff like that. He's out east of town on some big property in the desert. People say he builds big metal animals, but he doesn't let anyone in to see them. I wonder if Todd knows him. He knows everyone."

"I'll look him up." Arch tried to hold down the hope inside. The guy could say no. Would probably say no.

"I'm putting it on the list. Now. Church. You can come with me if you want."

"Church?" She had to be nuts. Or really religious. "I'm not a believer."

She drilled him with that determined look again. Tinker Bell on a mission. "You want to show people you've changed, right? Going to church is a great way to do that. And who knows? You might even like it."

Arch thought of Pastor Doug. How he spoke of God without all the blame and shame. "I'll consider it."

"Good." Mandy added it to the list. Arch was relieved to see she'd put a question mark at the end of the word. "Do you need to make amends?"

She said it matter-of-factly, as if she was asking if he needed to do his laundry. He bought time by washing his last bite of muffin down with a gulp of coffee. "Absolutely, but what do I do? Walk around town telling everyone I'm sorry?"

"I don't really know. It just seems like it might be important. Does it bother you? What you did when you lived here before?"

Arch stared into his coffee cup, swirling the liquid left at the bottom as if the simple answer she expected might be in there. "Sure it does. But sometimes it seems like that guy that did those things isn't me. Except, of course, I know that he *is* me. Or, at least, a part of me." He glanced up, trying to see if she understood. Her encouraging nod had him trying again. "I do want to make amends. But I also want to move on from that guy, as fast as possible."

He was stumbling on words, saying too much. Her quiet listening drew out thoughts he didn't even realize were inside him. He endured the answering silence. Finally he looked up, bracing himself for the pity in her eyes. And saw something that looked like respect. Which made no sense.

"I'll put it on the list," she said quietly. "I know you'll figure out what you want to do about it."

There it was again. That faith she had in him. Faith he couldn't possibly deserve.

She wrote down one more thing. He read it upside down.

"Fun?"

"How long has it been since you had any?" She tore off the paper and handed it to him. "Here you go! Not a long list. Doable. Just put it in your pocket and add to it if you think of anything."

"Right." He took the list and folded it, suppressing the urge to laugh at her naive belief that his problems could be fixed by a simple to-do list. But he'd take it, because she offered. Because she was sweet and she was trying.

"Okay, then." She stood up suddenly. "Let's go."

"Go where?" he asked.

"Driving practice. Around the ranch. You want to check something off that list, right?"

He stood, too. "Sure."

"Well, the only way to do that is to get started."

She turned on her heel and headed out the kitchen door. Arch followed, feeling a little dazed, realizing maybe that he'd underestimated the power of Mandy's list.

She stepped lightly down the porch and the strangest dog he'd ever seen bounded up from a dog bed and followed her, running in circles in the morning sun. It was small and it looked a bit like a terrier, but long golden fur sprouted from its body in every direction. It jumped and bounced as if it was too happy to take note of gravity.

"Snack!" Mandy stopped and crouched down, letting the little dog rush up and plant a kiss on her cheek. Lucky dog.

Arch knelt down next to her and let the dog sniff his knuckles with its black nose. "Is this Lori's dog?"

"Yes, this is Snack. He's been in a state of total depression since she left. Seems like he might be snapping out of it a little."

Snack sat and offered Arch a tiny paw, his tail wagging in a blur of movement. Arch looked into the animal's dark brown eyes. "Pleased to meet you," he said, shaking the proffered paw solemnly.

"Let's bring him with us for driving practice." Mandy straightened and headed for the truck.

Arch followed, trying not to notice the way her jeans hugged her curves, how she'd tucked them into her brown cowgirl boots, how her blond hair bounced in a wave of sunshine down her back. He wanted to wrap his fingers in a golden strand. He wanted to put his hands on her perfect hips. But what he wanted didn't matter, because things that were golden and perfect had to be earned. And out of jail, on welfare, with no idea what he was doing with his life meant that he hadn't earned the right to even think about her that way.

Plus, Mandy would never feel anything for him. She'd probably be horrified if she knew how hard it was for him to pull his eyes away from her beauty. She was offering help and friendship because they were family by marriage, and because that was just how she was. She'd offer friendship to a hungry bear if it needed a helping hand.

He caught the keys she tossed his way and they climbed into the truck. "Hang on tight to that dog," Arch advised. "I'm a little rusty at this."

Mandy put on her seat belt and settled Snack on her lap with her arms wrapped tight around him. "Let her rip," she said cheerfully, shooting out a hand to catch herself on the dashboard when he pressed too hard on the accelerator and shot them forward. "You *are* rusty."

"As an old nail in a rainstorm," he rolled out, gratified to hear her giggle.

He eased the truck forward more carefully now and started them down the lane that ran east toward the high desert and some of the lower pastures that Mandy told him were mainly used in the spring. There were ruts in the dirt road, and Arch used them as an opportunity to practice slowing down, easing over the bumps and accelerating again. He'd have to travel about an hour south to the town of Bishop to get his license, so he wanted to make sure he passed the test the first time around.

"You're doing well."

Mandy was practically sitting in crash position. He wasn't really doing that well. "How'd you get like this?"

"Like what?"

"So supportive. Like you're everyone's personal cheering squad."

She smacked his shoulder lightly. Little-sister style. "It's not like that! I think I was just taught, growing up, to look for the good in people. And to help them."

"That must have been nice." It was hard not to be jealous. Most people took it for granted— being taught right from wrong. He saw it now for the gift it was.

"You were raised opposite."

"I was raised mean. It's how my dad was. It's what he taught my older brother, and me." The

road turned parallel to the Sierras. The view of
the mountains rolling south was spectacular, and
he stopped the truck to take it in.

"It just doesn't seem fair." Her voice held a
pinch of wistful and a cup of sad.

"It wasn't. But Nora and Wade had the same
dad. And they didn't end up like him. So I can't
sit here and blame him, or my screwed-up childhood. Two people in my family rose above it all.
I sank like a stone. There's a personal flaw that
causes that. And I have to accept that."

She wrinkled her nose a little. "Well, I guess
that's kind of the same in all families. After my
mom died, Lori became this big success. Did
great in school, went to college, and now she runs
the ranch. I got scared and started baking. And
here I'm still here. Baking."

"Are you still scared?"

"You've seen me." She focused her attention
on the dog on her lap, petting the fluffy fur on its
huge ears. Snack lay down with a sigh of bliss.

"I'm not just talking about the animals." He
cut the engine and turned on the seat to face her.
"You talk about baking as if it's something bad.
Or that you're doing it because you're too scared
to go do anything else. But you love it, right?"

"I do." Her voice went all happy and dreamy.
"When a cake comes out just right, or when my
croissants are that perfect combination of soft in-

sides and crisp, flaky layers, I feel like everything's right."

"So what do you want to do with that? Is the
baking business you have now what you want?"

She paled, looked out the window. "Sure."

He'd seen that cake. He knew her talent. "Do
you have other dreams?"

Her voice came out in miniature. "I think, sometimes, that I'd like to go to cooking school."

Somehow he'd known that was there. A big
dream. "So why not go?"

She shook her head. "Lori needs me."

"Lori has Wade now. I think she's okay." He
was pushing at her just like she'd pushed that
list at him this morning. Because she was smart
and talented and it was clear she was hiding out
on this ranch.

She stared out the window, and for a moment
he was hopeful that she'd agree with him. But
she shook her head, briefly, resolutely. "My life's
here," she said. "I don't need school to teach me
stuff. I can figure it out myself." She turned to
him and gathered the little dog close. "This view
is incredible."

Subject changed. He'd pushed too hard. He
watched her profile, wishing he could trace it
with his finger. Her nose was just slightly turned
up. Her chin small but resolute. Her lips full and
pink and stubborn.

She glanced at him. Solemn blue eyes the color of the flowers he'd seen growing outside the prison walls each spring. Chicory, someone had told him. "I don't know why I can talk to you. I've never talked to anyone. About any of this." She reached out for his hand and took it in her own. It was like being held by a flower.

He wanted to bring her hand up and kiss her petal fingers. He closed his other hand over hers instead. Cherishing it. Rumbling out through the feelings forming in his chest. "I'm grateful I can talk to you, too." It wasn't nearly enough of what he wanted to say.

"I'm glad we're friends."

He closed his eyes for a moment, taking the word in. So much there that he was grateful for. So much else he could still want. "So am I," he said, giving her hand a brief squeeze.

He let go, missing the feel of her immediately, and looked out at the view. "So much open space. Do you ever get out there? Go hiking in the high desert? Or climb one of these mountains?"

"I haven't much."

What was he thinking? Her mom had died out in the wilderness. Chances were she'd lost her taste for mountain exploration. But he had to ask, because he was selfish and because maybe it would help her. "You want to try sometime? With me?"

She smiled, but he could see the doubt in her

eyes. "Maybe." It was a fragment of a promise. "I'll see." She picked up Snack and cuddled him to her chest. "Ready to keep driving?"

The conversation was closed. That was clear. So he'd focus on his driving for now. But he saw so much in her that she couldn't. And he knew one thing for sure. If Mandy Allen would give herself the chance to shine, she'd be one of the brightest stars this planet had ever seen.

THE DAMN LIST was burning a hole in Arch's pocket. Mandy must have put some crazy good-girl voo-doo on it, because here he was, just twenty-four hours after she'd written it, standing in front of the Benson liquor store, trying to find the courage to go in.

Trying to face his first attempt at making amends.

A delivery truck turned into the driveway while he watched and pulled alongside the building. The driver unloaded some boxes and a couple of kegs at the side door, then went inside for a moment. Arch waited, hoping to catch Mr. Howell alone. Apologizing was hard enough. He didn't want an audience.

He wiped sweaty palms on his jeans as the truck driver pulled away. Took a few steps toward the front door only to see Mr. Howell step out the side door, where his supplies were stacked. Arch hit mute on the fears cautioning him to walk away and veered up the side driveway. "Mr. Howell," he called.

The elderly man looked up, his beige cardigan hanging loose around him. Mr. Howell had been old back when Arch had been so horrible to him. He was a whole lot older now. "Mr. Howell," he said again. "Let me help you."

"Thanks, son." Mr. Howell nodded and stooped to pick up a cardboard box.

"I've got it," Arch assured him, kneeling to lift it before the store owner could hurt himself.

"Thank you." Mr. Howell turned to hold the side door open for Arch. The color left his face. "You."

"Let me do this for you?" Arch paused by the threshold, waiting for permission. "It can't change who I was. Or what I did. But I'd truly appreciate the chance to say I'm sorry."

The older man's watery eyes narrowed behind his spectacles. "Okay." His voice was quiet. Accepting. "But I have security cameras now."

Arch winced. What had he cost this guy? "You won't need them on my account," he told him as he eased the box through the doorway.

Mr. Howell followed him into the shop aisles and pointed the way to a storage room.

Arch set the box down, took a breath and faced Mr. Howell. "I was horrible to you. I bullied you and abused you. If there was a way to take it back,

I would. But I can't. So I'm here to tell you that I turned myself in years ago. I went to jail and served almost ten years. And if you'll let me, I'd like to carry the rest of those boxes and kegs in here for you."

Mr. Howell leaned on the doorway of the store-room, watching him warily. "I was glad when you and your family left town."

Arch understood the unspoken question there. "I'm not staying. But while I'm here I'd like to try to do some good."

He waited, and finally Mr. Howell nodded once. "I'd appreciate the assistance."

Arch followed him back through the shop. He didn't blame the store owner for supervising him closely as he stowed the kegs in the big refrigerator in the back and hauled the rest of the boxes to the storeroom. Plus he was glad of the guidance. The amount of stuff for sale, the colors, smells—it was all a lot to take in. His senses had been muffled in plain beige prison walls for a long time.

When it was done, he thought about asking for a handshake. But didn't. It would imply that they were even, that what Arch owed was all squared away. And a few minutes of hauling boxes wouldn't fix years of harassment. So he just said, "Thanks for giving me the opportunity, Mr. Howell. I understand that it doesn't change what I did. But I hope it helps."

The older man stuck his hand out. Surprised, Arch took it, giving the frail man's papery grasp a quick shake. "It helps, son," Mr. Howell said. "Good luck to you."

"And to you." Arch walked out the side door and back to where he'd locked Todd's bike. Mandy's list was still heavy in his back pocket, but he could swear his shoulders felt a little bit lighter.

CHAPTER EIGHT

THE CARROT STICK in Mandy's hand was shaking like a leaf in a windstorm. She commanded her wrist to settle down, reminded herself that this was just a teeny, tiny donkey. But the carrot still wobbled.

The miniature donkey eyed the vibrating carrot suspiciously and took a careful step forward on its tiny hooves, snuffling at her knuckles. Mandy bit her lip to stop the squeak that almost escaped her lips. Her fear made no sense. The donkey was less than three feet high—the size of a golden retriever.

The donkey took another tentative sniff, its breath making two tiny clouds in the early-morning chill. It reached out with tickling lips and took the carrot.

Mandy ran a hand through the fluffy gray fur on its neck, relishing the softness. She offered another piece of carrot. "Good boy." She kept her voice quiet. He was as jumpy as she was. Slowly she reached for the tiny halter she'd picked up at the feed store and slid it over his nose. She slipped the other strap behind his ears, buckling by his cheek. One last carrot bite and she hooked on the lead rope.

It was a small victory. She hadn't run out of the pen, or climbed the fence, or cried. True, a miniature donkey didn't count as a large animal, but this was a start. And she'd done it all by herself.

The donkey rubbed his forehead on her thigh, sending her heart crashing into her lungs. Animals should sound a warning signal when they moved. Like trucks that beeped as they backed up. Mandy braced herself and let him rub against her. Once he was comfortable with her, she'd probably be his personal scratching post.

"Okay, enough," she told him when her heart had slowed enough to let her speak. "Let's go for a stroll." It was an overcome-her-fears kind of stroll. She was determined to make progress, even when Arch wasn't around.

She opened the gate, trying to ignore the goat's pathetic bleats from the stall. It clearly wanted to come, too, but she wasn't up to handling two animals at once. She led the donkey into the lane and turned toward the ranch house. He trotted obligingly next to her, happy to be outside his pen for the first time since he'd arrived last weekend.

Last weekend. It hadn't even been a week since the wedding, but everything about life felt different. Because of her newborn courage. Because of Arch.

But here she was, thinking about him again. And she shouldn't. Not in this pathetic, breathless kind of way. She needed to focus. Had to get used to hoofbeats so close by again. To herky-jerky livestock movements. It wasn't the time to be distracted by inappropriate thoughts of her ex-convict brother-in-law.

The donkey blew out a long breath. He nuzzled her leg. He was sweet. This was *fun*. It reminded her of childhood days spent at 4-H contests. She jogged, urging the donkey into a trot.

When they slowed, she let the donkey munch grass for a few minutes and then turned them back toward the pen. The other reason she'd forced herself to overcome her fears today was that his pen really needed cleaning. It was time to grab a shovel and wheelbarrow and do the dirty work.

She was just pushing the loaded wheelbarrow through the gate when Arch rode up on his bike. He was more confident now, sailing over bumps in the lane like a pro. "Watch this," he called, circling around and pedaling up a pile of dirt near the barn. He went airborne off it, standing on his pedals to land. He skidded to a stop and flashed her a grin that took the past ten years off his face. "I'm getting better, right?"

"Absolutely." She had that fluttery feeling she'd

had in sixth grade, when Danny Carver popped a wheelie for her after school. Apparently some things didn't change between boys and girls.

She was learning that now. Far later than most people did. Hiding out on this ranch meant she'd hidden from all the stuff normal people her age did. Like dating. Like sex. But now she wished she'd gotten herself some experience. If she had, maybe she'd be able to think more clearly around Arch.

Because Arch was definitely trouble. It was fine to help him get back on his feet. It was okay to be friends. But it was not okay to develop some kind of bad-boy crush.

"I'll be back in a minute." She shoved the wheelbarrow out into the lane and stomped to the manure pile behind the barn, frustrated with the way the whole world seemed a little brighter whenever Arch showed up.

Because it was wrong. Wrong to think about the electric current in the air when he smiled. Wrong to think about what it would be like to trace that barbed-wire tattoo with her fingertips. Wrong to think about how much she wanted to kiss him.

She crashed the wheelbarrow into the smelly pile with a vigor that sent the manure flying. There had to be a way to tamp down these thoughts. She wasn't a risk taker. And Arch Hoffman, ex-criminal, barely out of jail, was a walking, talking risk.

Yanking the wheelbarrow around, she started back. She'd hid out on this ranch, avoiding any chance of heartache. But it had come for her all on its own. She'd be an idiot to chase after Arch. So she'd just have to find a way to get over these feelings.

Arch had fed the goat and the little donkey by the time she got back. He'd taken off his blue bike helmet and pulled a gray knit cap over his head. It was the tail end of October, and you could feel it in the mornings. "You put a halter on Shrimp."

"Shrimp?" She set the wheelbarrow down.

"The donkey. I named him Shrimp the other day, during the wedding. Temporarily, of course. Maybe you'd rather call him Gus. Or Zeke. Or some other donkey-like name."

She looked down at the miniature fluff ball, chewing his miniature bite of hay. "Shrimp. I like it."

"And now you're an official donkey wrangler. That's a huge step. Congratulations." Arch raised his hand up for a high five.

She smacked his hand. "Why, thank you." His eyes met hers, and she thought she saw laughter there and something more. Affection. Connection. *No.* That was her imagination again. And right now her imagination was not her friend.

"I think it's a sign." He gave her a wink.

"Of what?"

"That you're ready to feed the horses with me. No more standing at the fence."

Her laugh had the jitters. "You must be seeing things in me that I can't."

"Come on." He took a step toward the barn, then stopped, holding out his hand. "Let's grab the hay and go for it."

"Let's grab the hay and I'll *think* about it." No way was she touching his hand, so she shoved hers in the pockets of her shearling coat and fell into step beside him.

He told her about his ride over while they went to the feed barn for hay—about how he'd seen a coyote hunting in a field alongside the road. It passed the time, because in moments they had the hay they needed and Mandy was peeking through the fence at the horses.

Dakota was doing better, thank goodness, her limp barely noticeable at all now. But walking into the pasture with her and her five roomies at feeding time was still intimidating.

Arch set the bale on the ground and handed Mandy a stuffed burlap sack. "I put a few flakes of alfalfa hay in here. You can climb up on the fence and toss them into the corral. That way, anyone who gets too pushy will have a distraction when we go inside with the rest of the hay."

Even though she'd helped Arch with the chores the past couple of days, her nerves were still on edge. But she *had* to get over her fears. Arch was keeping a grueling schedule to help her. Coming over here twice a day when he had Marker Ranch to tend to. She needed to step up so he didn't have to.

"Okay." She opened the sack and pulled out a flake of hay, wondering if anyone had ever cracked a rib with a pounding heart. "Let's do it."

"You've got this," he told her. "Just remember that fear is only one feeling among a whole lot of possible feelings."

She stopped and stared. "Very philosophical. But I'm not sure I can choose whether I'm frightened or not. Case in point." She backed away from the fence as the hungry horses approached.

Arch pinned her with a serious look. "When I was in jail, I had to choose my feelings every day. It was natural to choose the negative stuff, like fear. But I saw what that did to other guys. How it brought them down. So I learned to focus on better things. Like my plans for the future. Or a good book and a decent conversation. You can choose which feelings you give your time to."

He turned away, looking self-conscious, as if talking a lot was new to him.

But he had a point. In theory she should be able

to choose something besides fear. She'd done it this morning with the donkey, hadn't she?

She stepped up to the fence. And froze as the big animals jostled each other, tossing their heads, excited for feeding time.

"Throw the alfalfa as far into the corral as you can."

The command in Arch's voice was just what she needed. Mandy threw the hay, and the big gray horse veered off to get it.

"See? The rest are pretty calm. They'll just follow along. Throw the rest in a different spot."

She threw more hay, and soon all the horses were occupied. Arch led the way to the gate, opened it and led her inside.

It was ten steps to the feeder. Mandy counted each one. By step five she could feel horsey breath around her as a few of the animals left their alfalfa snack to accompany her and Arch. The horses embodied motion, muscle and energy, but thankfully they stayed a few feet away.

Arch opened up the bale and tossed the hay into different sections of the feeder so the horses each had their own space to eat. And that was it. The horses were munching peacefully, and Mandy hadn't had to talk to them or direct them or touch them. She hadn't had to interact with them at all.

Strangely, suddenly, she wanted to. Dakota was closest, and Mandy took a step toward her, reaching out to put a hand on her shoulder. The mare's muscles moved beneath the smooth silk of her coat. The motion was familiar and laced with that wonder Mandy remembered from when she was young.

Dakota shifted toward her, and Mandy backed away.

"You're doing great," Arch murmured.

The breath Mandy drew in was shaky but perfumed with horses. And that scent tugged at her, evoking warm summer days riding bareback with Lori. How fun that had been. What a carefree time they'd had.

"Are you ready to go?"

"In a moment." She stepped forward and put her hand on Dakota again. Ran her palm down the horse's strong neck. Tangled fingers in her long mane. "See you later, Dakota."

Arch didn't say anything as they walked out of the pasture. But once he'd latched the gate behind them, he put an arm around Mandy and pulled her into his side in a half hug. "I'm proud of you. That was a big thing you just did."

It felt good to lean on him. She'd been standing on her own for so long. "Thanks for getting me to try."

He looked down at her, pride glinting in his eyes. "How does it feel? Being someone who hangs out with horses?"

She laughed, looking up at him from her cozy rest under his arm. "I'm not sure a couple pats counts as hanging out with them. But it feels like progress."

"You're amazing." He leaned down, and for a moment of total inner chaos she thought he was going to kiss her. And she wanted him to, desperately. But he brushed his lips over the top of her hair and released her. "You'll be riding again before you know it."

Gratitude for this step, for the courage he'd helped her find, overrode her good sense. Her hand went up, almost as if it had a will of its own, to touch the rough stubble of his cheek. The bumpiness was reflected in her breathing. "Thank you, Arch. For helping me like this."

Something dark and soft altered his expression. His free hand traced a lock of her hair from forehead to shoulder. "It's good for both of us, I think."

She shouldn't kiss him, no matter how much she wanted to. Starting something with him would be an enormous mistake. He was wrong for her, and his life was in chaos. She managed to pull her gaze away from his mouth, but it took all her willpower. She had none left to resist the impulse to slide her arms around his neck.

She felt him start, stiffen, and then slowly he brought his arms down to wrap around her shoulders. Tentatively his head came down to rest against hers. He was warmth and strength, and Mandy wanted to cling to him forever. But instead she stepped back, shyness making it almost impossible to glance up at him. But she did, and he looked shattered, dazed.

Her hands went to her mouth. "I'm so sorry," she said. "That wasn't... I mean, I didn't..."

He held up a hand to stop her babbling. "No, I'm sorry. It was great. I just..." He shook his head, and it was odd to see this confident man at such a loss. She could swear there were tears in his eyes when his voice cut quietly across the awkward space between them. "Hell, Mandy, I don't know the last time someone held on to me like that."

The loneliness of it lanced her heart. "I didn't mean to make you uncomfortable," she blurted through embarrassed misery.

"That's not what I meant." He stepped closer, took her hand. "It just took me by surprise."

It was automatic to step back into his arms when he pulled her. To feel his strength around her and over her. To hear his heartbeat so steady and his breathing so strong. To hear him whisper a reverent *thank you*. She closed her eyes, inhaling him. Something spicy and sweet. The salt of his bike ride from Marker Ranch. Fresh air. Alfalfa hay. Arch.

And then he set her gently away and his dark eyes glittered. "Thank you, Mandy. You can't know what you just gave me."

What to say to that? *You're welcome* was weird. She nodded, mute.

He motioned to the barn. "I'm gonna go feed the cattle now." His voice had gravel in it. It was clear he needed space, and she could use some, too.

"I have baking to do."

"Right. So I'll just see you later." He turned, striding for the barn as if he was afraid she'd chase him.

There wasn't a chance of that. Any courage she'd mustered was all used up and fear was back and raging. Her feelings were never small. They were never shallow. When her mom died, Mandy's emotions had threatened to pull her under. It had taken her years to find a way to contain them. And now that she'd opened her heart to Arch, even for a moment, she was in danger of being overwhelmed again. She sprinted to the house, needing the solid feel of its familiar walls between her and the mistake she'd just made.

ARCH TOOK A pull from his water bottle and shoved it back into the holder on the bike. He tried to shove his thoughts away, too. *Don't think about it. Don't think about holding Mandy this morning.*

Or about the comfort, so unfamiliar, so seductive that he'd wanted to keep holding on until his lost soul got found.

But he'd set her away, put space between them, because finding himself might take years. And no way would he be Mandy Allen's burden—he had to deal with his own lost soul. So here he was, squinting through the afternoon sunlight at the simple metal sign on a post at the end of a dirt road. The cutout script scrawled the name Dalton Carter across steel mottled with blues and browns in the artist's signature patina.

He'd looked the guy up on the iPhone Todd had gifted him. There'd been a few articles, all mentioning how Dalton was reclusive, living way out here, an hour's bike ride east of Benson, immersed in the fantastic metal creations he sold in galleries all over the world.

Arch's hand went automatically to the phone, zipped safely inside his coat pocket. There'd been no such thing as an iPhone when he went to prison. He'd read about them while he was in there and seen one occasionally in the hands of a guard. He figured it would be years before he had the money to buy one. But thanks to Todd, he had his own rectangular piece of magic. A link to the world that he'd stayed up half the night exploring. Benefits, parole information, job descriptions, articles were all right there inside that amazing phone.

But it was one thing reading about stuff on the phone and another thing to track down Dalton Carter in person. Nerves wove tight in Arch's stomach, but he couldn't let them win. He had a dream, and the only way to reach it was to intrude on a man who reportedly hated visitors. To knock on his door and beg for a chance.

Arch put his boot on the pedal and started down the driveway.

Dalton Carter's house was long and low, with weathered wood posts and big plates of glass making it seem almost a part of the desert scrub surrounding it. It was a nice house, but it was the old barn that drew Arch's eye. All around it were sculptures, some finished, some only halfway there. Fantastical intricate flowers and trees, dragons and birds. Purposely rusted or iridescent with color. An installation off to the left was part windmill, part sculpture, with abstract colors and shapes weaving in and out of each other. A graceful dance in the afternoon wind.

In other words, Arch's definition of heaven. He got off the bike, took it all in.

A man walked out of the barn, a curved arc of iron in his hand. He was so intent on the sculpture he was heading toward that he didn't even notice Arch. He was older, with long graying hair in a ponytail past his shoulders. His denim shirt was tucked into khaki work pants. Steel-toed boots clumped in the dust.

"Dalton?" Arch called, but the word faltered in the vast sky around him. He cleared his lungs of road dust and tried again. "Dalton Carter?"

The man looked up, and even from this distance, Arch could see the lines of his face knit into a frown.

"Who the hell wants to know?" The artist didn't move. Just shaded his eyes with one hand, studying him.

"I'm Arch Hoffman. I was hoping to talk to you for a moment."

"Talk to my agent if you want an interview." He kept walking.

"No disrespect, but I didn't bike an hour for an interview." Arch pushed his bike closer.

Dalton Carter turned, his free hand curling to a fist. "I don't care why the hell you're here. I've got work to do."

"I want to learn from you." Arch stopped a few yards away. He could see the other man better now, the dirt on his clothing, the black on his hands, the mistrust in his eyes. He didn't want Arch here. Wouldn't help him.

But these sculptures, the beauty of them… Arch had to try. "I grew up around here. I just got out of jail. I served almost ten years' time.

I learned some metalwork there and it's what I want to do. Now that I'm out."

Dalton studied him, his hand on the metal piece clenched white. "Head up north to Reno. There are plenty of guys up there selling sheet metal. One of them will hire you."

Arch gulped down the doubt crawling up his throat. "That's not the kind of work I want to do. I want to create. There was a guy who came and taught workshops to inmates. You might know him. He goes by one name. Thorn? He said I had talent." Name-dropping was a desperate move, but he'd throw all he had at this chance.

"Thorn?"

It was clear from the disgust in Dalton's tone that Thorn hadn't been the right name to drop.

"That guy and his found-object art?" Dalton took a few steps closer and jabbed a finger toward Arch. "The guy welded a bunch of flea-market forks to a sheet of metal and called it art! Where's the skill in that? Where is the craft?"

Arch wondered if he should just get on his bike and ride away. It was bad enough that he'd blown his chance here. He didn't need his disappointment served with a side of tirade.

"That guy took an oil drum and cut a hole in it. Put it on display and said it represented environmental destruction!" Dalton was pacing now.

"He wrapped barbed wire around a garden hoe and said it was an indictment of big agriculture!"

Arch's disappointment was transforming to worry. Dalton's fury bulged his veins. He looked about ready to have a heart attack, and Arch had never learned CPR.

"I can understand your frustration with his art. He gave a slideshow of his pieces and I didn't love them, either. But he was kind enough to give his time to a bunch of felons and he taught me a few skills."

It worked. Dalton slowed down. Stopped. Crossed his arms. Waited.

"I'd like to learn more from you. I'll pay you back with chores, I'll clean up or do some basic welding. Whatever would be helpful."

Dalton tapped his blunt, stained fingers on the piece of iron, staring off over Arch's shoulder somewhere. It was Arch's cue to leave. It was hard to speak through the thick frustration. He'd tried not to get his hopes up. But that hug from Mandy this morning had felt like a miracle and had given him the idea that maybe the day would provide a second one, as well.

"Thanks for listening to me, Mr. Carter." He turned the bike, walking it back toward the lane. It was hard to keep his head high when it felt so heavy.

"So you were in prison?"

Arch stopped. Swung the bike around. "Yes."

"What did you do?" Dalton's growl was rough with suspicion, but at least he was asking.

"I did all kinds of petty crimes around here. Car theft, cattle theft—all kinds of theft, really. And I made meth and sold it, too."

The scowl lines carved deeper. "Did you take it?"

"Nope."

Dalton nodded slowly. "Well, at least it shows you have half a brain. You still doing anything illegal?"

"I drove my brother's truck once without a license. Scared me so bad I'm riding this thing now." Arch tapped the handlebar with the sticky palm of his hand. He needed this break. *Please.*

"So you're not here to run off with my copper or anything like that."

"No, sir." Arch reached into his back pocket and held out Steve's business card. "My parole officer. You're welcome to contact him."

Dalton took it. Studied it. Shoved it in his pocket. "Park that bike. Let's see what you can do."

Arch stared. "You're serious?"

"Can you weld?"

"Of course!" Arch rolled the bike over to the side of the barn and leaned it there. And realized that he'd been wearing the goofy blue helmet for the entire interview. *Great.* He yanked it off and turned to see Dalton disappearing into the barn. He followed and almost collided with a fireproof welding shirt, held out at the end of Dalton's arm.

"Put this on." Dalton's voice was back to a bear's growl.

Arch slid his arms through the familiar heavy fabric. "Show me what you want done."

Dalton threw two pieces of steel scrap on the table. "Join 'em. Right angle." He pointed to the welding torch and stepped back, arms folded. Making it clear that this was a test.

Arch pulled the helmet over his head. Slid the gloves over hands that shook a little. Put a piece of steel into the clamp at the edge of the table. Eyed it. Shifted it. Then he switched on the torch and everything else went dark.

Heat. Mesmerizing. Light and spark. Shutting off everything else. He guided the flame, watching for that moment when the bond was clear. *There.* He shut it off. Pulled off his mask and waited for Dalton's steel-toed boot to kick him out the door on his ass.

The older man creaked when he bent over. He eyed the weld from all possible angles. Arch tried to read his expression in the dim light, his future hanging on every squint of the artist's eye, every line of his downturned mouth.

"Again." Dalton set two more pieces of scrap on the table. "A forty-five-degree angle this time."

Arch clamped the pieces and pulled his face mask down. The flame burned, the sparks shooting in random celebration. Because Dalton Carter hadn't said no yet. And maybe that was the second miracle of the day.

CHAPTER NINE

ARCH BALANCED THE cat carrier carefully, but yowls of protest still emerged in outraged waves. A few shoppers on their way into the downtown market glanced his way. He was starting to regret volunteering for Mandy's cat adoption. "Where do you want the noisy one?"

"Here by me." Mandy pointed to the end of the table. "He'll need the hard sell."

Arch set the carrier down. The cat complained again. Arch couldn't really blame him. If he'd been living with Mandy, he wouldn't want to be adopted out, either.

He grabbed the tape and helped Mandy attach the poster-board sign to the table. It had Adopt a Cat Today! painted on it in purple letters. He couldn't quite believe he was doing this. The craziest part was that Mandy hadn't asked him to. He'd wanted to come along and so had volunteered.

Ever since she'd given him that sweet hug the other day, she'd been a little distant. And he missed their easy banter from earlier in the week.

When they'd finished the chores this morning, he'd wanted more time with her, hoping to get that ease back between them again.

"Dalton doesn't need you today?" Mandy set a cage full of kittens in the middle of the table.

Arch held out a finger, and a white paw batted at him through the cage door. "He said he needs his weekends to himself. I don't think he's used to having anyone else around. I get the impression that a few hours of me in the middle of the day is almost more than he can handle. I'm a little worried that I'll show up on Monday and he'll have changed his mind about taking me on."

"He doesn't seem like the kind of guy who changes his mind a lot, from what you've told me." Mandy gave him the shy smile he was starting to crave. "You're amazing. Everyone always said he was a hermit. I'm proud of you for going out there and talking him into hiring you."

"I still can't believe he's paying me. He said he didn't want things getting 'all personal' between us."

"I've seen how hard you work. I should be paying you, too."

"Nah." He pulled her in for a quick hug under his arm, to reassure her. And because he wanted to touch her. "You and I have a trade going on. We're square."

His heart sank a little when she pulled back

and busied herself straightening a stack of flyers. "I have a feeling I got the good end of the deal."

"Not true," he countered. "You've helped with my driving practice, made me a list of stuff to get done, and you're letting me give away stray cats, which might actually improve my reputation around town." He plunked himself down on one of the folding chairs and watched the way her smile started small, then spread across her cheeks.

His reputation. The thought stilled his enthusiasm. He suddenly realized he probably wasn't doing Mandy any favors sticking around for her adoption event. He stood. "This could be a bad idea. Having me here won't persuade people to adopt cats. Maybe the opposite."

Her smile faltered. "I hadn't thought about that." Then he saw the stubborn set to her jaw that he'd been getting to know lately. "If they have a problem with you, then they don't deserve one of my strays." She plopped down in the chair next to him, folded her arms and tilted up her chin, as if daring someone to make a comment about Arch.

He sat, too, but worry gnawed. He hadn't thought this through. Was he really ready to greet shoppers? On a busy Saturday? But if Mandy was up for it, he should be, too. He wondered what people's reaction would be when they realized that the town lowlife was back, only instead of pushing drugs, he was pushing cats.

It didn't take long to find out. A woman who looked vaguely familiar, maybe someone from high school, stopped by with her young daughter. She was all smiles until she saw him. Then she pulled her daughter away. "We'll look at cats another time," he heard her say when the little girl protested.

He was going to ruin this for Mandy. He touched her elbow. "I should go. No one wants to adopt a cat from the town criminal."

"No." Mandy shook her head. "Don't take it personally. It's her problem."

She was being stubborn, so he tried humor. "I have enough on my conscience. I don't need to add *keeping stray cats from finding homes* to my list of wrongs."

An older woman stopped to ooh and aah at the kittens, so Mandy just shot him a quick smile. Arch shifted in his seat, reaching his fingers through a crate to give an elderly black-and-white cat a scratch on the jaw. He was a sweet old guy. If Arch had a home of his own, he'd keep this one.

"You."

The hissing voice froze his hand in mid-scratch. He looked up to see an older woman clutching her purse to her chest like a shield.

"Ma'am?" He had no idea who she was, but she was staring at him like he'd just stepped off the screen of a horror movie.

"Don't *ma'am* me, you *loser.*" Her voice shook under its load of venom. Her eyes shifted away as if she was trying to come up with words bad enough for him. "You *scum.*"

Mandy intervened. "Mrs. Patterson, please calm down…"

The woman shifted her fury to Mandy. "Why is he here?"

"He's helping me today." Mandy's voice was mild as milk, but Arch saw the way her hands twisted the tablecloth, out of the woman's view.

Mrs. Patterson fixed her glare back on Arch. "You think a couple hours of charity work will make up for what you did?"

Arch had no idea what she was referring to, but he was pretty sure it wasn't a part of his past he wanted to revisit in front of The Downtown Market.

"You *ruined* my son's life. He's homeless now, somewhere out by the coast. You sold him meth. You got him hooked. He's lost to us now."

Arch stared, trying to remember her son. He couldn't. There'd been so many deals, most alongside dark remote roads. Just quick exchanges of cash and drugs.

Mandy's voice cut smoothly through the tension. "Mrs. Patterson, I don't think you can blame Arch for everything."

"Of course I can," Mrs. Patterson said. "And I do."

"Do you blame Mr. Howell at the liquor store when your husband drinks too much?"

Arch stared at Mandy. Her face was angelic as ever, but he saw the flash of justice in her eyes.

Mrs. Patterson's mouth was a shocked oval. Then she seemed to collect herself. She pointed an accusing finger at Arch. "Liquor is legal. What he sells isn't."

"He doesn't sell anything anymore," Mandy countered. "*He* turned his life around."

"Mandy, hang on." Arch finally found his voice. He stood to face Mrs. Patterson and the pain she, rightly or wrongly, blamed him for. "I am truly sorry about your son. And I wish I hadn't sold him drugs. I doubt that helps you much, but I want you to know it."

Mrs. Patterson blinked a few times, maybe with surprise, maybe with emotion. She cleared her throat. "Well. It doesn't, really," she said quietly and turned away. Arch watched her shuffle slowly down the sidewalk, apparently forgetting that she'd meant to go to the market today.

He swallowed hard and stole a glance at Mandy. She was still standing, her expression still determined. And her fingers were still fidgeting with the tablecloth's hem.

"Thanks for sticking up for me," he said.

"You didn't have to apologize to her," she said quietly.

"An apology was the least I could do. Maybe if I hadn't sold to her son, he'd have gotten his fix from someone else. Or maybe he'd have stayed clean. Either way, what I did was horrible."

Mandy fixed him with an indignant glare. "Of course you shouldn't have sold drugs. But it's also not fair for her to blame all her problems on you."

"True. But she's a mom who's devastated by what's happened to her kid."

"I guess I should be more sympathetic." Mandy sat down with a heavy sigh. "But I also know she cut her son off entirely when she first found out he was using. And I know that she's had over ten years to go to the coast and try to help him, but she never has. So, yes, you can take some of the blame. Just don't take all of it."

"Why are you defending me?" He should be grateful, but he hated this. The greasy tentacles of his screwed-up past were grabbing on to Mandy. "I'm not like these cats. You're not responsible for me."

Her smile surprised him. "Maybe you are a little bit the same. Your lives haven't always been fair, and you deserve better."

It was somewhat humiliating, but he knew she meant well. "I don't love being compared to a stray cat, but I can see that we're all lucky to have you on our side."

He looked out over the street, trying to take in what had just happened. With Mrs. Patterson and her rage. With Mandy, who viewed him like one of her strays. He'd thought when she'd hugged him a few days ago that maybe she felt more for him than that…

The main street of Benson was busy. People were walking around, doing their weekend errands like nothing was wrong. But inside each and every one of them were so many wounds. Mrs. Patterson had them, he did, and even Mandy did.

He glanced at her, surprised to see that she was watching him. She looked away, a faint blush warming her face. He wanted to lay his hand on her cheek, feel the heat there—

"Arch?"

That voice was low and husky. And totally familiar, even after so many years. His pulse skittered, high on dread and anticipation.

Arch looked up. Kit's black-lined eyes were wide with shock. Her red-lipsticked mouth was partly open. The past slammed into him, the impact leaving him stunned. Kit Hayes. His partner in crime. The girl who'd loved the man he'd been. She was still a gorgeous combination of black hair, white skin, crazy curves and cleavage.

"Kit." It wasn't much of a greeting, but he wasn't ready for this.

Kit's skin was going paler than pale. She looked like she might faint. Her huge dark eyes went from him, to the cats, to Mandy. She cleared her throat, and color splotched her cheeks, as if she was coming alive again. "You're back."

"You…" Arch's mind wasn't keeping up. "You always planned to leave. I figured you had."

Kit's lips pressed into a thin line. "Well, some things don't work out the way we plan, do they?"

It was a jab straight to the throat. He'd walked out on her. One more way he'd screwed up back then. "Yeah, I guess so."

She drew herself up. She'd always been tough. "How long have you been in town?"

"About a week." He should say more. But he was time warped—his mind going back to their last night together. She'd wanted them to go to dinner. He'd made her wait around the ranch while he drank a twelve-pack with his buddies. She'd read a magazine while they shot beer cans off a fence post. Then, when his friends left, he'd talked her into having sex. They'd never made it to dinner. Classic Arch Hoffman, selfish to the core.

"A week!" Her dark brows drew together. She

took a few steps closer. Her hands were shaking when she coiled them into fists.

Arch stood to meet her, keeping the table between them. This was the Kit he'd known. A ball of fire barely contained. "How *could* you?" Her eyes narrowed, blade thin. "How the *hell* could you just leave without telling me?"

"I'm sorry."

"That's *really* helpful." The smile she shot him was anything but cheerful. "That helps *so* much. In fact, I feel so much better, I'm going to do *this*!" She raised her arms and flipped him off in a double-handed salute. Then she turned on her high black heels and walked away.

Arch glanced at Mandy. She was pale, staring after Kit. He wondered what horrified her more—him, Kit or the ugly scene unfolding at her cat adoption table. "I'm just going to..." He nodded toward Kit, who was halfway down the block already.

She started. "Of course. Go ahead. I'm good here."

He jogged after Kit and caught up with her partway down the next block. She was in a hurry, walking too fast for her high heels, covering ground in small jerky steps. "Kit, please. Wait?"

Her middle finger came up behind her, and she kept her lurching pace.

"Kit, stop." He reached for the thick leather of her motorcycle jacket.

"Don't touch me!" She spun to face him and he saw tear tracks, gray with makeup, streaking her face. "Just leave me alone. You couldn't be bothered to talk to me for ten years. Why the *hell* do you want to start now?"

"Because you're here. We're here. And you're upset."

She brought her knuckles up to wipe her eyes. Her fingertips ended in black nail polish. "I'm *not* upset! Just surprised."

"Okay, you're surprised. So am I. Can I buy you a cup of coffee or something?"

"No."

"Can we at least talk for a moment?"

She shrugged. But she pointed to a small side street. "Fine. Let's go down here. There's a bench."

Walking by Kit's side was eerily familiar and yet not at all. There were new lines around her eyes, though nothing like the way his own face had hardened. Her hair was pinned up, and a thick gray scarf was knotted around her neck. She looked sophisticated, in a rocker chick–slash–goth girl kind of way.

The road ended at a field. Someone had created a garden there, with flowers and a few benches. Kit waited until he sat down on one of them. Then she slapped him hard across the face.

His head lurched back from the sting of it. He braced to take another. But the onslaught came in words.

"How the *hell* could you do that to me? We had five years together. How could you just leave without saying goodbye?"

Arch ran a hand over his jaw. His eyes watered. "We got word that the feds were on their way to arrest us. Dad told us to get in the car, and we went."

Tears swam in her eyes as she paced the gravel in front of him. "You couldn't have called? You always had a burner phone ready. Why didn't you use it?"

His ears were ringing. He tried to remember that no-headlight drive through dark desert roads. Heading south and east and south again. How overwhelmed he'd felt. How badly he'd wanted to be done with drugs and dealing and weapons and illegal money. "We took back roads that night. No reception. No stops. I couldn't have called."

Her hands opened in exasperation. "And what about the ten years of nights after that? Where *were* you? Did you really go to Mexico like everyone said?"

He stood there feeling helpless in the face of all her feelings. She was so raw, and he felt so numb. "Dad and Blake went to Mexico. I turned myself in and went to jail."

That slowed her down. Her eyes were huge, so dark like his that sometimes people used to think they were brother and sister. Whenever that happened, Kit would plant a long, slow kiss on him, just to shock.

"You went to jail, *willingly*? Why?"

He looked out over the field beyond the benches. The fall sun was so bright overhead that each shrub and rock and blade of grass stood out in vivid detail. A couple of cows grazed, their jaws rhythmic as they chewed. Arch breathed it all in, trying to find the words that would make her see.

"I think the idea had been growing in my mind for a while, but I didn't really know what to do about it. But on the way south, I knew I wanted, more than anything, to live my life differently. And that the only way to start new was to do my time."

She shook her head slowly, as if moving it would help her assimilate this new information. "And they don't have a telephone in jail? They don't have a piece of paper so you could write me a note and let me know where the hell you were? I've worried and wondered for a decade."

It would be hurtful to explain that prison monotony had made his memories of her blurry, like old faded postcards. Or that he'd survived incarceration by focusing solely on the future, and she'd been a piece of the past. He'd hurt her enough. "I'm sorry," he said again.

"You're an idiot." She smacked him on the shoulder with her palm. "I would have visited you. I would have been there for you."

Tears were brimming in her eyes, and he felt them in his chest. It made his words a hoarse whisper. "You should have forgotten me."

She pulled a tissue out of her big black purse and dabbed her cheeks. "Are you done now? Are you home to stay?" He hated the wobble in her voice. Seeing him again had obviously stolen all the fire that made her strong.

He shook his head. "I'm here for a while. So I can get on my feet. Then I'll move on."

"Where?"

"I don't know yet."

She stared at him with her dark, brimming eyes. "I have to go to work. I'm a bartender at the Dusty Saddle, in case you've been wondering what I've been up to all this time."

He felt the dig. "Of course I've wondered."

"I don't think you have." She paced a few feet away, then turned back, like a restless cat. "You know, I just don't get it. You came back to town and you didn't even try to find me? But you have the time to sit in front of the grocery store with some little blonde and a bunch of stray cats?" She glared at him and shook her head. "I can't believe this. After all this time…" Her voice trailed off.

He didn't owe her an explanation, but the pain in her eyes had him on the run.

"Mandy…the woman with the cats…her sister married Wade. They're away on their honeymoon and her ranch is understaffed. So I've been helping her out."

"And she needed help with her cats, too."

He couldn't lie. "I wanted to help. It's a good cause."

"Who knew you were such an animal lover." She let out a bitter breath. "I'd better go."

He tried to offer comfort. "I would have looked you up. I assumed you'd put Benson in your rearview mirror years ago."

"Ha. That sure didn't happen."

"I guess not." He eyed her warily, not knowing how to end this conversation. He needed to offer something, but he didn't know what. "So, I'll see you around?"

She nodded and turned as if to leave. Then she stopped. "Maybe it's weird to ask, but I've got a few people coming over tonight. It's really casual. Just pizza and hanging out. Want to come by? Around seven?"

He couldn't hide his surprise. "Do you really want me there? You're pissed as hell at me. For good reason."

"I *am* angry. But it's mostly people you know. They'll want to see you." There was misery in her voice when she added, "And I guess I want to see you, too."

He saw the way she chewed the corner of her lip, just like she used to, and that little piece of vulnerability wrenched at his resolve. He'd promised himself when he returned to Benson that he'd stay away from his old life. No old friends, no trips down memory lane. But this was Kit and she was hurting and he was the cause. If she needed this, then he could give it. "Sure," he told her. "Where do you live?"

"Do you have a phone?"

He was about to say no and then remembered that he did. He handed it to her. "I'm putting myself in your contacts." She tapped the screen for a moment. When she gave it back to him, it was with a single, shocking kiss on the cheek. "See you tonight, Arch."

Her kiss rooted him to the spot. He watched her walk away, her outrageous figure on full display in her tight black jeans and high-heeled boots. She was sexy as hell and all the memories of what they'd been together, and *when* they'd been together, flooded back.

By the time she turned the corner, Arch's fingers were dug into the palms of his hands. This trip to town had been a mistake. First Mrs. Patterson and her homeless drug-addict son, and now Kit and a whole bunch of confusion.

He needed some air. He needed to walk. He needed to find his sanity and forget all that dark promise in Kit's kiss. Arch knew that he should finish helping Mandy with the cats. But his feet took him the opposite direction, straight out of town.

CHAPTER TEN

MANDY FIGURED THAT some days were like cake batter. Sweet and smooth. Other days were like a recipe gone wrong, where even the good ingredients fell flat. She sat on the fence, watching the horses tearing into their hay, trying to stay positive. But it was difficult. Today had been a bad-recipe day.

Which made no sense. She'd just fed the horses all by herself. A week ago that had been impossible for her. So why wasn't she happy? Or at least somewhat triumphant?

She knew the answer and she hated it. *Arch Hoffman.* He'd disappeared from her cat rescue table to chase after Kit, and he'd never come back. And ever since, the day had felt all wrong.

The chill of the incoming night had her zipping up her jacket. Tomorrow was Halloween. And in November the weather east of the Sierras would start to get really cold. Usually Mandy didn't enjoy winter much, but after today she was looking forward to it. She'd hole up in her kitchen, work on new recipes and avoid ever seeing Arch and Kit together. Because they *would* be together. How could Arch resist? Kit was so exotic, so confident, so sexy.

Plus she'd heard stories about their romance. It was kind of legendary in Benson. Kit kept to herself nowadays, but apparently she'd been just about as wild as Arch when they were young. Of course Arch would want to rekindle that spark, now that he'd seen Kit again.

This was ridiculous. Why was she sitting on a fence moping about a guy she had a million reasons not to get involved with?

She was a mess. *But*…sometimes good things came out of the worst messes. What she needed was a list. A mental list of all the things she'd learned from her disastrous morning with Arch.

Number one was easy. She'd adopted out all of her cats once Arch had left. And no one else had yelled at her. So maybe him running after Kit was a good thing.

Number two, thanks to Mrs. Patterson, she was more familiar with Arch's drug-dealing history. It was a reality check she needed, to remind her of just how troubled he'd been. And maybe still was.

And then there was number three. The way Arch had stumbled off after Kit like a man in a daze. He clearly still cared for her, which was good to know. Especially when Mandy's thoughts were drifting to his gorgeous body, his craggy face and his dark eyes *way* too often.

A glimmer of movement in the still evening had her shifting on the fence. Arch was pedaling his bicycle up the lane. What would he do if he knew what she'd just been thinking? He'd probably pedal the other way as fast as he could. She watched him jump the bumps in the dirt road with a mixture of admiration and resentment. Though what did she have to resent him for? He owed her nothing.

He rolled to a stop and leaned the bike on the fence. Pulling off his helmet, he shook out his hair. She was surprised that he didn't look happier after his reunion with his ex. "Sorry I'm late—and also for what happened earlier."

"You don't need to apologize."

"I think I do." He took a few steps toward her, his mouth drawn flat with remorse. "I ruined your cat adoption. And I should have found you after I talked with Kit, to tell you I was leaving."

She flushed, because that *would* have helped, but she hated being his obligation. "It was fine. The cats got adopted. And I understand. You ran into an old...friend."

"Girlfriend. Kit was my girlfriend for years."

Hearing him say it aloud made it even more real. And reality was good, even when it stung.

"She had good reason to be angry," he went on. "When I left here, I never said goodbye to her. I just disappeared."

"That's a lot to deal with." Mandy tried to ignore the juvenile jealousy that pierced her skin when she thought of him with Kit. "Please don't worry about me. I was fine."

"Let me at least help you feed now," he said.

"I've already got all the horses fed."

"You're serious?" He reached up for a friendly high five. No hugs this time. She raised her hand to smack his.

"Yup."

"Well, come on. Let's see what you can do with the cattle."

Arch steered the truck smoothly down the dirt track toward the last pasture of the night. They'd worked efficiently together. And his driving was improving by leaps and bounds. His voice was abrupt when he said, "I'm going to Kit's place for a party tonight."

Mandy dug her fingers into her palms to stop the tears prickling her eyes. They were just hormones and loneliness combining and confusing her. And this ache in her chest was simply worry for him. Because spending time with people he used to know might cause him to backslide, when he'd come so far. "Okay," she told him. "I hope you have a good time."

He drummed his fingers lightly on the wheel. "I don't know if I'll have a good time. I don't know why she invited me. She's still angry. And I don't know what else to do. I've apologized, but it doesn't help." His mouth twisted in a wry smile. "I think I owe so many apologies to so many people that I need to order a T-shirt with *I'm sorry* printed on it, front and back. I'll wear it whenever I go into town."

"Useful. And stylish." She didn't know what else to say. She couldn't possibly give him unbiased advice about Kit. She'd learned today that she was very biased where Arch was concerned. Jumping in to defend him from Mrs. Patterson. Feeling her heart hurt whenever he mentioned Kit. She cared, too much, about his choices and his happiness.

Arch ran a hand over his eyes, across his forehead, as if trying to clear his thoughts manually. "Maybe I'm a coward. When I came back here, I didn't think I'd have to face Kit. She'd always talked about leaving Benson. I assumed she'd have moved on a long time ago."

"Well, she invited you to her party. So she must have accepted your apology."

"Maybe." Arch put his arm along the seat back and his fingers toyed idly with a piece of Mandy's hair. "I thought coming back home was a good idea. And parts of it have been so great. But after today, I don't know anymore."

Mandy didn't know what to say to that. Reading too much into his words was a bad idea. Arch was so intense, such a big presence. It would be easy to imagine that there was some kind of subtext happening.

But there wasn't. He was just a guy asking for advice about a woman he'd loved. "You'll figure it out." She turned away, and the movement pulled her hair out of his reach. "I'm sure you'll talk it all out with her tonight."

"Right," Arch said heavily. "I'm sure." He let out a breath full of tension. He must have so many feelings after seeing Kit again. Mandy couldn't even imagine.

They'd reached the pasture and he put the truck in Park. "Okay, enough about Kit. We have cattle to feed. And since you're now such a feeding expert, let's switch roles for this last group. *I'll* drive the truck into the pasture. *You* hop in the back and throw the hay into the feeder."

Mandy's stomach tightened. "I don't know…"

She stared out over the fence where the cattle milled in a black and brown blur. "Cattle are scary."

"Or maybe you're just looking at them all wrong."

She glanced at him, surprised. "Wrong? They look like a whole lot of cattle. How can that be wrong?"

"Don't look at them as a group. Try to watch just one of them." Arch pointed through the windshield. "See that one on the right, with the brown on its forelegs? It's bossy. It wants whatever its buddies have."

She waited, and sure enough, the steer in question spotted a neighbor nibbling at a clump of grass. He approached, head lowered in a threatening way. The other steer trotted off.

"Pecking order. Just like chickens," Arch said. "And see the one close to the gate? All black except for that bit of white on his forehead? He's pretty affectionate. I saw him nuzzling one of his buddies earlier."

"Okay, so I'm supposed to get in there and give him a hug?"

He grinned down at her. "Not unless you want to."

"No, thanks," she said quickly.

"I just thought it might help you to see that they all have different personalities. Some of them are a little more aggressive, and you *will* need to be careful around them. But most cattle are pretty calm. Kind of sweet, in fact."

She couldn't help but tease him a little about his lecture. "I had no idea you were so philosophical about cows."

"I am a man of many talents." His wide smile brought its own warmth. "But seriously, I wonder if in your mind, all horses are associated with the one who threw your mom. And all cows, too, because they're big, like horses."

She stared at him, astounded. Because it didn't actually sound that far-fetched. "How do you know this stuff?"

"I guess I had a lot of time to think in prison. And I had to learn to read people pretty well to get by in there."

He looked at the cattle and Mandy looked at him—the way his shoulders tensed and his jaw clenched every time he spoke of the past. Here he was, helping with her troubles, which must seem so small compared with the ones he'd faced in prison. She tried to lighten his mood. "So now you're translating those amazing people-reading skills into a new career in cattle psychology."

His mouth eased from its grim line. "I guess I am."

"So what about that one?" She pointed to a

light brown steer who was standing behind the others, head hanging low.

"He actually could be unwell." Arch tilted his head to get a better look. "Let's check on him in the morning, to see if he's feeling better. Or maybe that's just how he is."

"Because, according to your theory, he might just have a really relaxed personality," Mandy said. "Or slouchy posture."

"Exactly." He flashed a smile with a touch of triumph. "They're individuals. And if you can see them that way, maybe you'll end up liking them. Maybe you *will* want to give that one a hug."

The idea made her giggle. "Hmm…it's an interesting theory, but I still vote no on the hugging. No matter what their personality, they're still awfully large."

"Yeah, there's really no changing that," Arch said. "They are large."

"Too bad Lone Mountain Ranch isn't in the hamster-raising business. They're just about the right size for me."

His laugh rang out through the cab, good to hear after so much trouble today. "Hamsters are far smaller, but I'm not sure there's much of a market for them."

She could make silly jokes with him for hours, but the day was fading. She took a deep breath. "Okay. I'm going for it. Let's feed them."

He didn't let his surprise show for long. "I'm proud of you, cowgirl. Let's do this."

Mandy jumped out of the cab and walked to the gate. Heart bumping and skipping, pulse going double time. It was just adrenaline. A bunch of old, useless fear. She could ignore it. Arch had taught her how. She wouldn't focus on the fear. Just on what needed to be done.

Arch eased the truck up and hit the horn once. The cattle moved away and Mandy opened the gate, following Arch as he drove through. When she closed it behind her, anxiety sped through her system. She was on the ground, in the pasture, with the cattle. Deep breaths helped stay the panic.

Luckily, these cattle were creatures of habit. They completely ignored her, heading straight for their feeder. She climbed into the back of the truck, pulling on her gloves while Arch drove closer to the big metal rack.

Tossing the hay in was easy. Some of the cattle fussed or pushed at each other, but most just waited patiently, trusting there'd be plenty for all.

And just like that, the cattle were fed and Arch was driving the truck back out of the pasture. He was out of the cab before Mandy had even finished locking the gate. He picked her up and swirled her in a dizzying circle. "You did it!" He set her down and took her hands. "You, Mandy Allen, have earned back your official rancher status today."

Her smile was so wide her cheeks hurt. "Thank you!" She wanted to throw her arms around him and hug her gratitude, but that didn't seem right anymore. He was going to Kit's in a couple of hours. So she squeezed his hands and let go. "I'm so relieved. I never thought I'd be able to do something like that again."

"I knew you could." His smile slowly faded to something more serious. His gaze delving into hers. He brought up a knuckle and swiped it down her cheek, just the slightest touch. "I'm so proud of you, Mandy."

His attention was addictive. She'd only want more if she let this go on. She took a step back. "Well, everyone is fed. And you need to get going... It's getting late."

"Yeah, I've got miles of biking still to do. I'll say one thing for life on parole—I'm in good shape."

She was going to try not to think about that. "It seems like you might be ready for your driving test soon. Let me know if you want me to drive you down to Bishop."

"How'd I get so lucky? To end up with a guardian angel like you?"

She couldn't handle sweet talk. Not tonight, when he'd be spending the evening with someone else. "No angel. Just a friend." She walked to the passenger side of the truck and opened the door. "So drive us back to the barn. Lord knows you can use all the practice you can get."

"Hey! I'm getting better." He slid behind the wheel and nudged her with his elbow. "Watch me as I execute a flawless three-point turn."

Mandy clipped her seat belt on and clung to the handle above the door. "Ready!" she called, covering her eyes with her free hand.

His laugh rolled over her, rich, soothing waves that lapped at her soul. He wasn't hers. He wouldn't be hers. But this thing they had together was precious and life altering. And she was grateful for that.

He turned the truck. It *was* flawless. But she rolled her eyes and told him his execution was so-so, just to hear him laugh again.

CHAPTER ELEVEN

MANDY SAT IN the kitchen, staring at rows of black and orange cupcakes. The plastic jack-o'-lanterns she'd stuck in the icing looked manic, kind of like her mood.

She'd been doing what she always did when she felt troubled. Baking and cleaning. But it wasn't working. Because she couldn't stop thinking about Arch, at a party, at Kit's house.

Tomorrow was Halloween. So tonight Kit was probably wearing one of those sexy costumes that Mandy would never have the courage to try. A sexy nurse, or a sexy maid, or even a sexy cowgirl.

Mandy wore a T-shirt covered in orange frosting smears. Her church threw an annual Halloween bash for the Sunday school kids, and this year Mandy was in charge. She had four dozen cupcakes finished. Once this next batch was out of the oven she would go to bed. Tomorrow she had a haunted house to set up, volunteers to organize and kids to entertain.

It was good to be busy. Better than thinking about Arch and Kit.

She drummed her fingers restlessly on the table. Then realized she'd picked up the move from Arch. Whenever he was thinking, or worried, his fingers beat out a pattern on the nearest surface.

Her chair clattered across the wood plank floor when she stood. She needed to *do* something. Not sit here thinking about what she couldn't— and shouldn't—have. She glanced at the kitchen timer. The cupcakes wouldn't be ready for a few more minutes.

She left the kitchen and wandered through the living room. Normally Lori and Wade would be here, inviting her to watch a movie or play a game with them. But tonight it was just her and her new shadow, Lori's dog, Snack, who had caught up with her the moment she left the kitchen. He tailed her down the hall, past the study, out onto the porch and back into the house. A house that didn't quite feel like home anymore.

Mandy was thrilled that Lori had married Wade. She loved seeing her sister so happy. But things had been different ever since he moved in with them a few months before the wedding. Suddenly Mandy was the third wheel in Lori and Wade's new life. Living here on the ranch had always been comforting. But lately that comfort had been seeping away, as if the warmth was leaching from the rooms.

But she needed some kind of comfort to get

through tonight. To soften this hard feeling of not being chosen. To ease the longing for things she couldn't have.

In her head, she relisted all the reasons why she was an idiot to have feelings for Arch. He was an ex-convict. He had no idea who he was or what he wanted. He was just passing through. He was practically family. He was with Kit. It was a long list.

But there was another list. Of memories and images. Arch laughing when he swung her around after she fed the cattle today. Arch cleaning Dakota's hoof every morning, then walking the mare around the pasture to make sure her limp was getting better. Arch in a goofy blue helmet, riding his brother-in-law's bike for miles every single day to make sure that Mandy's chores got done.

Not that list. Don't make that list.

In her bedroom she sorted the pile of clean laundry she'd left there. She took her time, concentrating on making all the T-shirts perfectly square. When she put them in her dresser, she remembered the brochure at the bottom of the drawer. Her hands found the shiny paper easily. The colorful photos were familiar, she'd studied them so many times. Students in chef's uniforms, dishing up beautiful food. Would she ever have the courage to be one of them?

Culinary school. Her impossible dream.

Maybe the reason she was getting so hung up on Arch was because she needed a new purpose in her life. A goal that was bigger than this ranch or even her baking business. Arch had helped her find courage she hadn't known she had. Maybe she could use some of it to finally make her dream a reality.

Snack trotted after her as she plunged downstairs, grabbed the laptop from the study and made it back to the kitchen just as the timer chimed.

The cupcakes were ready. And she was ready, too. She pulled the pan out of the oven and opened the computer. It only took moments to search the internet for the application to the San Francisco Culinary Institute. Heart pounding, fingers shaking, she entered her name and address.

And then, as always, the doubts and questions started. They'd haunted her since her mother's death up in the mountains that day. *You made the wrong decision then. What if this is the wrong decision now?*

This *wasn't* a decision. It was just an application. Mandy's fingers hit the keys, filling in her basic information. But the old anxiety was back, hissing and crackling and distorting her thinking. *How can you know that this is the right thing to do? You've made bad choices before. Your mom died alone because you chose wrong.*

She forced her fingers to keep typing. Reminding herself, as she had thousands of times, that she'd done the best she could that day. She'd tried to stop the bleeding. She'd left to ride for help.

She'd made the wrong decision, and it had haunted her ever since.

Tears streamed and anxiety rampaged, but now Mandy had Arch's voice in her head, too. Reminding her that she could choose which feelings to listen to. This pain and regret were terrible, but they'd ruled her life for too long now. So she'd choose to listen to this other feeling—this newborn, deep-down need to finally pursue her dream.

For years she'd been living in a mire of self-doubt and fear. Now she might finally have the courage to heave herself out. To believe that her life could be a better, brighter place. And to fill out the application that just might take her there.

ARCH SIPPED HIS root beer and watched Kit's party unfold from his corner of the couch. Tomorrow was Halloween. He'd totally forgotten until he'd walked through the door of Kit's rented bungalow and seen the costumes.

Had Halloween always been this skimpy? Women in lingerie, in tiny witch costumes, in sexy devil outfits. Everywhere he looked there were legs, breasts, fishnet stockings, killer high heels, made-up faces, styled hair. It was dazzling, overwhelming, tempting and terrifying. Too much after ten years' forced abstinence. He caught himself staring, which was probably the idea behind those tiny costumes. But it seemed rude and wrong.

Ten years ago he would have known how to be cool with this. Would have tossed out compliments and suggestive comments. Would have flirted with these women as his God-given right as Benson's local badass bad boy.

But now he was off-kilter.

In prison, a local professor had volunteered to teach them art history. This party reminded Arch of one of the surreal paintings they'd studied, where everything was disjointed and not what it seemed. Where arms were too long, people were part animal or had heads made of flowers. Just like those paintings, this scene was too much to understand. His eyes didn't know where to look.

So he was here, in his corner, wishing his root beer was a real beer, trying to take it all in.

Even the men seemed surreal. So vivid after ten years of living with men stripped down to the bare basics of prison uniforms. Most of the guys at the party had brought masks. Rubber ones with gruesome, disconcerting monster faces. Now the beer was flowing and the masks had come off and Arch was relieved. It was hard enough to take in all of these old friends. The masks just added to his discomfort.

In some ways it was like the past ten years had never happened. Sure, all the guys were a little older, maybe a little thicker. A few had beer guts. Tank Lewis had lost a few fingers in a motorcycle accident. But minus their masks, pretty much everyone was still about the same. Tank was still telling dumb jokes. Bruce Anderson still wore his cowboy hat and earnest expression everywhere.

Denny Kirkham plunked down in the chair opposite Arch and took a pull of the huge bottle of beer in his hand. "So, Arch Hoffman. What the hell, man?"

Not sure how he was expected to answer, Arch just nodded. "Hey, Denny. How have you been?"

"Good, man. Good. I'm a trucker now. Doing some long-distance hauling."

"You like it?" Arch asked.

"It's a good gig." Denny nodded. "I've seen a lot of country." He took another drink from his beer. "So?" He leaned forward. "Tell me about life in the slammer."

Arch had been fielding this question in one form or another all night. He'd perfected his answer. "It sucked."

But Denny had always been persistent. "Did

you see fights? Did they put you in solitary? Did guys try to…?" He gave a lewd wink. "You know…"

Arch decided to ignore the last question. "There were fights. Not much time in solitary."

"Right, well…" Denny stood, obviously disappointed not to get more information. "Enjoy the party." He drifted off.

The thing was, Arch *wasn't* enjoying it. The cheerful chatter and laughter around him felt false, like everyone was trying too hard to have a good time. An image of Mandy from earlier today flashed into his mind, and it felt more real than this party. She'd been gripping the handle in the truck, assuming crash position, joking about his rusty driving skills. Giggling like crazy. *That* had been fun.

He smiled at the memory. Maybe part of changing was needing a different kind of fun. He remembered suddenly how Mandy had added "have fun" to his to-do list. He wasn't going to check that box off sitting here. He'd have more fun reading a good book, or sketching ideas for a metal sculpture in his notebook. He'd rather be out under the stars, or even fixing something back at the ranch.

He wanted to laugh more with Mandy. He liked the organic humor that fizzed between them. That comfortable understanding they'd had from the moment they met.

This…people drinking, the off-color jokes, the stories of trucks and fishing, it didn't fit him anymore. A favorite old sweater that had gone through the dryer and come out shrunken and itchy.

He stood and headed for the kitchen, where he'd last seen Kit. He'd say goodbye and go on home.

It was just Kit and a girlfriend in the kitchen, leaning on the counters, chatting, with ornate cocktails in hand. They looked exotic and artificial, like plants under grow lights. Arch leaned on the door frame and tried to take Kit in. Tried to reconcile this bombshell from his past with his current reality.

She was gorgeous. Always had been. Her black hair fell in thick waves down her back. No costume for her tonight. Just a dress, skintight and black, held up by tiny straps. Sometime in the years between them, she'd had a tropical flower tattooed in vivid pink and yellow across her shoulder. They'd gotten their first tattoo together. A rattlesnake for her, barbed wire for him. He suddenly remembered how she'd been so tough that day, slamming down bourbon from a bottle while the artist did his painful work.

Kit's friend, a pretty redhead, spotted him

leaning in the doorway. She said something to Kit, who turned to look at him. Her brows arched but her voice stayed husky and casual. "Arch. I still can't get used to you being here. How are you enjoying the party?" As if she hadn't slapped him today. As if he hadn't betrayed her horribly so many years ago.

Suddenly the dynamics in the room felt like those in a prison yard. An artificial veneer of peace over a seething undercurrent of animosity, secrets and wounds. "It's a good party. Thanks for having me. I'm taking off, though."

Kit's eyes widened. "You're leaving? I thought you'd like seeing so many familiar faces. You used to like Halloween."

"It was nice of you to invite me," he said quickly, before he hurt her feelings any more. "Really kind. It's just…a lot. The most people I've been around since I got out."

Kit's friend sauntered toward him in a tiny minidress. As she passed him to leave the kitchen, she glared up at him with big green eyes. "You're such a jerk," she whispered for his ears only. And walked out the kitchen door to join the rest of the party.

Arch's skin went hot. He understood the woman's animosity. He'd hurt her best friend. But he was done trying to make it right when there was no way he could. He was ready to be out in the cold night, pedaling his bike home under the stars.

But he should talk with Kit a little first. She was trying hard to be nice to him, when he absolutely didn't deserve it—as her friend's whispered words had made so very clear.

"So I bet you've been wondering what I've been doing all these years." Kit's voice was as sultry as she was. She leaned against her kitchen counter and took a dainty sip of the cocktail in her hand.

Arch's gaze followed the path of the glass to her lips. They were painted red and full of memories. Memories he shouldn't think about now. His glance jolted away and caught on her pinup girl cleavage. *A very bad idea.* All his years of abstinence were betraying him right now.

He looked at her eyes instead and willed his gaze to stay there while she told him about her life, bartending at the Dusty Saddle. The owner, some guy named Chris, wasn't around much and had entrusted her with a lot of responsibility. "I'm practically running the place now. I do all the ordering, I book the music, I decide what bar food we'll serve. I make the staff schedule. It's almost like having my own place."

"That's great." It eased the edge off his guilt to know she'd found something she liked.

"I've even been setting aside a little money

each month. Thinking maybe I can buy the place when Chris is ready to retire." Her plans were bubbling over. Her face lit up when she spoke about work, and she looked different than the furious woman he'd met earlier today.

"I'm happy for you. You've found something you love."

She nodded, but her mood downshifted. "I never meant to stay here in Benson. But my mom left my dad a few years ago. I felt like I couldn't leave him, too." She swallowed hard, shot him a nervous glance. "And maybe not knowing where you were made it a little harder to leave, also. Like if I left, then I'd know for sure that I'd never see you again."

His mouth was open. He shut it abruptly, but she hadn't noticed because she wouldn't look at him. She was staring into her drink, swirling the liquid in her glass. Two bright pink spots on her cheeks told him she regretted her confession.

He regretted it, too. She'd *waited* for him? It had never occurred to him that she would. He hadn't thought it possible to feel more guilt, but there it was, leaden inside him, making it hard to say what he should. "I'm sorry the way I left made it hard for you to move on. To go after what you wanted."

"Don't." She looked up then, her dark eyes sharp. "Don't pity me. It was stupid of me to say that about us. I'm fine. I like my life the way it is."

Arch studied his boots, and the linoleum around them, still trying to breathe through the guilt. "I'm honored that you thought of me that way." He looked up at her. "I didn't know."

"Didn't you think of me at all? Didn't you wonder?"

"Of course I did. But…" He tried to find the words that would make her see how things had changed. "My whole focus in jail was to make a new start. So I tried not to think too much about the past. It was like I had a door in my mind and I closed it. I spent all my time learning. I read books and studied every trade they offered. All I wanted was to come out with a whole new set of skills."

She took another sip of her drink. "And did you?"

"I think so. I actually just got a job working with a metal artist. And that's what I want to do, more than anything. Work with metal."

She stared at him for a long moment. "I guess I really don't know you anymore. I had no idea you were interested in art."

"I didn't know it, either, until prison."

She crossed the kitchen toward him then, and Arch wasn't sure what she meant to do until her arms were up around his neck and she was giving him a hug. Her spicy perfume filled his mind. "I hate you for leaving me," she said low in his ear. "But I'm also proud of you. Facing jail time must have been really scary. But you had the guts to do the right thing."

He had no words to give back. Her breath moved on his ear. Her fiercely feminine smell tangled his thoughts. She'd loved him. These were old feelings between them, but at least they were *feelings*. Something other than just getting by, day after day. The familiarity of her invaded his system like a drug.

It had been so damn long since anything felt familiar.

He inhaled. And all the loneliness, the years of total isolation, welled up in every cell, yearning to feel someone there who knew him.

She looked up, and he saw something similar in her dark eyes—that same old longing—and it was too much. He was as weak as a parched man at a desert oasis. Maybe the water here was poison, but he'd take that risk for a drink, even a sip.

He stopped thinking, stopped trying to decide which part of his brain to listen to.

She went on tiptoes, one hand sliding through his hair. The other clinging behind his neck. Her eyes, her skin, her mouth, all of it connecting to his dusty, discarded memories. Bringing them

back to life. She'd been his girl so long ago…
Underneath the perfume she still smelled the
same.

Her mouth tilted up and caught him in its own
luscious gravity. His lips came down hard over
hers. He kissed her with ten years of hunger. Her
mouth opened, so soft, welcoming him to lose
himself. But under the surface desire, unease
slipped its cool hands.

All this contact was inundating his senses,
overpowering his system. He had to be smart,
had to find a way to wake up his brain and *think*.
He needed air and found a little more of it when
he straightened, ending their kiss.

Kit looked up at him, and what he saw in her
face stilled him. A promise that this night could
end however he wanted it to.

Sex. He could have it with her. That close-
ness, that incredible release. He'd dreamed of it
for years.

"You want to stay tonight?" She reached up
and pushed back the hair that had fallen across
his forehead. "We should be together."

Should. The word was the cold shower he desperately needed. He *should* be thinking hard, not
jumping into something just because it was familiar. Familiar was a warning signal. Familiar

was danger. His familiar ways had landed him a decade in jail.

And under it all, he suddenly knew. No matter how seductive Kit was or how incredible their kiss, going back to her would be a huge mistake. A tear in his carefully knit resolve to move forward. And one torn thread could so easily weaken all the others.

He stepped out of Kit's siren arms. "I don't think that's a good idea."

He saw her face shutter, her emotional armor instantly deployed. "Suit yourself." She backed away to the other side of the kitchen and reached for her drink.

He might not know her well anymore, but he knew enough to see the pain behind the mask she'd put on. "Kit, you have to understand. I'm so fresh out of jail. Just two months. We're told, over and over, not to rush into anything. I don't know who I am. I don't know what I want."

"But you know you don't want me." There was a weariness in her voice. "If you'd wanted me, you'd have gotten in touch years ago."

He swallowed hard to contain the churning emotion. "I put you through way too much. You shouldn't want me now."

Her shoulders lifted in a resigned shrug. "Feelings don't make much sense, do they? Plus, you keep saying you've changed."

He nodded. "I have. Enough to know that you deserve better than a guy who treated you like I did. Who just got out of jail and has nothing."

She smiled faintly. "How about you let me be the judge of that?" She emptied her glass and set it down hard on the counter.

She'd held on to him for ten years. He couldn't let her keep holding. "Don't wait for me, Kit. Don't put a minute more of your life on hold for me."

She refilled her glass with straight vodka and raised it in his direction. "I'm fine, Arch. I've always been fine."

He had a feeling that wasn't true. But he needed to be away from her, from the pull of the past. And if she was broken, he wasn't the one who could fix her. He had no answers. He was desperate for air. He slipped out of Kit's house by the back door.

His breath ghosted white around him. He pulled on his gloves, a wool cap, and zipped his jacket as high as it would go. He had to get his driver's license before the weather got much colder. But the cold was a relief tonight, after the close air of the house and the mistake he'd almost made.

Because something had become clear to him in that kitchen. Something he hadn't had the courage to say out loud. The truth was, if he was going to be in a relationship with someone, it wouldn't be Kit. It would be with the woman who brought him laughter and felt like hope. It would be with Mandy.

CHAPTER TWELVE

SHRIMP THE DONKEY had the world's softest nose. Mandy was pretty sure it had healing powers. She was sitting on the porch steps, wrapped in a down parka because the weak early-morning sunlight wasn't really warming anything. Shrimp was supposed to be trimming the grass that had gotten long by the steps, but instead he was nuzzling her cheek. Each swipe and snuffle took away another piece of the angst she'd woken up to.

Frustrating angst. Last night's leftover heartache. She'd thought sleep would help, but Arch Hoffman was the first thing on her mind when she opened her eyes.

Lucky for her, the skittish donkey had somehow decided Mandy was his new best friend. Or maybe he just really appreciated his morning walk. Whatever the reason, he chose nuzzling her over eating, and that had to be the highest compliment a donkey could give.

At least *someone* had chosen her.

She ran her hand over the fluffy hair on his neck, appreciating this stolen moment of quiet in what was going to be a chaotic day of kids and Halloween. But at least one worry was off her mind. Her ranch hands were over their stomach flu. Ely had shown up this morning, thinner and lankier than ever, and taken over the chores. And he said Juan was planning on coming back tomorrow.

Things were suddenly heading back to normal. It was all she'd wanted a week ago. So why was she at such a loose end now?

"It's my favorite donkey. And my favorite person."

Mandy looked up to see Arch walking up the lane from the barn, not far from where just over a week ago she'd dropped the cake and he'd shown up like a miracle to rescue it.

There was new energy in his step. His arms swung a little, like he couldn't wait to take on the world. Mandy's heart took a dip toward the steps beneath her. She'd heard great sex made a person feel that way. He must have had a good night with Kit.

"I think Shrimp likes me best now." She buried her face in the donkey's soft fur to hide her blush. What would he think if he knew she was pondering the details of his sex life? Ugh. She *had* to get rid of this stupid crush.

Arch sat down on the step next to her and held his knuckles out for the little donkey to sniff. "I can't fault him for that. Are you ready for chores?"

"I'm sorry." She smacked her free palm to her forehead. "I should have called you. Ely showed up a few minutes ago and he's taking care of everything. And apparently Juan will be back by tomorrow. So you are officially free of me." It was a relief to say it. She needed distance between them. She didn't want a front-row seat at his reconciliation with Kit.

Arch looked out over the dry lawn. When he spoke, his voice was quiet. "I'm not sure I'm ready to be free."

Mandy froze. Wanting his words to mean what she hoped. But there was no way—after all, he'd just shown up from Kit's. She waited, watching Shrimp, who'd finally decided to do his job and eat the long grass by the steps.

"I like doing chores with you. I like spending time with you."

"I like it, too." Mandy's breath stuttered.

"I know we've only known each other a week, but it feels like longer." He glanced at her, a question in his eyes. "I feel like we're good friends."

And there it was. *Friends*. Stated clearly, out loud.

"We *are* friends." She deserved a special award for keeping her voice so neutral. "But you've got work with Dalton every day during the week.

Plus your own chores at Marker Ranch. You couldn't keep doing chores here anyway."

"I guess you're right." He sat a moment, seeming glum. Watching Shrimp. Then he brightened. "But I can still help you ride again, right?"

She stared at him. "What? Ride a horse? No! I'm not going to ride."

Confusion drew his brows together. "Oh. I just thought... Isn't that the next step in getting used to big animals again?"

"Maybe. But that doesn't mean I want to take it." Just the thought had her staving off a full-blown panic attack.

He nudged her gently with his elbow. "I'll be with you every step of the way."

Ugh. He was so confusing. But she'd promised herself to stop reading meaning into his words anymore. She'd surely get it wrong anyway. "I don't think I can learn to ride again."

"Are you sure? Because I'd really like to teach you."

"It's impossible for me."

"Why?"

She picked at the end of Shrimp's lead rope. Maybe because she'd fought through her fears last night, she finally wanted to tell him. "It makes me panic. Because I feel, sometimes, like I killed my mom."

He set his hand on her arm. When she glanced

at him his olive skin was ashen. "You didn't. Mandy, you can't take the blame for an accident."

"There would never have been an accident if I hadn't begged her to take me riding. She'd been up late the night before at some charity thing at our church. She was tired. But I wouldn't leave her alone until she agreed to a ride."

Arch whistled low. "I can see how it would be hard to live with that. But it doesn't mean you're to blame."

"I think it does." The guilt was suffocating. The regret, too. "I wish I'd just stopped nagging her."

Arch reached for her free hand and folded both of his over hers. "You were a kid who wanted to go riding. All kids push for what they want."

"But there's more. We got up into the mountains and I asked to go to this place called Ten Lakes Overlook. Do you know it?"

Arch shook his head. "Nah, we didn't do too much stuff like that growing up here."

Another reminder that he'd lived down the road, but in another world. "It's a treacherous trail. And kind of a long way. But I was taking photography at school and I wanted to get pictures of the view."

His hand came up and he smoothed her hair, tucked it behind her ear. His voice was gentle. "There's nothing wrong with you wanting that."

"I was competitive in school. I wanted to have the best photos in my class." Emotion, rising like a tide inside her, almost blocked her next words. "So I talked her into riding all the way out there. And then some bird swooped down, suddenly, right at the overlook, and my mom's horse bolted. My mom fell. Her foot caught in the stirrup and she was dragged. It's all granite rock on the ground up there."

She had to turn away from the pity in his eyes. The rest of the story tumbled out with tears streaming. "I finally got her horse stopped and her foot free. She was still alive, but hurt badly. I didn't know what to do. I wanted to stay with her and comfort her, but I had to get help. I wrapped extra clothes around all her bleeding parts. I covered her with my coat. I kissed her and told her I'd be back, and I rode like hell down the mountain." Sobs tore her next words out. "When search and rescue got to her, she was dead. She'd died all alone up there after I left."

"Oh, hell, Mandy." Arch pulled her in, wrapped her close in his arms and gave her the comfort of his big body. But the safety he offered made her sobs come harder. He ran a hand over her hair, again and again in a soothing rhythm. His quiet voice was steady in her ear. Letting her know that it wasn't her fault. That he was there for her.

A soft nose pushed against her cheek, breaking up her sobs.

"Shrimp is trying to help," Arch murmured.

She could feel the donkey's breath on her neck. "Nothing helps." But the sobs slowed a little, allowing her to finish what she needed to say. "All I could think of, at Lori's wedding, was that my mom should have been there. That she *would* have been there, if I hadn't made her go riding that day. Or if I'd gotten help faster."

"Do you really think you could have gotten down a steep Sierra trail any faster than you did? And every kid asks their parents to do things. And I bet your mom was happy to help you with your project."

Shrimp tried again, this time with a delicate nibble on her hair. "That's enough, Shrimp," Arch said. "Go eat some grass."

The miniature donkey huffed out a breath and compromised by nibbling grass right at Mandy's feet.

"That donkey has decided you're his person." Arch cocked his head so he could see her face. "Are you doing okay down there?"

Mandy sniffed and scrubbed her hands across her cheeks. Wished for a tissue and used her sleeve across her nose instead. "I'm so sorry." She tried to steady her quavering voice. "You came here in this great mood and I totally destroyed it. I was just trying to explain why I don't want to ride. I didn't mean to cry all over you."

"I was in a good mood because I was looking forward to seeing you. And I got to see you and talk to you about real stuff that matters. Which I like. But I pushed too hard asking about the riding. I'm the one who should be apologizing."

"You don't need to. I never told you the details of the accident. You couldn't have known."

"You went through something I can't even imagine. You're a strong person, Mandy."

"Ha!" She shook her head. "Lori's the strong one. I'm the sister who fell apart and started baking."

He smiled down at her. "Nothing wrong with that. Especially when a person bakes like you do." He pulled her in close under his arm and Mandy let herself relax against his warmth and strength. She could hear Shrimp chewing and the slow steady rhythm of Arch's heart.

She was due at the church soon. It was hard to break away, but she shouldn't get used to him like this. "I have to get going."

"Are you sure? We could go for a walk up one of the canyons behind here. All the aspen have changed color. I bet they look incredible."

What was with him wanting time with her today? Maybe he felt sorry for her. Or maybe Kit was busy and he was worried about spending a weekend day alone. "I can't. I'm putting on the Halloween party for all the kids at my church. I've got to finish loading my car and get down there to set up."

"You want some help?" Then his eagerness faltered. "Actually, after the cat adoption fiasco, you probably don't."

How awful that he felt so unwelcome. "I'd love the help. And it's a church event, so people will be happy to have you there."

"Why would they be happy to have someone like me helping with their kids' Halloween party?"

"It's church," she reminded him. "Jesus? Welcoming sinners? Forgiveness? All that?"

He flushed. "I guess I'm not too familiar with the Bible. I got to know a pastor in prison. Pastor Doug. He talked about Jesus sometimes. But mostly he just talked to us about staying clean when we got out."

She couldn't resist a little teasing. "Remember when we put church on your list of things to do? It might be good for you. Maybe you could learn to forgive yourself for some of your past choices."

He gave her a long look. "And you think church will help with that?"

"Yes." She'd been born and raised to believe church could help with most things.

"But you go every Sunday. And you haven't forgiven yourself for what happened with your mom that day." He pulled her a little closer into his side. Like he was trying to soften his words with his touch.

Mandy let his words sink in. He was right. What had all those Sunday mornings been for if she'd missed out on that lesson? She craned her neck to see his face and caught the way humor creased his smile lines deeper.

"Seems like maybe we both need to work on that forgiveness thing," he added.

"I guess so." She shook her head, amazed. "Here I was, feeling guilty that I'm skipping the church service today so I could set up the party. But I guess it's okay, because I'm hearing my sermon from you."

His grin took on mischief. "Maybe I found my new calling."

It was hard to look away when he smiled like that. She shouldn't try to make this more than it really was. But the idea of spending the day together was too tempting. "Do you really want to help me with this party?"

"Sure." He stood, stretching as he unfolded his big body from the steps. "And I won't even need a costume. Being Arch Hoffman back in town seems to scare people plenty, all on its own."

She smiled. "We'll put you in the haunted house."

He held out his hand, and Mandy took it, a

little wave of wonder rippling through her as he pulled her to her feet. She'd known that life delivered lots of unexpected heartache, but she hadn't known about unexpected friendship. Just over a week ago, she'd been lonely and teary over a wedding cake. And now here she was, pouring her heart out to Arch Hoffman. Walking along between him and a tiny donkey. Taking small steps into a world where everything seemed a little brighter than it had been before.

CHAPTER THIRTEEN

ARCH TIPPED HIS head back to take another look at the ceiling of the parish hall. Streamers and spiders dangled everywhere. He'd climbed up on the tallest ladder and used every inch of his height to get them taped to the rafters.

The party was just getting started. Kids were running into the hall in costumes, eyes wide at the decorations and different activity stations. Parents greeted each other, laughed and chatted.

He grabbed some tape and secured the paper monster Mandy had made to the wall behind him. People said hello or smiled as they walked past. No one seemed to care that Arch was crashing the church Halloween party. Maybe Mandy had said something to them, or maybe they really were just good folks. Whatever the reason, besides a few surprised looks, no one had said anything to Arch except "nice to meet you."

It was easy to be here, and after yesterday's drama, he had a new appreciation for easy. He'd ridden home from Kit's party last night feeling heavy with the knowledge that she still cared. And scared by how fast he'd slid right back into old patterns. She'd kissed him. He'd kissed her back. And he'd almost lost his way.

He'd woken up today wanting only to see Mandy. She was the opposite of Kit for him. Where Kit brought worry, Mandy made him feel grounded and whole. Something about her was healing, even the sadness and tears she'd shared with him this morning. She was filled up with a light she had no idea she had.

He wanted her to know what she meant to him. How much she mattered. He'd tried to show her today, to be the steady friend she'd needed to help her through her regrets. But he wasn't being completely honest, because she felt like a whole lot more than just a friend to him.

It troubled him. He wanted to look after her. Protect her. Keep her safe. But he knew now that he also wanted more. He wanted to love her. Which made no sense. He was an ex-con with little to offer. The kind of guy he should be keeping her safe from. Because she deserved so much more than what he could give.

He looked across the church hall to where she was running a game of pin the tail on the monster. Her black witch's costume was totally unconvincing with her huge blue eyes and blond curls peeking out from under the tall hat. Plus she giggled whenever one of the blindfolded kids veered off course.

In total Mandy style, she stayed right by the kids when they got confused, steering them gently by the shoulders so they could pin their monster tail in the right place. She'd do a lot to make sure the people around her were successful, and he was one of the fortunate recipients of her help.

She glanced his way and caught him looking. Graced him with her sweet smile. He gave her a thumbs-up, because he knew that otherwise she'd worry. He'd realized today how worry followed her always, breathing murky breath down her neck. Just like it did with him. They both had their traumas hitching along for the ride.

"Can we try?" A little kid and his sister, dressed as matching pumpkins, were eyeing the bucket of so-called eyeballs on his table with giggly apprehension.

"Teeckets pleease," he said in his best Count Dracula accent. He had on a black cape courtesy of Mandy and she'd drawn some ugly scars on his face with makeup.

Each child gave him a ticket.

"Now, eef you dare, you can deeg your hands into these vonderful, though rather slimy, eyeballs."

He gave the mildly evil laugh he'd been practicing and the kids burst into full-blown giggles.

"Here. Let me demonstrate." He pushed up his sleeve and plunged a hand into the peeled grapes. "Ew. Slimy," he said in his normal voice. "I mean, how vonderful!" he corrected in his Count Dracula voice.

The little boy was laughing like crazy and stuck his hand into the grapes as soon as Arch had pulled his out. "Vonderful!" he mimicked. His little sister wasn't so sure and started to back away.

Arch pulled a grape out of the bucket and knelt down in front of her. "Would you like to just hold one eyeball?"

"Yes, please," she said solemnly and took the grape, rolling it back and forth in her hands. "It's a grape, right?"

Arch nodded. "But I think on Halloween it's more fun to pretend they're eyeballs."

She smiled. "Me, too."

"You're a natural with kids."

Arch glanced up. It was the pastor. Mandy had pointed him out earlier.

"Thanks." Arch looked down at his grape-eyeball-slimed hands. "I'm Arch Hoffman. I'd shake but…"

"You're busy," the other man finished for him.

"Doing God's work. I'm George Brennan. Pastor here."

"Mandy brought me," Arch explained. "I hope that's okay."

"Of course. Are you new in town?"

Pastor Brennan looked pretty young. Maybe he'd come here recently and missed out on the Hoffman era. The brother and sister pumpkins were done with their eyeballs and gave a wave as they moved on to the next activity, so Arch shared the truth with the pastor. "I grew up in this area. I caused a lot of trouble when I lived here. I served almost ten years for theft, drug manufacture and dealing, and some other stuff. Nothing violent, though I did fight a lot." The guy deserved to know. It was a kids' event, and he had every right to kick Arch out if he wanted to.

But the pastor just looked a little surprised. "I appreciate you being so up front about all that. And I appreciate your help. If there's anything I can do to support you, just let me know. I hope we'll see you at church on Sunday." And then he smiled and moved on to say hello to the women working at the cookie-decorating table. As if he and Arch had just talked about the weather. As if he trusted that Arch was fully capable of behaving like a normal, non-jail-attending citizen.

Maybe there was something to Mandy's church after all.

"Mr. Dracula? Can we please touch the grapes?" Three little boys were holding up their tickets.

"Grapes?" He flung his cape around him. "Zeez are not grapes. Zeez are eyeballs. Monster eyeballs. And only the bravest of the brave will dare to put their hands on them."

"Cool!" said the smallest boy, pushing up the sleeves of his Superman costume. "I'll go first." And he dipped his hands in with a squeal that had heads turning all over the hall.

Arch grinned, joking with the other boys about their costumes while they waited for the mini superhero to be done with the eyeballs. He thought about the crowd at Kit's party last night. About the sexy costumes and gruesome masks and beer. How it had all seemed so surreal and uncomfortable.

But these laughing kids, these kind people, these slimy grapes, *this* felt fun. This felt right. So maybe, after all his work and study and help from Pastor Doug, he really had changed a little. Maybe he'd even grown up. He'd already known he wanted to let go of the past. But maybe tonight was proof that he was ready for whatever came next.

"I'VE GOT IT." Arch took the table from Mandy's hands and tipped it on its side, flipping the legs up. He carried it to the pile stacked against the wall. "Is that it?"

Mandy turned in a slow circle, surveying the empty parish hall. "It's hard to believe, but I think we're done here."

"The kids had a great time. So did I."

"We had a good turnout. At least thirty families, and we raised almost five hundred dollars for the local food bank."

"You're a star."

"No, I think *you* were the star of the night, Count Dracula. The kids couldn't stop talking about you and your eyeballs."

"I'd never done anything like that before," he admitted. "It was fun. My favorite Halloween ever."

"Really?"

He pretended to think for a beat. "Well, the ones in jail were pretty great, but this was a close second."

She laughed, a tired sound. She'd already taken off the witch's hat, but now she pulled the black robe over her head, revealing her usual jeans that hugged her in the best places. And a pale blue long-sleeved T-shirt printed with a bunch of cartoon dogs and cats and the words *Adopt Don't Shop* across the chest. She was adorable.

"Oh, wait!" She ran into the kitchen and disappeared for a moment. Then came back with a cupcake in her hand. "I saved you one. As a thank-you."

He almost moaned. It was chocolate with white and orange icing, and when he sank his teeth in it was like eating a sweet cloud. "It's incredible. Thank you."

"It turned out okay?"

He stared at her. "You didn't try one?"

"I wanted to save them all for the kids."

"You're nuts. If I knew how to make something like this I'd have a rule. For every dozen I made, I'd get to eat at least one."

She giggled. "I'd be huge."

He held the cupcake out. "You have to share this with me."

"No! You jumped in and made the night great. It's yours."

He pulled the plastic orange pumpkin off the top and used it like a scoop, then handed it to her. "At least try the icing."

She slid the icing into her mouth. He saw the bliss wash over her.

"Best frosting ever, right? Have some more." He broke the cupcake apart and handed her half, then savored the glow of pleasure on her face as she nibbled her piece. "Now can you admit that you're an incredibly talented baker?"

She giggled. "I can make good cupcakes. That's all."

He stilled. "You've got so much talent, so much kindness. You organized this whole party and made it look effortless. You gave a bunch of families a great night *and* raised money to feed a bunch more. You're the most beautiful woman I've ever met, inside and out. Why can't you see that?"

As the last words echoed around the empty room, he realized what he'd said.

She was staring. Oh, hell. She was probably freaking out. Thinking that the last thing she needed was an ex-convict coming on to her. Especially one who was also her brother-in-law. He cleared his throat. Looked around for a distraction and found it in a bunch of balloons hovering in a corner. He pointed. "Want me to go pop those?"

"No." She was still staring, but now a slight smile creased the tiniest thumbprint dimple into her soft cheek. "I'm glad you said that. About me. It was nice of you."

"I wasn't saying it to be nice. I was saying it because I feel…" He searched, but the words weren't there. The feeling was, though. He tried again. "Last night when I went to Kit's, it was weird. I didn't feel like I belonged at all, even though the room was full of people I used to know. So I left. Because I realized I'd much rather be at the ranch, reading a book or watching the stars. And because I realized that if I could have whatever I wanted, I'd be doing those things with you."

Her skin had gone paler than ever and her eyes were wide. This was a bad idea. They were all alone in an empty hall after dark. Was she scared of him? "It's okay if you don't feel the same way. I'll be quiet about it from now on."

"I like you." Her voice was a quiet lifeline in the shadowy room. "I do. A lot. It's all so new, though."

He took a step closer and reached for her hands, wrapping them carefully in his. "I barely have a job, I'm almost broke and I can't drive yet. I'm on parole. I have no right to ask, but you're all I've been thinking about. Would you go out with me? On a date?"

She nodded, her eyes wide and solemn. "I'd like that."

Nerves rushed in. She'd said yes. Now he needed to think of something fun for them. Something perfect. "Just be patient with me. I'm a little rusty on the dating front."

Her burst of laughter took him by surprise. "Hey, it's been ten years…" he tried to explain.

"No, it's not that." She reached up with her sleeve and wiped the laughter from her eyes. The dim light of the kitchen allowed him to see that she was beet red. "It's just that…well, there probably isn't anyone on this planet rustier than me."

He tried to fathom what she was saying. She was gorgeous and funny and smart and good at everything she put her hand to. "You're perfect. Any guy would want to ask you out. How can you be rusty at dating?"

"Um…" She looked around the room as if hoping that someone else would show up and answer his question. "I've never really been on a date."

He was staring. And silent. Then some guy instinct kicked him in the shins, telling him to say something, anything, because his silence was going to make her feel horrible. "Why?"

"I guess I never really wanted to before." Her hands wafted up from her sides, palms out. "After my mom died, I withdrew from a lot of things. I haven't left the ranch much. Just for church, or to do errands. I thought you realized…"

He was staring again. But it was hard to fathom, after years of being locked up, that someone with freedom would want to just stay in one place. But then he remembered her tears this morning. She'd been trapped, too. In grief, in guilt, in the dire consequences of the decision she'd been forced to make on the mountain that day. Locked up in her own sorrow just as surely as he'd been locked in his cell.

"High school?" he asked weakly. "You dated then?"

"I had a boyfriend my freshman year. We'd meet up after school and kiss a little. But then my mom died and everything changed."

"So if I kissed you right now…" He knew the answer before she gave it.

"It would be my first kiss in a very long time."

"Right." They both stared. At the floor. At the ceiling. At anything but each other.

"So it's not like there's any pressure or anything," Mandy finally deadpanned.

His laugh came out a little hollow. But he was grateful that she'd eased things. "Yeah." He shoved his hair back with an uneasy hand. "So this kiss. Do you have any expectations I should know about?"

She put a hand to her cheek as if she was thinking hard. "Well, I'd always imagined it would be from a tall, dark and handsome guy. In some dim room where no one else was. And that his mouth would taste sweet. Like cupcakes."

His heart thudded to a halt. Started up again. "You want that kiss *now*?"

She shrugged as if they were talking about ordinary things. "I think we should get it over with. Otherwise, when we go on a real date, it might be stressful. Because we'll both be worrying about it."

"Very logical." He kept his voice light, but his heart seemed to have taken up residence in his throat. Everything was sped up. His pulse battering in his neck, his hands feeling shaky. Like her first real kiss was his first, too. He took a step closer, watching her body language, not wanting to frighten her or get this wrong in any way. "I *am* tall. And dark."

"And handsome," she breathed.

He was so close to her now. He took her hands in his. "I can't promise it will be perfect, but there's a good chance I taste like cupcakes." He slid his hands up to her shoulders, which were only chest height for him. She was so tiny. When they hugged he'd felt like he was engulfing her. But she seemed even smaller now, fragile and vulnerable, and he wanted to do this so well. He wove his fingers into her soft hair, tipped her chin gently up and brought his mouth to hers.

The touch of her lips made him forget about getting the kiss right. Because this was right. *She* was right. He savored each soft second, not wanting to push her too far. But her mouth explored his with a curiosity and a wonder that dissolved his careful intentions. At first her kiss was a nibble, the briefest touch, as if she were getting her bearings. And then it was more. Like she'd found her way. Her hands went to his shoulders and she drew him down. She sought his tongue with hers, igniting a longing so intense it almost dropped him to the floor.

Fueled by it, he cupped her jaw with his fingers, tilting her head, slanting his lips over hers. She gasped, her fingers digging into his biceps, and she didn't seem so fragile anymore.

He pulled away, overwhelmed by the depth of his desire for her.

"Do that again." Her whispered command sent heat across his skin and he brought his lips back to hers, allowing himself another kiss, teetering close to the edge of his control.

Want snaked through his blood. He grabbed on to a shaky breath, trying to stay calm, trying not to rush. He opened his eyes, taking in her arched brows, her long lashes, her porcelain skin. She was so beautiful. He never knew that people were made this perfect.

A sharp heat behind his eyes had him blinking, pulling back. Tears? Not cool. He looked past her, willing his emotions to settle. It was just a kiss. But he knew that was BS. It was a lot more. Something soul deep, and he'd never even been certain he had a soul. She tasted like cupcakes. She tasted like Mandy. But more than that, she tasted like home.

He wanted to be strong for her, but he stood breathless and shaking, one hand still in her hair, one hand on her hip.

"Hey." Her low voice trembled. At least he wasn't the only one who felt something big. "Are we okay?"

He wrapped his arms around her, breathing in the faint floral scent of her hair. "I think we're more than okay," he answered. "But I'm not the one who just had my first adult kiss." He stepped back and set them apart so he could see her face. "Be honest with me. Was it okay?"

She looked at him for a long moment and he worried until he saw laughter crinkle her eyes at the corners. She was torturing him on purpose. "It was all right," she finally said. "But I think you might need a little more practice."

His laugh came out long on relief. "And would you consider helping me out?"

The giggle she'd been holding back burst through. "I could share my extensive expertise with you."

"All right, then." He took a step in and brought his mouth down to brush his lips over hers. "Let the lesson begin."

MANDY HAD THOUGHT a lot about kisses. She'd read novels, she'd watched movies, she'd imagined what it would be like to kiss someone many times. But none of it prepared her for Arch's mouth on hers. The buzzing promise of all that harnessed energy, dialed lower for her.

Potential energy. She remembered the term, suddenly, from high school science. Arch was potential energy, keeping it calm, keeping it sweet, while the arm he slid protectively around her back was pure power and hard muscle. While the fingertips that pushed back her hair used just the tiniest amount of their strength.

She brought her hands up to frame his big shoulders, to wrap as far up his neck as she could reach, and she kissed him beyond gentleness, looking for an intensity that matched her feelings, that could somehow express the longing she felt for him so deep inside.

There was so much restraint. She slid her hands down his sides, hooked her thumbs in the waistband of his jeans. She was tired of restraint.

With a low sound that was almost a growl, his control faltered. His arms banded her back, his fingers coiled strands of hair, and he took their kisses from warm to searing. Mandy couldn't get enough of that heat, pulling him closer, wanting the feelings he stirred to incinerate the last of the fears that had held her still for so long.

But he pulled back, his breathing rough. She was breathless as well, but she didn't care. She just wanted to throw herself back into those flames where there was all heat and no air.

"There's so much wrong about this," he ground out, holding her away when she tried to pull him close again. "I'm your brother-in-law. I'm a hell of a lot older than you. And I'm fresh out of jail."

She tried to keep it light. Wanting only to get back to their kiss. "Exactly the kind of guy I've been waiting for. I'm picky like that."

He brought his forehead to hers with a laugh strung taut with desire. "Be serious. I know you're what I want. But I also know you deserve better."

She stepped back. "Don't do that."

"What?" His stricken look went right to her heart, but she had to make this point.

"Don't try to protect me. I'm tired of it. All I've done, for over ten years, is protect myself. And I almost suffocated in the process. You came along and helped me find the courage to take risks. So please don't try to take that away from me now."

"I just... I know what people will say. What Wade and Nora and your sister will say. They won't like this."

"I don't care. I could have dated. I've been asked out a few times, but I didn't want to go. But I *do* want *this*. I've wanted it since I met you. Maybe this is a huge mistake, but it's *my* choice and I want to take the risk. You're not responsible for that."

His dark eyes studied her face and maybe he saw the answer he needed, because he reached out and ran the side of his hand softly down her jawline. "Stubborn."

"It's that little donkey. His personality is rubbing off."

"I like it," he murmured. "Especially when you're being stubborn about kissing me." His arms crushed her close, his mouth came down hard and he clearly wasn't worried about her being fragile anymore. Exalted, she kissed him back, trying to show him she *was* strong, she was brave and she didn't give a darn who thought what about her and Arch Hoffman. All she cared about was this feeling between them, this desire that roared through, muffling all the sound but their breathing...and the footsteps coming down the hall.

That thought registered just in time, and she shoved Arch back, grabbed a few of the bags scattered near their feet and made a show of handing them to Arch just as the pastor walked into the room.

"All done in here?" he said brightly. "I was just going to lock up."

Arch looked dazed. He glanced at Pastor Brennan. "All done. We'll just carry these last bags out to the cars."

Mandy's cheeks were so hot she wondered if the pastor could feel the temperature in the hall rising. She grabbed the last bag and scooped up the witch's hat from the table. "Good night, Pastor. Thanks a lot."

"See you in church," the pastor called, locking up cabinets with keys that dangled from an enormous ring. "And I hope we'll see you, too, Arch."

"Sounds good," Arch replied and nodded to Mandy that she should walk out ahead of him. Her face still glowing red, she led the way to the parking lot.

"I brought the ranch truck. Put your bike in the back and I'll give you a ride home."

He kept a hand on her shoulder during the entire drive to Marker Ranch. A warm reminder of how things had changed between them. And at the ranch, when he'd unloaded his bike, he came to the truck window and kissed her one more time. "Can I take you to dinner tomorrow night? On a real date?"

Holy cow, she would raise more than a few eyebrows if she went out on the town with Arch. But she didn't care. "Absolutely. I'll pick you up from Dalton's."

She drove away, his final good-night kiss ringing through her veins. She'd tried to act casual when she said goodbye. But it was impossible to maintain once she was on her own. On the main road she pulled over, rolled down her window and sent a squeaky whoop out into the crisp night.

Then she sat in the dark, hugging her arms

across her body, trying to contain the joy and desire going off like fireworks inside.

She tilted her head out the window to get a better look at the stars, scattered like glitter across the sky. Every cell in her body felt like one of them. Alive and glowing and finally free.

CHAPTER FOURTEEN

IT WAS A perfect fall morning. Clear skies, crackling cold, bright aspens decorating the lower slopes of the Sierra like a gaudy skirt on a granite hula dancer. An ideal morning for a stroll around the ranch with Snack. Because Snack needed it. Or at least that was the story Mandy told herself.

But the underlying, itchy truth was that Mandy had post-kiss jitters that made it hard to focus on anything except what it had felt like to kiss Arch Hoffman. Just those three words together—*kiss, Arch, Hoffman*—sent the jitters rattling up her spine all over again. Walking, fresh air, nature's beauty—they were all legendary in their ability to clear a person's head. So why was hers still spinning?

It was Arch's fault. His bone-melting kisses after the Halloween party last night kicked off a wild emotional ride that had her hanging on for dear life.

It was her fault. She'd barely kissed anyone. Never practiced. Choosing to kiss Arch Hoffman was like using a race car to learn to drive.

She'd loved his kisses. She wanted more. And she intended to get them tonight. Todd had agreed to feed the animals at Marker Ranch so she and Arch could have a real date.

He wasn't the kind of man she'd imagined herself with. But now that she knew him, she couldn't imagine herself with anyone else. She couldn't wait to see him again.

Snack pulled on his leash like a fish at the end of a line. He was heading for the barn, probably hoping to find Lori there. But to Mandy's surprise, the little dog bypassed the barn and went straight for Dakota's pasture. He put his paws on the lowest rail and barked once. Dakota's ears pricked forward and she jogged over to sniff at him through the fence. Mandy was relieved to see that the mare's limp was completely gone, her weight even on each hoof.

"These two are a riot together, aren't they?" The creaky voice had her turning around.

"Jim!" Mandy took his hand, excited to see the ranch manager. "I got your message that you'd be back today. How are you feeling?"

"Good as new." The weathered rancher squeezed her hand in return. "I've got a few years in me still."

"Well, please take it easy. Juan and Ely are both back now. Make them do all the heavy lifting. And if you want to work part-time for a while, that's fine, too."

Jim's grin creased the gray-stubbled cheeks beneath the brim of his hat. "Listen to you. A rancher's daughter after all. How'd you get by? I heard we had all the boys out."

"Arch Hoffman helped me. Wade's brother?" She tried to control the flush that warmed her cheeks.

Either Jim didn't notice or he had the grace not to say anything. He just nodded. "I'd heard he was back. Is he giving you any trouble?"

"No! The opposite. He's been extremely helpful. He did most of the chores, morning *and* evening."

Jim nodded sagely. "I figured he had it in him to make a change. Wade and Nora are good people. Some of that smarts must have rubbed off on their brothers."

She wanted to keep talking about Arch. Wanted to hear his name. But that was silly. "Dakota has been limping. We found a stone in her hoof...well, Arch did, and he got it out. But we could see a bruise. It seems to be healing, though."

Jim nodded. "I hadn't noticed her favoring it, but I'll check it out." He walked over to the fence, leaning on it to take a look at the mare. "You know, it's nice to see you down here. I've missed having you at the barn. There was a time when you spent twenty-four hours a day with the horses."

"There was."

"You were a great rider, you know." Jim shot her a grin with a bit of the devil in it. "Better than your sister. Don't ever tell her I said it. She's a great rider, too. Totally fearless. But your riding was all grace."

Her face got hot. "I loved it."

"I helped teach you to ride. If you ever want to get back on a horse, I'll teach you again."

"I don't know if I can." She let out a regretful breath. "Horses are just so wiggly. You think they're going to move one way and instead they go the other. And why do they have to be so darn big?"

His laugh sounded a little like Shrimp the donkey when he got noisy. "You just have to get used to them again." He pointed over the fence. "Do you see that little palomino over there? That's Ava. Just like Ava Gardner. The actress?" He got a distant look on his face. "That woman was the love of my life."

Mandy giggled. "I had no idea." It was odd to think of Jim in love with anyone, even an old Hollywood star.

"God's truth. Anyways, Ava, the horse, came from a family I know. They lost their property last year due to this drought. She's older. They used her to teach all their kids to ride. You couldn't get a smoother, more predictable ride if you saddled up your couch. If you want, you can start on her."

Mandy watched Ava. The mare was standing on three legs, resting one of her rear hooves. Her head hung down. "Is she asleep?"

"She's just real relaxed." Jim cocked an eye at her. "You want to try it?"

Mandy's heart bumped into her throat, obstructing her answer.

"I'll just grab a saddle." Jim winked at her. "Then you can decide."

This was nuts. No wonder she'd stayed away from the barn all these years. She'd forgotten how persuasive Jim could be. He'd known her since she was tiny. Put her up on her first pony. He'd never mentioned it, but she was sure he knew exactly why she no longer rode.

Yesterday she'd told Arch she'd never ride again. But that was before she'd cried all over him. That was before she'd said all of her fear and worry out loud. And it was before she'd kissed him. Maybe she was finally learning how to get through the heart-pounding moments.

Jim moved quickly for an older man with a hurt back. He plunked a saddle on the fence and went into the corral with a halter. Moments later he came through the gate with Ava. Mandy backed away, but Ava plodded right on by and stood like a rock while Jim tied her to the fence.

Jim handed Mandy a brush. "Go ahead and clean her up real quick."

It was like being a kid again, down here at the stables learning under Jim's steady hand. She brought the brush up to Ava's neck, and if Jim saw the way it was shaking, he didn't say anything. Ava was oblivious, too. Mandy ran the brush unsteadily down the mare's neck and her skin didn't even quiver.

Mandy looked down at Snack, who was sitting a few feet away with his ridiculously fuzzy ears perked up. "Stay there, boy," Mandy said and tied his leash to the fence. She quickly ran the brush over Ava's back and flanks, removing any debris.

"Looks good," Jim said and tossed a pad and the saddle onto Ava's back. Mandy froze at the sight of the tooled leather. The silver embellishments. "My saddle!"

Jim's shrug was matter-of-fact. Refusing to acknowledge that the last time Mandy had used it was the day her mom died. "I saved it for you."

He'd kept the leather spotless. The silver polished. Mandy swallowed hard. "Thank you," she managed.

He nodded once, and Mandy was pretty sure she saw some extra moisture in his eyes. "Well, you're all set." He untied Ava and backed her up.

"I'll lead her, if that's okay. That way you can focus on your seat."

His easy manner and the baby steps he offered made it all seem simple. Her heart flooded with anxious adrenaline, as if reminding her that this was impossible. But she'd been listening to that anxiety far too long. She concentrated on Jim's advice instead.

"Remember how to get on? One hand on the pommel, one on the seat. Foot in the stirrup, and up and over."

The familiar words gave her courage. Deep inside, she knew the steps. Ava stood like a sleepy statue and Mandy was up on her back in an instant. Her feet sought the stirrups just as they always had. Heels down. Toes in. Her body remembered it well. Which was good, because she needed her mind to handle other tasks. Like breathing.

"Ready?" Jim asked. "Hold the horn until you get the hang of it again."

Mandy grabbed on. Jim made a clicking noise and Ava swung into a walk alongside him, moving with predictable, plodding strides. A rocking-chair horse. Mandy's body adapted, her legs heavy in the stirrups. She let go of the horn and put her hands on her thighs. Jim led Ava up the lane toward the upper pastures, but before the land got hilly, he turned her around and led them back to the corral.

Mandy had forgotten how magical the world looked from the back of a horse. Good memories flooded in. Of how much she'd loved to ride. Of the movement, the collaboration, the understanding between horse and rider.

At the corral, Ava stopped by the fence, not even flinching when Snack barked a welcome. Mandy leaned forward, gave the mare a pat on the neck and slid off, amazed and grateful. She'd ridden a horse. And she'd survived.

Jim tied the mare and turned to Mandy, a tight smile on his face. He cleared his throat. "Well?"

Her own voice had gone thick, too. "That was really nice. You were right. She's the perfect horse for me. Thanks, Jim."

"Anytime you want to do it again, you just say the word."

"I will." The tension, the fear, the relief were all balling up in her chest.

He seemed to sense it. "I'll get her unsaddled. I'm sure you have a lot to do. I'll check in with you later."

"Sure." She bent to untie Snack and stumbled toward the house on a wave of emotion and elation. Elation that she'd ridden—that she was overcoming the fear, step by step. But also emotion. Her anxiety might have crippled her, but it had also allowed her to stay frozen in time, holding on to the past. Hiding out in her mom's house, in her mom's kitchen, doing the chores her mom had once done, had made Mandy feel like they were still connected. Like she hadn't completely lost her mother on the Ten Lakes trail that day.

Changing, moving on, reaching for a future, meant that connection might weaken.

But Mandy knew her mom wouldn't want her to be stuck forever.

In the kitchen, Mandy opened a drawer and pulled out her mom's old apron. The pink flowered cotton was starting to fray. Her mom's scent was long gone. But she hugged it anyway. It wasn't nearly enough, but it was all she had.

Looking out the kitchen window at the view down toward the barn, it struck her that if there was a heaven and her mom was an angel, maybe she'd sent Arch Hoffman to catch the wedding cake that day. Because since he'd arrived, everything had changed. Letting go of the past was bittersweet, but for the first time in years Mandy felt hopeful.

She'd ridden a horse today. And she couldn't wait to tell Arch all about it.

ARCH SAT ON a bench behind Dalton's studio, filing the edges of some sheet metal pieces he'd cut earlier. It was monotonous work, but he didn't mind. He had plenty to keep him busy.

Like wondering what the hell he'd been thinking, confessing his feelings to Mandy. All the things wrong with that decision would fill several of Mandy's carefully printed lists. That she was his younger sister-in-law could go right at the top. Next would be the fact that he'd just gotten out of jail and that he was crashing temporarily at the family home in a town where no one wanted him.

Let's see, and add to the list the fact that Mandy was completely inexperienced with men. Yep, he should have stopped everything between them the moment he'd learned it. Instead he'd kissed her. And it had blown his heart wide-open.

That was what worried him most.

"You look like you've got problems piled a mile high." Dalton squinted at him in the bright afternoon sunlight. "You didn't even hear me say your name."

Oh, crap. Now he'd blown it with Dalton. "I'm sorry. I was in my head. Can I help you with anything?"

Dalton shook his head. "Let me guess. It's a woman."

Arch flushed. "How did you know?"

"Isn't it always a woman that gets a guy lost in his own brain?"

"I guess so. It's someone I really care about. But I don't feel like I have a lot to offer her at this point. I'm just out of jail and barely on my feet." The need to talk to someone overrode his caution. "I'm taking her out for dinner tonight. And I want it to be perfect."

Dalton shaded his eyes with his hand and looked out over the desert that stretched out from his house in endless gray-green and brown. "You should make her something."

Arch looked up at his mentor. "You mean, now?"

"Yes, now. If she matters like you say she does, make her something special to remember this night by." He gestured to Arch to follow him inside.

"Put that here." Dalton pointed to a workbench. Arch set the file and metal down.

Dalton paced back and forth, rubbing his hands while he thought. "This will be a good chance for me to see what you can do." He stopped abruptly. "Make something that reminds you of her. Grab some paper and draw it out and show me what you've come up with. You have fifteen minutes. Go."

Heart hammering, Arch scrabbled for paper and a pencil. So far he'd only done the most menial tasks for the artist. Now Dalton wanted him to design? In just a few minutes? He needed to think.

Needed to get his head in the right place. He went back outside to the bench in the sun.

His mind was as blank as the paper in front of him. Dalton Carter was going to see this design. Was going to judge what he came up with.

He wished he'd brought his own notebook. He had a bunch of ideas scribbled in there. Too bad he couldn't think of a single one of them now.

Frustration surged. He leaned back against the wall. Closed his eyes. The desert was so quiet. He could hear the faint hiss of the afternoon wind moving sage and sand. Dalton clanking around inside the workshop. He pictured Mandy. The way the sun caught her hair, and how her mouth felt on his. Her cuddling that donkey and sitting in front of the grocery store surrounded by cats, a determined glint in her eye.

His pencil hit the page and he drew.

Ten minutes later he stood in front of Dalton, one hundred percent schoolboy, complete with shuffling feet and hands shoved in pockets. Waiting for the verdict.

Dalton stared at the drawing. Tipped it one way, then another. Leafed through the other pages, where Arch had sketched out the pieces of metal he'd cut for his creation.

"Well, what do you know?" Dalton finally said,

handing the pages back to him. "The kid's got talent."

"Seriously?" Arch stared at the papers, then back at the artist. It took every piece of his will-power not to fist pump the air or bust into some kind of end-zone dance. This was Dalton Carter. He had to keep it together. "You're sure?"

"What? You want me to give you a gold star?" Dalton clapped him on the back and shoved him toward the workshop. "Come on, grasshopper. Now you have to actually make it. No more wasting time. Get in there and get to work."

ARCH FINISHED JUST a few minutes before Mandy was due to arrive. He brought his creation out of the workshop and set it on one of the wooden tables Dalton had outside.

Dalton followed him and they both stood looking at the delicate California poppy. The papery petals and lacelike leaves were cut from steel and burnished a dull silver.

"Holy hell." Dalton's voice was quiet. He knelt down, looked at the flower from eye level. Picked it up and turned it over in his hands.

"Is that good or bad?" Arch swallowed hard, bracing himself for the artist's critique.

"It's organic." Dalton ran a work-blackened finger over one of the leaves. "It makes you wonder how something so fragile grew from such a heavy metal."

Arch finally breathed. Dalton didn't hate his work.

"It's truly unique. I see more of these in your future. Because, clearly—" Dalton handed the flower back to Arch "—you have a future."

Arch's knees almost buckled at those last four words. It was just a statement, but it felt like a blessing. He had a future. Arch couldn't contain the grin spreading across his face. Or the relief that weakened his legs. He sat down on the bench by the wall, trying to take it in. One of the most successful sculptors in the country thought that he had a future. Doing what he loved the most.

MANDY COULDN'T STOP staring at her flower. The petals were layers of metal so thin they truly resembled the fragile poppies that decorated so much of California in the spring. The steel leaves were so delicate they looked like they'd bend in a breeze.

She loved her gift so much, she'd insisted on carrying it into the Mountain Café, the inexpensive home-cooking restaurant where she'd brought Arch for their dinner date. The food was good here, and since it was on the edge of town, it had a view all the way to the mountains.

"I can't believe you did this with steel." She

looked across the table at Arch, who was trying to look like he didn't care about her praise. But she could see from the way his mouth twitched at the corners that he was holding back a big smile. "I had no idea you could make things like this."

"I learned a fair amount the last few years. But today was special, because I made it for you. And because Dalton put the pressure on."

"He seemed pretty excited about it when I picked you up."

"Yeah, I think it's the longest he's gone without insulting me."

She loved his understated humor. "He's a legendary local curmudgeon, so any praise from him is something to cherish."

Arch took a sip of his water. "He told me I have a future."

It was the best news she could have heard. She hopped up from the table, came around to his side and slid next to him in the booth to hug him. "I'm so, *so* proud of you!"

He wrapped his arms around her. Pulled her close and spoke against her cheek. "I'm proud of you, too. I can't believe you rode a horse! I wish I'd been there to cheer you on."

She pulled back and looked up at him. "I guess we both have things to celebrate."

"Good thing we're having dinner." He leaned down and brushed his lips over hers. Her breath caught. She wanted more than that tiny taste. She kissed his lower lip and he brought his mouth to cover hers in response.

"You've *got* to be kidding me."

A woman's voice. Mandy jerked away to see Kit, clutching a container of takeout, her eyes like bruises, there was so much hurt in them.

"Kit." Arch's voice was lined with regret. What exactly he regretted, Mandy wasn't sure. But an ache started in her chest.

"I guess after ten years locked up, it must be hard to keep your hands off women." Kit's tone was raw agony.

Mandy stared at Arch, horrified. His dark eyes were shuttered, but she saw the guilt there. She might not know much about relationships, but she could do the basic math here. It was hard to speak through the humiliation. "You're seeing Kit?"

"No." Arch turned away from Kit and took Mandy's closest hand in his. His eyes were pleading with her. "I'm not. Mandy, everything I've said to you is true."

"Ha." Kit's hollow syllable held all of Mandy's fears. "I don't know what the hell he's been saying to you, but I know what he's been doing. Two nights ago he was in my kitchen, kissing the hell out of me. So you can decide which to believe. His words or his actions."

She was lost in some kind of bad-dream soap

opera. Glancing around, Mandy saw several tables of people staring, riveted to the unfolding drama. All these eyes, Kit's accusations, Arch's obvious guilt… Mandy reached for her purse with her free hand. "I'll leave so you two can talk."

"Mandy, please don't go." Arch's grip tightened on her hand. "It was one kiss. One slip back into old habits." Arch looked stricken as soon as the cruel words were out. Through her own misery, Mandy actually felt sorry for Kit.

One kiss. She jerked her hand away from Arch.

"Old habits?" Kit's voice wasn't loud, but the hurt in it silenced the room. She straightened, threw her shoulders back and pointed a finger at Arch. "The way you kissed me was a lot of things, but it sure as hell wasn't a *habit*." She paused and Mandy watched the tears glitter in her narrowed eyes. "You said you'd changed. You said you were *different* now. But you're not different. You're still a liar, still a con artist. The only difference is that now you're conning the people who care about you. And I can't think of anything lower than that."

Kit shoved her hands forward and the container of takeout struck Arch full in the chest, splattering food everywhere. A burger landed in Mandy's lap. There was coleslaw sliding down her arm.

When she looked up, Kit was gone, the glass exit door swinging in her wake.

"Mandy, I'm so sorry." Arch grabbed napkins from the metal holder and started swiping at the coleslaw.

"Don't." She'd believed he was interested in her. *Just* in her. That they had a special connection. What delusional part of her brain had even thought that was possible?

The waitress rushed up, her hands filled with cleaning rags. "I need to ask you to leave."

Mandy slid out of the booth and stood, letting the burger fall where it would. Opening her wallet, she dropped a couple of twenties on the table to cover the food they'd ordered. The silent, fascinated regard of the other customers melded into one blinding spotlight. She stumbled away from the table.

A hand caught her arm. It was Miss Carmen, the organist at church. The elderly woman swiped at Mandy's coleslawed sleeve with her napkin. The kind concern in her eyes was one more bit of mortification. "Mandy, are you all right? Can I do anything?"

Maybe it was best to take a cue from Kit, minus the food throwing. Shoulders back, chin up. Ignore the tears as they start to spill. "Thank you, Miss Carmen. But I'm fine." She allowed herself one last glare at Arch. "Happy to see things clearly now."

Giving the older woman's hand a squeeze, she whispered, "Thank you," and then turned for her own grand exit out the door—except she pulled on it instead of pushing. One more aspect of dating she hadn't yet mastered. She shoved out into the night air and ran for her car. Arch could walk home. He could hitch. He could go shack up with Kit or the waitress or whoever. She didn't really care right now.

Except that she did. She really did. And that was the worst part of all.

CHAPTER FIFTEEN

MANDY LOADED CANS of cat food into her cart, trying to blend in with the Wednesday evening shopping crowd at the downtown market. The trouble was, Benson was a small town, and by now, a couple of days after her disastrous date, everyone had heard about the food-throwing love triangle drama at the diner. Five people had stopped her already to express their dismay or to share their opinion that Kit and Arch had always been wild together. To remind her that she could do better.

It was sweet that they were outraged on her behalf, but the truth was, she wished they weren't. Because she didn't want to do better than Arch. She just wanted him, without the Kit-kissing part. And definitely without the Arch-is-a-player-and-Mandy-got-played part.

She felt stupid for missing Arch so much. It was torture ignoring his calls and texts. But every time he reached out, the ache started up in her heart and she pressed Delete. Too bad she couldn't delete the way she missed him.

The cans dropped into the cart with an extra-loud thud as her anger simmered. Why hadn't Arch told her about his kiss with Kit? If he'd let her know right away, she could have decided not to kiss him. She could have refused to go out with him. She could at least have made an informed choice about how much she wanted to risk with him. Because now she'd risked too much, and it hurt.

She reached for another can and froze. Kit was here, at the market, standing at the check-out stand. Adding insult to injury, her high black heels and tight black pants showed off her gorgeous figure.

Rolling her cart carefully, Mandy about-faced so she could sneak away. But her own cowardice stopped her. She couldn't let Arch's idiotic kiss change her entire life. She and Kit lived in the same town. They were going to run into each other. It was better to collect the tatters of her self-respect and face this head-on than to skulk away. No matter how tempting skulking might be.

If she didn't talk to Kit, their awkwardness would haunt her. She'd dread the possibility of running into her every time she came to town. And fear would rule her life once again.

Plus, despite her anger at the flying burgers

and coleslaw fiasco the other night, Kit's devastated face haunted her.

Mandy abandoned her cart and turned to see Kit on her way out the door. She followed and caught sight of her partway down the block, just about to get into a red Jeep. "Kit!" she called.

Kit heard her, looked and turned back to her car.

"Kit, wait!" Mandy increased her pace, knowing she looked foolish jogging after someone who obviously didn't want to speak with her. But it worked. Kit stopped and waited, an arm draped casually over the vehicle door.

Mandy arrived breathless. This had seemed like a way better idea back in the store aisle.

"What do you want?" Anger and hurt still laced Kit's voice.

Mandy swallowed the lump in her throat that blocked her words. *Courage.* She'd been riding Ava all week. If she could do that, she could do this. "I want to talk."

"We have nothing to say to each other."

"Yes, we do." Mandy kept her voice firm. She wouldn't back down now, especially when a few locals were eyeing them with interest.

"You want an apology," Kit said.

"That would be nice. I also want to make sure that you're okay."

Kit snorted. "Why do you care? You won. You have him. It's obvious."

Mandy tucked that information away to ponder later. Telling herself she couldn't care less. That it wasn't causing that tiny rise in her pulse. "I won't take up too much of your time. Can we just talk for a minute?"

With an eye roll visible from space, Kit closed her door, leaned on her truck and folded her arms across her chest. "Sure."

It wasn't exactly encouraging, but Mandy stumbled on. "I didn't know something had happened between you and Arch."

Kit let out a long breath and some of her rigidity softened. "I know. I mean, I realized, once I had time to think it through."

"Okay." Mandy waited a moment but Kit didn't say anything more, so she filled in the gap. "I don't want it to be awkward when we see each other around town. I also don't want you to throw food at me again."

Kit flushed. "I feel terrible about that. I'm really sorry. I was aiming for Arch."

Mandy surprised them both by giggling. "Maybe you need more practice. On a target or something."

Kit's mouth tugged up at one corner, in a hint of a smile. "Probably."

There wasn't much else to say. But at least Mandy felt a little better. The air between them wasn't exactly clear, but it was less cloudy. "Well, thanks for talking."

She stepped back to leave, but Kit put up a hand. "Wait." She met Mandy's eyes as if suddenly resolved to say something. "I don't think anything *did* happen between me and Arch, honestly. I keep playing it back in my head. *I* kissed him. He stopped it. And he tried to tell me he wasn't interested. But I didn't want to believe it."

"I'm sorry." Mandy's relief was mixed with guilt. Kit was so clearly heartbroken.

"It's not your fault. It's mine." Kit's fine black brows creased in. "He left town without saying goodbye all those years ago. If that doesn't show someone's true feelings, I don't know what does." She paused, and her next words came out in a rush. "I thought I'd moved on. But maybe in the back of my mind, I was waiting for him. Hanging on to this idea of what we were. All young and wild. It's just…" She faltered, looking past Mandy, like she was trying to piece the words together. "It wasn't always easy being with him. But it was exciting. He's larger than life, you know?"

Mandy did know. The way Arch had caught the cake that first day, like some superhero out of nowhere. How he'd made the chores look so easy, helped her be brave, made her laugh. "It rubs off on you," she said. "I get it."

"I used to be what he wanted." A sheen of tears

gave Kit's dark eyes extra depth. "It was an amazing feeling to be wanted by him. But you're everything he wants now. You're good. Sweet. Wholesome. That's the life he's after. And he's *always* gone after what he wanted. Even if it meant breaking the law. Even if it meant hurting someone else."

Mandy tried to balance Kit's words with the Arch she knew. She couldn't. "So you're saying he's only interested in me because I represent something to him? That I'm a part of the life he's trying to acquire?"

Kit was quiet for a moment. As if she were wrestling between possible answers. "No," she said. "Maybe that's part of it, but it's not all." Big silver rings adorned all of Kit's fingers, and she twisted them as she spoke. "Arch cares for you. And I can see why. You followed me today to try to make things right. Not many people would do that." She regarded Mandy with her huge sad eyes. "I guess I'd just tell you to be careful. Arch casts a big light. When it's shining your way, you see the world in high definition. When it's gone, things can feel pretty dark."

"I…" Emotion clogged Mandy's throat, making it hard to get the words out. "I just need to know that you'll be okay. I hate that I'm a part of what's hurting you. I've had a lot of hurt, so I know what it's like."

"I'm fine." Kit's expression hardened, as if she'd pulled the walls of a shell back around her. A shell made of makeup, black leather and silver jewelry. "I've always been fine. Seeing Arch back in town threw me off, that's all."

Their moment of connection was clearly over. "I appreciate you talking to me," Mandy said. "I really do."

Kit turned to open the door of her Jeep. Then she paused, looking at Mandy again. "Just do me one favor," she said.

"Of course."

"If you're out with Arch, don't come to the Dusty Saddle."

Mandy's heart lurched for the other woman. "I won't. I promise."

Kit nodded, slid into the driver's seat and closed the door between them.

ARCH WAS KICKING the mud off his boots when a truck turned into the driveway of Marker Ranch. He studied it, his vague apprehension turning to relief when Nora pulled up to park alongside the porch.

He went down the steps to help with her door, but she waved him off. "Hey, Arch."

"You're back in town already? Is everything okay?"

"I had a couple days off. I wanted to see Todd."

"I like your husband. You married a great guy."

She smiled. "I heard you two are buddies now. Are you enjoying that mountain bike? Todd sent me that video of you wobbling around on it your first day. You sure were rocking that shiny blue helmet."

He laughed. "It's a good look. Seriously, Todd has been a great friend to me. I don't know what I'd have done these past few weeks without him. He's even taking me down to Bishop for my driver's test." Arch ignored the disappointment weighing those words down. He'd looked forward to taking that trip with Mandy. But she hadn't returned his calls since their messed-up date. He couldn't blame her.

"I'm glad things are good. And how about here at the ranch? Todd's your biggest fan and says you have everything running smoothly, but I promised Wade I'd make sure things were in order."

"I get it." She was a good sister. And in her way, she was looking out for Arch, too, by making sure Wade's expectations were met. "Let me take you on a tour and you can see for yourself."

Arch showed Nora the lumber he'd salvaged from one of their dad's old sheds and how he'd used it to patch the barn and several fences. They toured the cattle and horses, already fed for the evening and happily munching. He showed her the broken gate he'd welded, the leaking trough he'd sealed, the shiny engine on the tractor that he'd cleaned with advice from Todd. And then he brought her back to the house to show her the windows he'd caulked and the faucets he'd replaced.

"We gave you a huge list of projects," Nora said in wonder as she tried out the kitchen faucet. "I can't believe you did them all. And this thing doesn't drip anymore. It's a miracle. Wade and I tried to change the washer a few different times."

"It needed a little more help than that," Arch said.

"Wait, what is this?" Nora reached for the poppy he'd made Mandy. After she'd left it behind on their date, he'd set it on the kitchen windowsill. Nora turned the flower over and over in her hands. "This is gorgeous! Where did you get it?"

He explained about Dalton and the work he'd been doing there. He meant to leave Mandy out of the story because it was such a big mess. But Nora was listening and asking questions and really wanting to know. And leaving out important details had caused this disaster with Mandy and Kit in the first place.

So he finally asked Nora to sit down at the kitchen table, got them each a root beer from the fridge and told her everything. How he felt about

Mandy, how he'd made her the flower, how he'd hurt Kit and Mandy all at once.

"I feel like I'm floundering," he confessed. "Barely getting by. Messing up my good decisions with bad ones."

"Well, let's face it. You haven't had much practice with making good decisions. And everyone messes up sometimes."

He hadn't expected her to be so understanding. "Can I ask you what you think I should do?"

"You have to fix it. It's only a disaster if you leave it all messed up, right?" She sighed. "You know I'm at fault in this, too. I should have warned you about Kit. I saw this coming months and months ago. She and I talked and I could tell that she still cared for you. In fact, it was her willingness to forgive you and to try to understand you that helped me see past the conflicts I was having with Todd. That's kind of strange to think about."

"It is." He couldn't imagine wild Kit advising capable Nora.

"I guess maybe I was hoping you two would have some kind of happy ending together." Nora paused, then shook her head. "No, I take that back. You two were never good together. You were way too volatile. Lighter fluid and a match."

Arch smiled at the description. "We were. We had fun, but we pulled each other down. I don't want that again. And I don't love her anymore. Which feels awful to say."

Nora nodded. "You can't love someone just because they love you. It doesn't work that way. But you do owe Kit a conversation. And an apology. You should never have dated Mandy without telling Kit first. That is where you really messed up. You need to own that part of it."

"You make it sound so easy."

"Easy doesn't factor in when you need to apologize."

"You're right." He set his root beer on the table with a resolute thump. "I'll go see her tomorrow and try to set things right."

Nora took a sip of her soda and studied him for a moment. "You really have changed, Arch. I see how hard you're trying, and I don't want you to get derailed." She picked up the sculpture that lay between them on the table. "This is your calling. It's so obvious. You need to chase it with everything you have."

"I plan to."

"I know you've got feelings for Mandy, but please don't let that get you off track." She touched one of the steel petals. "This matters more than anything. *This* will keep you on the right path."

Arch nodded. "I'd like to try to have both. If I can."

Nora smiled gently. "I get it. Love is awesome. But stay true to this. It's a gift."

"High praise coming from you."

Nora sighed. "I've thought a lot about it. There are so many things you did that I hate. And I will always hate them. But if you're not doing them anymore, I don't want to spend my life angry at you." She shoved her chair back. "I need to get home. Thanks for all you've done on the ranch. Wade will be thrilled when he sees it."

"Thanks for taking a chance on me. For letting me stay."

"I'm sure you can stay here as long as you want. Wade will be living up at Lone Mountain Ranch with Lori and managing his cattle from there. It would actually be great to have someone living on the property."

"I'll check in with him when he gets back," Arch said. "I hope he'll feel the same way."

Nora put a gentle hand on his arm. "Welcome home, Arch. And good luck with Kit. And Mandy."

"Thanks, sis." He walked her to the door and watched her drive away into the dusk. And stayed there, watching the stars appear one by one. Almost two weeks on the ranch and this moment each evening, when he watched the sky change, still felt like a miracle. Like freedom. Sixty-seven days since he'd left prison, and he was still figur-

ing out what that word meant. So far his definition included this open sky with its endless stars,
his sister's forgiveness and that metal poppy on
the table inside. And the way his heart felt every
time he thought about Mandy Allen.

ARCH PULLED OPEN the door of the Dusty Saddle
and crashed into a wall of memories. He and Kit
used to hang out here all the time. Long nights
of beer and pool that ended in booze-blurred sex
back at her place. Crazy that she worked here
now, that she chose to spend her days and nights
behind a bar. But Kit had always loved a good
party. She still did, if her pre-Halloween bash
was any indication.

The bar was empty at eleven in the morning.
Hazy sunlight filtered through the high windows,
casting the tables and chairs in a glow that made
the old place look somewhat cheerful. Arch heard
the clip of high heels on the wood floor and Kit
stepped through a door behind the bar. She froze
for an instant when she spotted him standing
there, then walked around the bar to meet him.

"So many times I imagined you showing up
here. So many times I wanted you to. But now I'd
rather you just left." Her voice was more husky
than normal and he knew it was emotion. Emotion that he couldn't help her with. He had nothing to give in return. Not with her. Not anymore.

"I should have told you I was going to ask Mandy out. I wish I'd told you."

The anger from the other night, the burger-throwing rage he'd expected to find, wasn't there. Instead her voice was resigned. "I think you tried, sort of, at my party. But I didn't want to hear it."

"I should have been more clear. I like her. A lot. That kiss between you and me was a mistake." They both winced at his blunt words. He was terrible at this. "I mean, you're a very attractive woman. But I want something else."

"Why?" She took a step closer. "We still have all this chemistry. I felt it that night. You did, too. Why can't we try again?"

He took a step back. "You're attractive. It was a great kiss. But it felt all wrong. This thing with Mandy, it's different."

"Yeah." Kit ran a hand through her black waterfall hair in a bleak gesture, like it was all too much to take in. "I guess I just keep getting stuck on why different is better. Why you want different and I want the same."

"The same scares me down to the bone. We have some good memories, but they feel like they'll pull me back to that person I was. And I can't go back. Not one step. Not one inch."

"So sweet little Mandy Allen is your answer?" Her voice shook a little. "You can't become a good person just by holding someone nice close to you."

"It helps."

"So you're using her."

"No." He didn't want to say it. Not when the words would cause her more pain. But she was pushing him into a corner. "She means a lot to me. It feels very…" He tried and failed to find the word he wanted. "Special."

"You barely know her."

He took a deep breath. Honesty was brutal, but it was needed here. Total honesty to set them both free. "I fell for her. Pretty much the moment we met. I know that deep inside—as sure as I know anything. I want to be with her."

Kit's eyes went wide. "You mean, forever? Like, you want to marry her?"

"Please don't ask me that. Don't make me say things that will hurt you."

She turned on him then, her frustration visible in the clenched fists at her sides. "Don't you get it? I *need* to hurt. I *need* to break apart this idea of us that I've carried around for years." She paused as if trying to find her breath. When she spoke again her voice was small. "I didn't even know I was carrying it. I've had boyfriends. I thought I'd moved on. But seeing you again? It all came back. All the feelings, all the ways I've missed you.

I thought I was strong and you made me weak again. So just say it. Do you want to marry her?"

She was asking for a brutal remedy. An amputation with blunt truth. "I don't even know if she'll go out with me again after the other night. But someday, if I can figure out how to be the man she deserves, then, yes, I'll ask her to marry me."

Kit stilled, a thick wall of silence around her. Then she let out a long, slow breath. "Thank you. I needed to hear it."

"Will you be okay?"

"Of course." Her mouth was a tense line that told him she was willing it so. She walked past him, to the door of the bar, with quick, jerky steps. "And now I'm ready for you to go. I appreciate you coming by. And I'm sorry I threw that food at you the other night."

"And I'm sorry I didn't give you a heads-up about Mandy."

"Well, now I have one," she said with false brightness. "I'll see you around, Arch."

"Sure." He walked past her and out into the morning sunlight. When he turned to say a final goodbye she was already closing the door behind him. He heard the snick of the dead bolt sliding home, and she flipped the sign on the window

to Closed. The staccato of her high heels clicked
away from the door. He knew, without seeing or
hearing her, that she was crying.

CHAPTER SIXTEEN

MANDY SET THE vase on the dresser in Lori's room. Lori and *Wade's* room now. She tipped the sunflowers back and forth until the bouquet looked balanced. It was hard to believe it was Saturday already. Almost three weeks since the wedding. Lori and Wade were due home later tonight, and Mandy wanted the house looking spotless.

Though Lori and Wade were the people she knew best in the world, she was nervous. They'd had three weeks on their own. Would they resent coming home to her? Would they wish she didn't live there so they could continue honeymooning?

Mandy's nerves had her scrubbing the old house until it gleamed. Even Snack got a bath, indignant and spluttering. Now he was hiding in his dog bed in the corner of the room.

Cleaning also helped take her mind off Arch. She hadn't seen him since their terrible attempt at a date almost two weeks ago. She missed him. Sometimes she'd catch herself glancing at the driveway, hoping she'd see him pedaling her way with flowers or an apology. But…nothing.

Though maybe that had something to do with her refusal to return his texts and calls. He'd hurt her, yet she missed him, and that scared her. So she'd continue hitting Delete when she saw his name.

She clattered down the back stairs to the kitchen. The tea she'd brewed a few minutes ago was ready. She pulled on her jacket, grabbed a blanket and went to sit on the porch swing to watch the storm come in.

It was late afternoon and clouds were piling up on the peaks. They were supposed to get snow by tonight. Maybe even a few feet of it. She crossed her fingers at the thought. An early-November storm could mean a long winter. The drought-ending kind of winter that brought heaps and heaps of snow.

The noise of an approaching truck had Mandy glancing down the lane. It took her a moment to recognize it. Wade's ancient Chevy. The one he drove before he'd bought the new Ford he and her sister had taken to the airport. Her heart bumped when she recognized Arch at the wheel.

She stood as he climbed out of the truck. "You're driving."

He covered the ground between them in a few long strides and was up the steps before she knew it. He held out the metal poppy. "You left this at the restaurant. I'd love for you to have it. If you'd be willing to, that is."

Mandy took it, wondering anew at its fragile beauty. "Of course I want it."

"And I have some other things to show you." He held out a piece of paper. "Todd took me into Bishop last weekend for my driver's test. I passed. This is my temporary license."

"Congratulations." She took the paper. "Archer *Cash* Hoffman?"

"My mom had a thing for Johnny Cash. Dad probably just liked any reference to cash."

Mandy shook her head in mock dismay, but the truth was, she'd missed his lame jokes.

"And one more thing." He pulled an envelope out of his pocket. "Look inside."

She peered in, surprised to see a bank statement from the local credit union and a couple of pay stubs from Dalton. She handed the envelope and the license back to him. "Why are you showing me all this?"

He gestured to the swing. "Will it hold both of us?"

"I think so." She sat on one end, and he took the other. The old wood let out a groan of protest at his weight.

He grimaced. "Uh-oh. Here I am hoping to make amends. It's not gonna help if I bust your pretty swing."

She pulled her blanket close and waited. Because she had no idea what to say. She still believed he should have told her about Kit. But it was hard to stay upset when her heart was rising like a helium balloon in her chest, wanting to float the rest of her up with it. He was here. And it was just so good to see him.

He cleared his throat. Glanced at her. "I should have come sooner. But I wasn't sure… You haven't answered my calls. Or texts."

"I know. It was rude."

"No. Rude was what I did. Putting you in that situation with Kit. Not telling you." He paused and shifted on the swing so he was facing her a little more. "You know what bothers me the most? That this whole time I've known you, I've been telling you to be brave. To overcome the things that frighten you. But I didn't even have the guts to tell you about Kit."

She nodded. It bugged her, too.

"I came out of prison so sure I'd changed. But what happened with Kit has been a wake-up call. I haven't changed as much as I'd like to think. It's like the day I drove without a license. I wanted something, and because of that, I felt entitled to break the rules. Since I wanted you, and mentioning Kit might have got in the way of that, I just didn't mention her. That guy I was, who thought he was above the law, is still in me."

He looked so miserable that she tried to soften

it for him. "You're trying. Maybe some things are easier to change than others."

"I don't want to excuse what I did. Not when I hurt you with my actions." He rose from the swing to stand in front of her. But he was so tall, he knelt on a knee to make eye contact. "I swear to you, I will tell you the truth about everything from now on. That's why I brought these papers. I want you to know everything about me. From my middle name to my income. And anything else you have questions about."

Mandy finally found the thing she needed to say. "I want you to tell me things up front. No matter how uncomfortable they might make you. No matter how hard they might be for me to hear. If you can't give me that, I can't be in your life."

His eyes were intent on hers. "I will tell you everything."

"You promise."

"I promise." He took both her hands in his. "So here is everything. I spoke with Kit. I apologized and made it clear that I don't have feelings for her and that I plan to be with you, if you'll have me."

Mandy felt her cheeks flush warm in the cold night.

"I want to spend as much time as I can with you. You make me laugh and you make me hope. You make me want to work hard and be a better person. So I'm asking for a second chance to date you."

Mandy thought about what Kit had said. That Arch had a light that lit the world up. It was here now, a spotlight of words and conviction. It wasn't easy to live without it. But in the days they'd been apart, she'd learned that it was possible. The world hadn't stopped. She hadn't crumbled. Because he'd helped her discover her strength.

"You can have the chance," she told him.

His smile was a mixture of relief with a good dose of Arch Hoffman dazzle. "Really?" He straightened and pulled her up from the swing and into his arms, pressing her close against him. She held tight, inhaling his scent, relishing his strength. He buried his face in her hair and whispered, "I've hated this time away from you."

She pulled back to study him. Wanting to see his face close-up. Needing to see honesty in his eyes. It was there. "Me, too," she whispered.

He wrapped his arms around her and they stood that way, watching the layers of cloud come down over the mountains. But even Arch and her blanket couldn't keep the cold at bay. Mandy shivered. "It's supposed to snow."

"I can't wait." Arch pulled her in tighter. Looked down at her. "Would you want to go snowboarding next weekend? If we get a few feet, Todd said the resorts would open. Maybe not down here, but up near Lake Tahoe for sure."

"I've never been snowboarding," she told him. Another piece of life she'd let slip by.

"Me neither. We can learn together."

It was one thing to say she wanted to date him. But to go away with him? Mandy shivered again. "I'm not sure."

"You're cold." He wrapped the blanket snug around her shoulders like a cape. Held it closed under her chin and bent to kiss her.

She brought her lips to his in a delicate scrap of a kiss. Seeing how it felt to be close to him again. When he parted his lips, she tasted his warm mouth and wanted more.

She ran her hands up onto his huge shoulders, trying to pull him closer than a kiss. Pull him into her skin, into her body with all longing she'd felt for him while they'd been apart.

"We have to get you warm." His words were a vibration against her mouth. She was cold, but she'd choose freezing over ending this kiss now.

"Come inside," he whispered. He turned her, walking her backward. Kissing her softly with every step until her back was against the door of the house. She fumbled for the handle but the screen was in the way, so she gave up and reached for his hair instead, weaving her fingertips in its silky ends.

His arms wrapped around her, pressing her body up against the length of him. The heat from him traveled over her skin and through her bones and she clung to it.

Every part of her was on alert to the newness of this. The wild undercurrent that she knew would be there if either of them dropped their restraint. His arms trapped her between him and the door so she could feel the power of him, the height, the breadth of muscle. His kiss scattered her senses. One coherent thought flitted. That she'd had no idea kisses could be like this.

A car door slammed somewhere in the back of her mind. And then closer now a voice rasped out, "What the hell?" and suddenly Arch was gone, jerked away, leaving behind cold air and the smack of bone on bone. Arch staggered back a few steps, his forearm over his jaw where Wade had hit him.

Lori, wide-eyed and beach-tanned, ran up the porch steps. She stared from her husband to his brother to Mandy in horror. "Mandy, are you okay?" And then to Arch. "What the *hell* do you think you're doing to her?"

Mandy emerged from her shock in time to step between the two brothers. "He wasn't doing anything *to* me. We were kissing."

"I could see that," Lori fired back. "Have you lost your mind?"

"No! My mind is fine," Mandy retorted. "Leave him alone."

"You don't know my brother," Wade said. "He takes what he wants and to hell with the consequences. Stay away from her, Arch."

"I love her." Arch's voice cut a quiet slice through their outrage.

"You don't even know her." Wade raised his arm as if he was considering hitting Arch again. "So what's your angle? Are you thinking that if you get with her then you can have a free ride around here?"

Mandy couldn't stand it for one more second. "Stop it! Everybody calm down!" She opened the front door and pointed inside. "Kitchen. Now!"

Arch tried to smile at her bluster but winced. His jaw must really hurt. She was still stunned from his declaration. He loved her?

Mandy followed the small group into the kitchen, amazed that they were all listening to her. "Sit," she commanded, pointing to the scarred old pine table in the middle of the room. They did, her sister staring at her and Wade glaring at his brother.

She tossed Arch an ice pack from the freezer, put the kettle on the stove and pulled mugs and plates out of the cupboard. Then she fished a tub of homemade chocolate chip cookies out of the pantry and planted it in the center of the table.

She held up a hand when Wade started to speak.

"Hear me out before you start making pronouncements about my life. Arch and I care about each other. We've helped each other out the past few weeks. We've decided we want to date. Evidently, you think that's a bad idea, and you're entitled to your opinion. But I want you to know that it's *my* idea. He's not taking advantage of me, or preying on me, or anything else you seem to think he's doing."

"He's a felon, Mandy," Lori said.

"Oh, really?" She kept her voice mild. "I hadn't realized."

"Don't be sarcastic. You've never dated." Lori was in full-on big-sister mode. "You don't know all the things that can go wrong."

Mandy resisted the urge to throw a cookie at her sister. She sat down at the table across from her instead. "I haven't had a boyfriend, true. But I'm not a naive idiot, either. I know that a lot of relationships fail."

Wade cleared his throat, obviously trying to calm down. "Arch, I left you in charge of our ranch. I trusted you."

"And I think you'll find that everything is in great condition," Arch said.

"But you *can't* date Mandy," Wade went on.

Arch stared at him and Lori. "You two act like she's twelve years old. Mandy is an adult, as well as a very strong person. Do you even know her?"

He glanced her way and Mandy mustered a faint smile, trying to show that she appreciated his vote of confidence. "She's a donkey-wrangling, cake-baking, cattle-feeding, horseback-riding, cat-rescuing wonder woman. And I'm sure she can be trusted to figure out who she'd like to spend her time with."

"But you just got out of prison," Wade said. "You need to focus on getting your life together."

"I do," Arch said. "And I have been focusing on that and will continue to do so. I know it's soon. Mandy knows it's soon. But we want to be together. It's the only way I can explain it." He turned to Mandy and she saw that familiar humor tugging at the corners of his mouth. "Hard to believe there's all this fuss and we haven't even gone on a real date yet."

She giggled. "I know. We're already causing so much trouble."

"You haven't gone on a date yet?" Lori ran her hands over her face, as if trying to wake up from a strange dream. "Why were you making out on the porch when you've never been on a date?"

"Excellent question," Arch said. "We'll be going on a lot of dates in the near future to make up for that. If that's okay with you, Mandy."

"That sounds great. How about the High Country Sports Bar this week? I saw a sign that said they have a DJ on Wednesday nights." Mandy glanced at her sister. "Maybe you and Wade would want to come, too? You could chaperone since you're so worried."

Lori glared at her. "Maybe."

Wade was still solemn. "Arch, I just don't want to see Mandy hurt."

"I'm not planning on hurting her," Arch assured his brother.

"I'm right here," Mandy reminded them. "We don't have to talk about me in the third person."

"How are you going to pay for these dates?" Apparently Wade was not going to let this drop, but Mandy was tired of the interrogation.

"Arch has a job working with Dalton Carter, the metal artist, who thinks he has incredible talent. He's got his driver's license already. He's taking care of everything he needs to do. So just cut him some slack, please." She stood to catch the kettle before it whistled. Popped a tea bag into each mug and poured water. Handed everyone a cup. She didn't care if they wanted tea or not. She just wanted them to calm down. Tea was good for that.

There was silence. The uneasy kind. During which Lori and Wade had some kind of secret newlywed conversation conducted with raised eyebrows. Arch looked mildly amused.

Mandy knew one thing. Any doubts she'd had about going snowboarding with Arch had resolved in the face of this conflict. She was so tired of everyone tiptoeing around her. Maybe she'd been broken. But she wasn't anymore. "Look," she said softly. "I've been doing great. Better than I've been in a long time. So judge all you want, but Arch and I will be spending some time together. In fact, Arch invited me to go snowboarding next weekend. And I just happen to have a gift certificate to a really nice lodge that I won at the church silent auction last year. If this storm drops as much snow as they say it will, Arch and I will be heading toward Lake Tahoe first thing next Saturday morning."

The slow smile breaking across Arch's face cracked something inside Mandy's heart. And out of the crack poured anticipation, of time together, of the chance to know him somewhere other than here, where they both had so much baggage.

"I just hope you know what you're doing," Lori murmured.

"I'll kick your ass if you hurt her," Wade added.

"Stop it with the third-person thing," Mandy said.

Arch grabbed a cookie off the plate. "I have to get to the chores over at Marker Ranch before the snow starts." He leaned down to Mandy and brushed a light kiss over her mouth. "If the snow isn't too thick, can I take you to church tomorrow?"

Mandy couldn't help but steal a glance at Lori and Wade. Both were studies in disbelief. Probably never thinking they'd hear those words come out of Arch Hoffman's mouth. Neither had she. Maybe he was just trying to stupefy Wade and Lori, or maybe life was offering up a lot of miracles today. "That would be great," she told him. "Can you be here by nine thirty? If the roads aren't too bad?"

"I'll be here."

"I'll walk you out."

He offered his hand and she took it, following him out into the dusk.

"Don't forget your poppy." Once outside he handed her the small sculpture they'd left on the railing.

Mandy turned the work of art in her hands. "Thank you for sticking up for me in there. I hate that they think I'm so weak."

"They'll see that they're wrong." He pulled her close and kissed the top of her head. "Thanks for sticking up for *me*."

"How's your jaw?" She brought a fingertip up to brush it, but he caught her hand and kissed it.

"I've had worse. It's okay. I'm glad my little brother is looking out for you. Even if it makes him somewhat violent."

"He's pretty upset."

"Hopefully he'll come around. Wade has so many reasons to think I'm a bad idea. Reasons I gave him." Arch stepped close and pulled Mandy in. Kissed her gently on the mouth. "I can't tell you how much I love doing that," he murmured.

"You can do it anytime." She kissed him back, wanting endless time for more kisses like this.

"You're serious about going snowboarding?" he asked.

"Yes. Are you serious about church?"

"Absolutely. Anywhere with you." He kissed her gently. "I'd better go or I'll be feeding cattle in the dark."

"See you later, then." She kissed him again.

"See you."

Mandy waved him off and then took her poppy inside. Lori and Wade were still sitting at the table with their tea. "What is that?" Lori asked.

Mandy set the poppy in front of her sister.

"It's amazing," Lori breathed, running her fingers over the delicate stem. "It looks real."

"Arch made it."

"On his own?" Wade asked.

"He's a talented guy." Mandy picked up her tea and took a gulp. It was strong. Just what she needed.

Wade and Lori stared at the sculpted flower.

"It's weird." Wade's voice was hushed. "He's my brother and I don't really know him at all."

"Maybe you can get to know him now," Mandy suggested.

"Are you okay?" Lori pulled her gaze away from the poppy and fixed it on Mandy. "This thing with Arch. Is it making you happy?"

"I think so," Mandy said. "But this is my choice, good or bad, and I need to do it my way. Wade, I know you have a lot of bad memories of your brother. But that's not the guy I've gotten to know."

"We care about you, Mandy," Wade said.

"I know. And I'm grateful. *Now*, there's soup for dinner, and some roasted chicken. We'll eat in an hour. So why don't you two go get settled in? And over dinner you can tell me all about your honeymoon."

"You're really not going to let us talk you out of this?" Lori asked, biting into a cookie. She closed her eyes in exaggerated bliss. "God, I've missed these."

"No," Mandy said, pulling a salad bowl out of the cupboard. "And I need you to be supportive of me right now."

"I'll go check on the animals," Wade said. He grabbed a cookie and headed for the door.

"I guess I'll start unpacking." Lori stood. "Where's Snack?"

"Upstairs in your room. Sulking after a bath."

"Okay, then." Her sister paused as if she wanted to say more. "You're being *careful*, right?"

Mandy stared, trying to figure out the overemphasis on the word *careful*. When it hit her, her cheeks went scarlet. "Oh, *that*. No! Yes. I don't know! We're not at that point yet."

"I'm dumping a box of condoms on your bed when I go upstairs. If you get to that point, use them."

She might sink through the floor. "I'm twenty-four years old," she reminded her sister. "I've got this."

"But you're also my little sister. And I get to worry."

Mandy laughed at that. "Oh, no, I've got the worry department covered. Now go cheer up that dog of yours."

She heard Lori calling for Snack as her sister clumped up the stairs. Mandy started pulling ingredients from the refrigerator, feeling happier and more excited than she could remember feeling, ever. Arch Hoffman was back in her life. He was taking her to church tomorrow. She'd faced down her sister and Wade's disapproval. And snow had started falling outside the window. Big fat white flakes covering the parched autumn ground.

CHAPTER SEVENTEEN

IF THERE WAS any one moment that illustrated how much Arch's life had changed, it was sitting in church with his brother. Wade was even wearing a suit because he'd volunteered to be one of the ushers.

Arch wished he could take a photo of himself and his brother, sitting in this pew, and send it to their dad. It would be the best revenge for all the ways he'd wronged them. Arch would caption it. *You tried so hard to make us be like you. Look how that turned out.* Not a very charitable thought. Nor a practical one, since he had no idea where his dad was. But fun to think about.

Mandy slipped her hand into his and Arch glanced down to catch the smile she gave him. He wanted to kiss her, but this was church, so he simply squeezed her hand and tried to pay attention. He didn't know much about religion. Didn't know anything about the story that the pastor was referring to. But he did know words like *forgiveness* and *redemption*. So he held on to those and sent up a prayer that he might be worthy of them and of the beautiful woman sitting by his side.

When the service was over, Lori and Mandy had to help with the coffee hour. Arch and Wade snagged coffee for themselves and a couple of doughnuts and headed out into the covered hallway that ran alongside the snowy courtyard. It was cold out here, but better than the crowded hall full of church members.

Arch didn't like crowds anymore. He'd lived in them for ten years. "One of the best things about being out of jail," he told Wade, "is that I have the ability to leave a room if I don't want to be in it. I can come out here and watch the snow and breathe the good air. I can walk out through that gate over there and turn in any direction I want. And walk for as long as I want. Or I can stay here and eat this awesome doughnut."

"I guess I understand it some," Wade said. "When you're in the army, you're not free to just go somewhere, unless you're on leave. When I got out, it was awesome to go where I wanted, at any time. I'd take walks, or go into a store, just because I could."

Arch nodded. "It's all new to me. Living without walls. Making choices all day long. For some reason, the place I get the most overwhelmed is the grocery store. I stand in the aisle at the Blue Water Mercantile and debate three different kinds of macaroni and cheese. That guy sells about a million flavors of soup. And there are so many different kinds of milk now. What the heck happened to just good old-fashioned cow milk?"

"I know." Wade grinned. "Dan, the guy who owns the Blue Water, is a good friend of mine. He's kind of a health food nut, so he's got some crazy products in that store. Like almond milk. How the heck do you get milk from an almond?" He put two fingers together and mimed squeezing a tiny nut.

Arch busted out laughing at the image. "I know. And what's up with hemp milk? Isn't hemp just another name for pot?" He could barely get the words out, he was laughing so hard. "It's really weird, after going to jail on drug charges, to see grocery stores selling milk made out of pot plants."

He was joking, but it was such a relief to talk to someone who understood a little. His laughter settled. "Man, you disappear for ten years and the world changes."

"It sure does," Wade agreed. "Like this. Us. I can't believe I'm saying this, but I'm glad you're home, bro."

"That's nice to hear. I told you on your wedding day that I'd work hard to earn your trust. I want you to know that I'll keep working at it."

Wade sobered. "I've been thinking about that, a lot—you earning our trust. You weren't all bad, Arch. When we were young, I remember you trying to keep Dad away from me. He'd go to hit me and you'd stand between us. And then he'd beat the crap out of you instead."

Arch hadn't been expecting this. Wasn't prepared for the memory of his dad's fists crashing down. Splitting his lip. Blackening his eyes. Of Wade cowering in the corner. "Hey," he croaked through the emotions threatening his composure. "It's better not to think about that stuff too often."

"Sometimes it's important, though," Wade said quietly. "Like now. Because I want to thank you, for trying to protect me."

"I was a piece of work." Arch could taste the bitterness of it. "One minute protecting you, the next bullying you myself."

"That's how it works, right?" Wade put a hand on his shoulder. "Abuse is a cycle. But we're breaking it now."

Arch nodded. Not trusting himself to speak.

"I'm married, Nora's married, you've got a thing for Mandy… We're changing it all up. Our kids will never be treated the way we were."

Arch smiled at the thought. "I hope so, bro. I really do."

"Treat Mandy well and it could happen," Wade advised. "You really care about her, don't you?"

Arch felt the weight of it settle across his shoulders. Warm responsibility. "I do."

Wade laughed suddenly. "I could never have predicted this. Arch Hoffman. Brought to his knees by Mandy Allen. The lion captured by the lamb."

"What?" Arch had no idea what his brother was talking about.

"It's a church thing," Wade said. "Stick around here long enough and you'll catch on." He turned to the door. "I've got a couple things I need to do. Thanks for the talk, bro. I'll see you later." He pushed inside and the rumbling of the coffee room voices poured out into the quiet courtyard. And then the door shut behind him and it was peaceful again.

Arch leaned against the wall, watching the snow fall, trying not to think about the memories Wade had dug up. There were a lot of memories just like it, and he tried to keep a tight lid on them all. His dad had been unstable, terrifying, a physical, emotional and psychological abuser.

The snow made a soft patter on the courtyard cement. He closed his eyes, pushing the past away, trying to focus on the present. He had so much to be thankful for. The humor and connection with his brother. His work. Mandy's forgiveness. And the possibility that if he kept trying hard enough, he wouldn't mess things up with her again.

MANDY DUCKED BEHIND the snow wall she and Lori had built and frantically scooped more snow into a ball. "I've got you now!" she yelled and dived over the wall, rolled through a drift and jumped to her feet. But Arch had disappeared.

She could see Lori off to her right. Her sister had launched herself onto Wade's back and was trying to shove snow down his jacket. Snack was jumping around at Wade's ankles, looking like a scraggly bunny popping in and out of the snow-drifts. But Arch had been here a split second ago and now he was… "Yikes!" she squeaked as he appeared from behind her and scooped her up.

He ran with her in his arms and dropped her into an untouched snowbank and flopped down next to her. "Snowy enough for you?" he asked, raising a cocky eyebrow.

"Not yet!" She still had her snowball and she rolled over so she was lying on top of him and then tucked it under his collar.

Arch was up on his knees in an instant, throwing her off as he reached into his jacket in a frantic attempt to get it out. "That is *cold*!"

Mandy used the distraction to scramble away, but he caught her by the ankle and pulled her back.

Snow was going up her jacket, so she pushed herself onto her knees and giggled as she tried to pry his fingers off her ankle.

It wasn't going to work. Especially once Arch removed the snowball intact from his collar and threatened to slide it under her scarf. Mandy scooped up loose snow and showered him in it, giggling the entire time. And then he grabbed her and kissed her, pulling her down on top of him and rolling them over and over.

And when they were too cold for more kissing, they raced each other to the porch to pull off their damp coats and boots. Inside the kitchen, over mugs of cocoa, Arch pulled a very battered list from his pocket and showed it to Mandy. And put a check by the word *fun*.

ARCH GRABBED THE drinks off the bar, nodding his thanks to the bartender. Looking out over the busy dance floor, he made a note of who he knew in the High Country. Kit wasn't here, thank goodness, but he'd already run into Bruce and Tank. He'd exchanged a few words and moved quickly on. It was his second-chance date with Mandy, and he wouldn't blow it by giving either of those two an opportunity to regale her with stories from his sordid past.

Mandy had run into a few girlfriends who were here on a night out, and she was taking a couple of minutes to catch up with them. He made his way toward her. She was listening as one of her friends went on about something that required a lot of giggling and hand waving. Arch placed her drink in her hand with a small glow of pride. She was stunning and she was here with him. And he was the luckiest guy on the planet.

He stood quietly, content to wait on the outskirts of the group while Mandy's friend wrapped up her story.

A hip-hop song came on, low beats throbbing in startling contrast to the country music they usually played here. Arch glanced over at Mandy to see how much she was going to hate it and was surprised to see a wide grin on her face.

"Let's dance!" One of her friends took Mandy's glass and placed it on a nearby table. The other girls were setting their drinks down, too, and heading for the dance floor. Mandy looked at Arch uncomfortably, caught between her date and her friends' invitation.

"Go ahead. It's no problem," he assured her.

Her brows rose in invitation. "Want to come?"

The bright blue of her eyes was visible even in the dim light of the bar. There was an extra sparkle there tonight. Maybe it was the cocktail she was drinking, or maybe, possibly, it was being out with him that put it there. He didn't want to take it away trying to bust lame moves on the dance floor. He had no idea how to dance to music like this. "You go with your friends. Have fun."

"If you're sure…"

"I am." He wanted her to be happy. To remember this night as special.

She gave him a quick kiss on the cheek and disappeared into the crowd. Arch tried to follow her progress, but people were crowded around the edge of the dance floor, cheering on their friends' attempts at old-school break dance moves.

Arch took a sip of his soda to wash away the feeling that he didn't fit—could never fit—into the lighthearted camaraderie around him. There was too much inside him that was dark and raw.

A loud cheer from the dance floor caught his attention. The crowd parted around two women who were dancing together. One was dark haired and the other blonde, like Mandy. It *was* Mandy. Dancing back to back with her friend, pulsing seductively on the downbeats.

Mandy pushed her hair off her face and Arch swallowed hard. Just that gesture was a mix of grace and sensuality he wasn't prepared for. Mandy's friend said something and Mandy laughed and dropped down against the other woman's back with knees bent, the guys in the crowd going wild at the sight of the two gorgeous women now slowly working their way back to standing.

Arch hadn't realized he'd gone closer until he was at the edge of the dance floor. He was in a daze watching this side of Mandy. A side he'd barely allowed himself to think about. But how could he not think about it now, watching her dance with her friend like this?

Her thighs. They were muscular and taut, and when she raised her hands up high in the air, the hem of her short dress went up even higher, and he swore he heard the collective intake of breath from every guy in the room. Or maybe he just imagined that, and it was really his breath whooshing back into his lungs after Mandy had stolen it.

She certainly wasn't the shy, scared Mandy he'd met on the ranch. She wasn't the prim Mandy he'd courted at church. She was all legs and blond hair and killer moves, and he took another swallow of his drink, trying to steady himself, unable to look away as she danced close to her friend, inches apart, and they did this sexy, in-your-face shimmy, and then burst out laughing.

Arch had never imagined—well, maybe he'd imagined—but he'd never *thought* that he'd see Mandy like this, liberated, sexy as all hell and not afraid to show it, reveling in the music and her friends, and accidentally turning on at least half the population in the High Country Sports Bar.

He was determined to play the gentleman, to show her that he could take her out and have fun with no expectations, but *damn*, he wanted her. He wanted her like he'd never wanted anyone, with an intensity so deep he felt tears spring behind his eyes. Because it wasn't just the way she'd totally abandoned herself to the music—though that was beyond hot. It was that he knew *her*. Her sweetness more sustaining than any cake she could conjure, her forgiving nature and her generosity and her heart stuck right out there on her sleeve, caring for every stray that came along. Including him.

But to know now that her sweetness was tempered by this sexy edge, this openmouthed downbeat joy, well, he could feel himself sliding. Like when he was a kid and he and Blake would climb the steep hill behind the barn with old baking sheets when the snow got icy. And he'd sit on his tray and push himself off and get some speed and careen down that hill, totally out of control. Never knowing for sure if he'd manage to stop before he hit the barn wall.

He was on that baking sheet now and he was going down that hill and there was nothing he could do about it because he was falling for

Mandy, falling hard that if and when he hit the barn it was going to hurt like hell.

The music ended, the DJ put country music on again and there was a migration on the dance floor as the hip-hop dancers made their way out and the line dancers went streaming back in. Arch spotted Mandy coming toward him, stopping to nod or smile at something some guy or another said. His protective hackles went up as he watched to make sure none of them tried anything. He was glad when she was back with him again.

"That was so fun!" Her smile was wide, her skin glowing, and she reached for her glass and took a long drink.

"You're a great dancer," he told her. Though that didn't even begin to sum it up.

"I haven't danced like that in ages." She looked at him resolutely. "And here's something else I haven't done in a long time. Or ever." Her hands slid up along his jaw, fingers twining in his hair so she could bring him down toward her. She was going to kiss him, Arch Hoffman, town loser, right here in the middle of the High Country. It was crazy, but he went with it, lowering his face to hers, mesmerized by the determination in her eyes and the heat pounding through him.

She tasted like lemon cocktail and felt like silk, and when her lips claimed his there was nothing tentative this time. It was a strong, clear message of desire. He kissed her back, forcing himself to keep it calm. They were in public, and she'd had a drink or two. If he trod lightly, she'd have no regrets.

"I want you," she whispered against his cheek, and he damn near passed out when her meaning sank in, and then she was kissing him again and his mouth was lost in the softness of hers and the wonder that she wanted him, flawed and messed up as he was.

He wove his fingers into her hair and kissed her harder, and she sighed against his mouth, right there in the bar. *Right there in the bar.* What the hell were they doing?

It took every piece of willpower he had, all the discipline and restraint he'd learned in prison, to end that kiss. He set Mandy away from him with firm hands on her shoulders, the wild-eyed, plump-lipped confusion on her face telling him she'd felt the passion between them, too.

"Mandy, we can't do this. Not here, in a bar. Drinking. That's not how it's gonna be between us."

She bristled at that. "Why do you get to say how it's going to be?"

"Because of me, our first date became something you regret. I won't risk that happening again. When we kiss like that it's going to be you and me, sober as hell and fully aware of what we're getting ourselves into."

"I know what I want, Arch. I want to kiss you. It's simple."

She reached her hands around his neck again, and pressed herself against him. Suddenly he knew what people meant when they talked about weak knees, because if she kept this up, his were going to send him right to the floor.

He set her away again, more firmly this time. "This thing between us, since the moment we met, hasn't been simple. And no way am I letting you stumble into *complicated* with a few drinks in your system. So no more of those kisses until you're stone-cold sober."

She studied him for a moment, her wide blue eyes taking him all in. He watched a slow smile spread across her face as if she'd just realized something good. She took his hand and pulled him through the crowd to the bar. "Bartender," she called. "Got any coffee?"

The laugh she inspired drew the tension out of him. She was funny and beautiful and had just kissed him into complete oblivion. And it was better than anything he'd ever thought life could deliver to a guy like him.

"You wanna play pool?" he asked, handing a few bucks to the bartender to cover her coffee.

She added cream neatly and picked up her

mug, leaving her half-drunk cocktail glass on the bar. "Sure," she said and flashed him a sweet smile full of promise. "Because apparently I've got some sobering up to do."

CHAPTER EIGHTEEN

MANDY WATCHED ARCH trudge uphill through the thick powdery snow, his snowboard tucked under one arm. He flopped down next to her on the slope. "I made it halfway down the hill. I guess that's an improvement," he said.

"It's impressive," she assured him. "I'm pretty sure I've fallen more than I've actually stood today. Though I guess that's mathematically impossible." Looking down the bunny slope, Mandy could see other beginners teetering on their boards. A few lay on their backs in the snow, postfall, looking like haphazard snow angels.

A little boy skied by them on a leash held by his dad. Mandy wished someone would hold her on a leash and make sure her innocent-looking snowboard didn't turn into some kind of board of death, shooting her flailing down the hill until she finally crashed into the lodge below, taking innocent bystanders down with her.

Inhaling, she tried to clear away the vivid image, courtesy of her anxiety.

"I could sit here all day and take in this view."

Arch gave her a friendly bump with his shoulder. "I'm glad we came up here."

"It's incredible." The resort was at the top of high Sierra peaks. From their seat on a snowbank at the edge of the bunny slopes they could look east and see the deserts of Nevada rolling into the hazy distance. They could look north and see Lake Tahoe, gleaming like a sapphire so far down below.

"It's strange that I'm already starting to take views like this for granted," Arch said. "When I was in jail I would imagine sitting somewhere like this and it seemed impossible that I'd ever be out in such a wide-open space again. But here I am, so focused on learning to snowboard that I forget to even look at the view."

"You must be getting used to your new life," Mandy said.

"I am. And the best part of it is spending time with you."

He pulled her in close and kissed her forehead. Which irritated. Ever since their date earlier this week, he'd been a little distant. Avoiding the kinds of kisses they'd shared before. Maybe she'd come on way too strong. Maybe she'd worried him somehow.

She wanted to ask him about it, but they'd already had so many serious talks. They needed to have fun. To keep things light for a change.

So she'd kept quiet, hoping the distance would just pass.

"Ready to try again?" His smile was all encouragement. There was no fear in his eyes. And why would there be? For him this was pure fun— just one more part of the world to sample now that he was free to be a part of it. He was done with prison and loving life.

She reached for her snowboard. "You're not scared at all?"

"I might be if I was on one of those hills up there." His black-gloved hand waved vaguely toward the steeper slopes above them. "But this is a bunny slope. Designed for practice. And if these little squirts can figure out how to get down it, so can we."

"I don't know." Mandy felt worry tug at her confidence. "I stand up and suddenly everything our teacher said in class this morning floats out of my brain."

"Hang on." Arch sat back down and loosened his boots from the straps on his board. He stood up and jammed it end down into the snowbank so it couldn't slide away. Then he offered her both his hands. "I'll stand in front of you. You just practice going and stopping, with your body facing downhill. If you know how to stop, you'll feel way better."

"How do you know that?" She stood, upright but shaky.

"Because I know you." He leaned in and kissed the tip of her nose. "And your anxiety. Have I mentioned how cute you look in a helmet and goggles?"

She giggled. "A few times."

"You were meant to snowboard. No one can look this good in their snow gear and not succeed." He took a step backward. "Remember, bend your knees a little. Keep your upper body straight."

Mandy gripped his gloved hands in hers and tried to find her center of gravity, which was hard to do when the board was already sliding. She shifted her weight back and it slowed. Tipped her weight forward and slid again.

"You're doing it!" Arch said.

Mandy inched her way down the hill, starting and stopping. About halfway down the slope, Arch let go of her and stepped aside. Heart thudding in her ears, Mandy bent her knees and allowed the board to slide a little more quickly. Dug her heels in and stopped. All on her own.

"That was it!" Arch came bounding up and high-fived her. She smacked his hand, lost her balance and sat down hard in the snow.

"Ouch!" She grabbed his offered hand and

stood up again. She would conquer this. She wouldn't let her anxiety win.

Without a word to Arch, she gave a little hitch with her body that sent the board heading downhill again. She tried to remember everything they'd been taught in their beginner's class this morning. Suddenly she could hear the instructor's words. *Look where you're going. When you want to stop, turn your hips hard.* She was picking up speed. Her pulse was speeding, too. *No*, she told the anxiety thundering her way.

She kept her eyes on the lodge below. Counted to three and then wrenched her hips around to face front. Snow shawled up around her ankles. She'd stopped! She raised her arms over her head in victory and turned her head to look at Arch. He was running down the hill toward her, whooping in triumph. "I did it!" she shouted. Her front edge caught, slamming her into the snow face-first.

"Mandy, are you okay?" Arch helped her get to her knees and sat her back on her rear in the snow.

There was snow in her goggles, snow in her scarf, snow down her front. But she was okay. She'd slid. She'd stopped. She'd face-planted. She was a real snowboarder now. "I'm fine!" she assured him.

He brushed the snow from her face with a gentle touch of his gloved hand. Kissed her once on the forehead.

"Are *we* okay?" she asked. He was kind and sweet and fun. But he wasn't the same in-love Arch he'd been on their date earlier this week.

"Sure," he said. "We're great."

But the remote look on his face said otherwise.

She was so tired of waiting for him to come back to her. She'd take her cue from snowboarding and just go for it. "We don't seem great. You're being kind of distant. If your feelings for me have changed, just tell me and get it over with."

He sat down in the snow next to her. "What are you talking about? You think my feelings have changed?"

"Yes. You barely kiss me or touch me. You worked late at Dalton's all week, so I hardly saw you. So, yes. It seems like everything's changed since we went on that date."

"I worked late at Dalton's so I'd have money for this weekend. You took care of the hotel with your gift certificate, which is great, but I want to take you to dinner tonight."

"Oh." It hadn't occurred to her. She'd assumed she'd pay for dinner. "That's nice."

A shy smile tilted the corner of his mouth. "I thought it would be."

"And everything else is okay? You haven't gotten sick of kissing me?"

He leaned over, pressed his lips to hers, lingered there until her breathing hitched. "I could never get sick of kissing you. It's just…" He looked away, out over the incredible view, as if gathering his thoughts there. When he met her eyes again, a flush warmed his cheekbones. "I just figured, after that date, when things got so intense between us, that you'd want some space. To think things through."

"Wait, you think I might want space from you because we had a good time? That doesn't seem very logical." She studied him, trying to figure out what was really going on.

He shook his head. "I'm saying the opposite. Not very well, apparently. Look. Something shifted on that date. And I think it shifted for you, too. The way we were together, well…it heated up. A lot. And I know you haven't…you know…" His face went ruddy.

"You're embarrassed!" It was the first time she'd ever seen him so flustered. "You're worried about sleeping together?"

He nodded, looking relieved that she'd caught on. "On our date it hit me just how much chemistry we have. How much I want to be with you, that way. But I guess I'm worried. It's your *first time*. Are you really sure that you want it to be with someone like me?"

"No. I want it to be with *you*. Not someone *like* you. Arch, you're not making any sense. Ten years ago I was an awkward fourteen-year-old with braces on my teeth and a Harry Potter book in my hands. Would you want to date or not date me now, based on who I was then?"

"That would be weird."

"Exactly." She picked up a mound of snow and tossed it his way. "So why would I care who *you* were ten years ago?"

He watched as she scooped up more snow. "I think you're oversimplifying," he said. "I don't want you to regret being with me. A parolee. A felon."

"Now you're trying to scare me with labels. Look, what if you were young again, and living with your father, but you knew everything you know now? Would you still follow in his footsteps?"

"Absolutely not."

"So that's my point. You aren't that same guy." She unstrapped her board and stood up. "Now come on. I'm not ending this day until I can get all the way down this bunny slope without falling."

His smile reached his eyes for the first time all day. "Challenge accepted." He stood and grabbed his board under one arm, held out his free hand to take hers. "Let's do this."

At the top of the slope, they stood on their boards and looked at the long stretch of snow below. Arch glanced at Mandy. "You ready?"

She exhaled a shaky breath. "I think so."

"Courage," he reminded her.

"Courage," she echoed, and pushed off. Her board hissed over the packed snow. She angled across the slope as it picked up speed. Adrenaline bubbled, but she tamped it down and kept her focus. Standing solid. Looking where she wanted to go. Trusting that even if she crashed, and even if crashing hurt, she'd probably be okay.

CHAPTER NINETEEN

ARCH WATCHED MANDY'S expression as she looked out the window at the snowy nighttime mountain. The resort left some outdoor lights on to give diners a view of the picturesque pines, their branches tipped in snow. Mandy's eyes were big, taking it all in. She was incredible. Dainty and refined, sipping the lemon drop she'd ordered at the bar. "I could get used to this," she said.

Arch grinned. "Me, too. Snowboarding all day, eating an awesome meal with you afterward. Drinking a nip of something really good." He took a small sip of the scotch he'd ordered. He was taking it slow. It was the first time he'd had alcohol since before prison. Steve had given him the okay to drink, last time they'd talked, but Arch had still stuck with water at dinner. It was only after their meal, when the reality of sharing a room with Mandy loomed, that he'd craved a few drops of liquid courage.

They were in the vast bar, not ready to go up to their room just yet but not wanting to monopolize a table at the busy restaurant. A fire crackled cheerfully in the large stone fireplace close by. Mandy looked up at the huge beams supporting the roof. "I could live here."

So could he. Dinner had been perfect. There was candlelight and white tablecloths. Hushed waiters and soft music. And most of all there was Mandy. Looking so pretty in a blue sweaterdress. She'd paired it with high-heeled black suede boots that had the power to destroy his concentration if he looked at them too long.

They'd talked nonstop through their meal. Mostly about travel. They were both eager for it, after her sheltered life and his incarcerated one. First they'd made their top-ten list of countries they'd like to visit. But that wasn't enough, so they'd chosen their top ten national parks, top ten American cities, top ten art museums and top ten tropical destinations. They were going to be on the road a lot if they really visited half of the places they'd named.

Then they kept the game going. Foods they wanted to try. Sports they'd like to play. And through it all he learned that Mandy was a lot more adventurous than he'd realized. Though she drew a line at skydiving, apparently.

He'd had a glimpse of her daring side, seeing her perseverance on her snowboard today. But watching her blue eyes sparkle when she talked about visiting Paris, he knew her adventures were just beginning. And he felt proud that he'd played a small part in helping her find that spirit again.

There was a cover band playing in the next room. Even though he wasn't much of a dancer, he now knew that Mandy was. "Want to dance?"

She set her drink down with a grateful smile. "Yes, please."

He took her hand and led her through to the dance floor, stepping on it just as the band started their version of a Tom Petty song. It was from his pre-prison days and Arch was grateful he knew it well. He was no dancer, had pretty much never danced, but he gave it his best shot, rewarded by the wide smile on Mandy's face. She reached up and put her hands on his shoulders so they swayed together.

He couldn't resist the proximity. He slid his lips across hers. The first kiss he'd given her since they'd finished their day on the slopes. He ducked his head lower, took the kiss a little deeper and felt her lemon-drop sigh against his mouth. She pressed closer, and he put his arms around her back. Elation took hold of him, and disbelief that he was allowed to do this with her. He breathed in her floral scent.

God, he wanted her. He was trying so hard not to have expectations. To be okay with whatever was comfortable for her. But the hope of sharing a bed with her, of holding her, of maybe even making love to her had been there, heating his blood all day. Especially after their talk on the slopes.

He closed his eyes, breathed her in, tried to be content with just this, her body against his, her arms around him, swaying to the song.

After a few moments she looked up at him, her eyes smoky in the dim light. "I think we should head back to our room."

They were the best words he'd heard in pretty much forever.

MANDY GLANCED AT Arch as he stood next to her, waiting for the elevator. Maybe the darn thing was slow, or maybe she was just nervous, but it seemed like they'd been standing there a long while, suddenly awkward with each other.

Arch caught her looking and put an arm around her shoulder, kissing the top of her head. But he said nothing. Mandy leaned against him, pulling from his warmth and confidence as her nerves ran relays around her mind. What if she was terrible at this? What if she had no idea what to do? What if she did it wrong?

Suddenly the whole idea of holding off on sex until she found that special person seemed like a terrible idea. She should have found someone, anyone, to practice with. Arch mattered. So much.

She didn't want to make a fool of herself. She didn't want their first time together to disappoint.

The elevator doors finally opened and they stepped in. Mandy closed her eyes briefly, thinking about all the bits and pieces of the day that had led to this moment. The way Arch had looked, so confident on his snowboard. The way he'd helped her with hers. The way he'd sat up on the snowy hill, taking in the view and talking about freedom. The relief on his face when she'd assured him that his past wouldn't scare her away.

He couldn't have known that she'd made up her mind to sleep with him days ago. Everything had changed for her that night at the High Country. Maybe it was dancing with her friends, knowing he was watching, and realizing that she wanted, so badly, for him to see her differently than sweet, scared little Mandy. Or maybe it was playing pool afterward. That moment when he'd helped her make a shot, his body aligned with hers, his big hands helping her grasp the pool cue. Whatever it was, it had woken something inside her, a buzzing desire and an excitement that still simmered under her skin.

She opened her eyes and found him watching her. "Will you kiss me?"

"In this elevator?" His eyes narrowed. Homing in on her.

"Yeah," she said, feeling her cheeks go warm at her own boldness.

"Yes." He reached for her hand, tugged her close. His jacket smelled good, like fresh air and leather and spicy cologne.

She tilted her head up and saw the clear intent in his eyes and felt it ripple over her. He cupped her jaw with his fingertips, brought his mouth down to hers, and kissed her with an intake of breath that resonated in her entire body.

He tasted like scotch, a heady flavor for their kiss. She sought out more until her hands were tangled in his hair and his mouth was ravaging hers, blocking out everything else so when the elevator doors opened, they stumbled out, still entwined.

Mandy pulled away, her breath ragged, her legs shaking. It wasn't just her desire for him that overwhelmed. It was *his* desire for *her* that tipped her over the edge. The way his breath caught in his throat. The way he tried to stay gentle but then forgot for a moment, his hand grasping her hair, stilling her, as he shifted closer and claimed her mouth as his. The way he'd tilted her head back and found her throat, his hot mouth sliding and branding.

"Come on," he said and pulled a room key from his pocket. At the door he kissed her again, their breathing audible in the quiet hallway, hers coming in short gasps when his hand found her bare thigh between her dress and her boots. "I've been wanting to touch you there all night," he murmured, pulling back to put the key in the lock while she leaned against the wall for support.

"So touch me," she challenged, and with a frustrated groan he abandoned the lock and scooped her up, holding her easily against the wall with one arm while his free hand roved from knee to thigh. His fingers slid along the edge of her panties and she gasped and somehow he got the key in the lock. He shoved the door open and stumbled with her across the room, setting her down on the bed.

He sat down next to her, shrugged off his jacket and regarded her with a slightly bemused expression. "You're still good with this?"

"I'm good. Just kiss me. Please."

His mouth was warm and reassuring at first. But she didn't want that. She wanted to lose herself, to disappear into what he could give her. So she tugged them both down to lie side by side on the bed. He took the lead, leaning over her to take the kiss deeper. And any lingering fears dropped away, erased by Arch's mouth, his soft lips, his rough stubble, her name when he whispered it against her lips.

She ran her palms down his chest, not prepared for the heat she felt when her hands shaped the contours of his muscles. Tugging his shirt out of his jeans, she trailed her fingers over the taut skin of his torso.

The hoarse sound he made in response stopped her.

"I'm sorry… Is that not right?"

He buried his face in her hair, his laugh vibrating against her scalp. "It's very right. It's just been so long since anyone touched me."

"Tell me what you need," she whispered. "I have no idea what I'm doing."

"That makes two of us." He propped himself up on one elbow. Ran a hand over her dress, tracing each curve. The sensation crashed through her body. Her pulse was running rabbit fast.

"How do you feel about clothing?" he asked.

"Um…" The cowardly part of her wanted to suggest they keep it all on. But then she wouldn't feel his skin against hers, and she wanted that more than anything. "Let's take it off."

He sat up, grabbed his shirt and yanked it over his head. She'd never seen him shirtless and she sat up, too, and stared. The muscles of his torso and arms were sculpted and defined by the shadows of the lamplight. The barbed-wire tattoo she'd seen when he lifted hay bales coiled around the top of one bicep.

He kicked off his boots and socks. Slid down his jeans. Regarded her carefully as he sat before her in black briefs and nothing more. He was so much. He was hard to take in.

"Your turn," he said softly.

Her face went hot, but she'd started this. She slid her boots and socks off. Pulled her thin sweaterdress over her head. Saw his eyes go wide at her black lace bra and panties.

"You're so damn beautiful." His tone was rough, but the hand he ran down her arm was tentative. "You're an angel. I don't know why I get to be with you."

"Because I want you." She was going to burn up, and they were barely touching. If she reached out to trace his tattoo, she might actually melt.

His hand slid down her arm, brushing the side of her breast, his gaze following its progress, drinking her in. "You amaze me," he said softly. "In my most desperate dreams in prison I never thought it could be like this. That I'd be like this, with someone like you."

She understood. Though *her* prison had been self-imposed. But now she was ready. She wanted to step beyond fear and right up to the wild edge she'd sensed between them. She kissed him, infusing it with all the loneliness she'd felt, all the unarticulated desire for something deeper. For something more.

With a low noise in his throat he pulled her roughly to him. She straddled his lap, writhing under his hands as they roamed over her skin, driving her past her nerves, past fears and into someplace molten and consuming.

She knew she should pay attention. That it was her first time. Their first time. She tried to notice the details, but his hunger didn't let her. He was so big, he was everywhere, his skin on hers, his mouth on hers, his hands seeking the places that would drive her up and over the edge. His arms holding her tight when she shook with the pleasure he gave.

And all the while he held himself back, letting her gain confidence, giving her time to get to know her body and his. Until he coached her with gentle kisses and heat stoked so high that there was only bliss when he entered her, only longing and sensation that grew and rose and imploded, leaving her limp in his arms. Her first time ever. His first time crying out her name. Her first time seeing tears brimming up in his eyes.

CHAPTER TWENTY

MANDY WAS TRYING to arrange the new comforter. Arch was trying to kiss her. He knew he was making it hard to finish their project, but who could blame him? She was so totally kissable.

When she'd offered to help him fix up his old bedroom on Marker Ranch, he'd jumped at the chance. The room was ugly. Ugly with the past, and ugly with the broken-down furniture, mossy-green paint and bad brown carpet.

"You have to stop." She giggled as he wrapped his arms around her to plant another kiss on her cheek.

"But it's so nice in here. I can't help it."

Earlier in the week, he'd pulled up the carpet to reveal the original hardwood planks. A little sanding, a little varnish and the floor looked a million times better. You could see that the room had nice bones now. With its peaked roof and the bench he'd built under the dormer window, it was starting to look more like one of the fancy rooms Mandy had shown him on her computer.

Yesterday was Saturday and they'd spent it

rolling the walls with a gray-blue color. They'd painted all the trim bright white and the shabby pine bed frame a soft cream. And this afternoon, with the new sheets and a colorful comforter they'd just put on the bed, it was looking way better in here.

"It is nice, isn't it?" She stepped away from him and looked around with a satisfied smile.

"You are the grand mistress of low-budget decor." He pointed to the bowl of huge sugar-pine cones she'd put on top of the dresser. "I'd have never thought of doing that."

She reached for the large framed map leaning against his bedroom wall. "We just need to hang this up and we'll be done."

He shook his head. "I'm not ready to be done. I like having you in my bedroom. Did you know you look beautiful with a hammer in your hand?"

She put soft hands around his neck to pull him down for a lingering kiss. "That's very kind of you to say," she murmured.

He'd felt that kiss all the way down his spine. "I don't think we can hang that map until we test out the bed."

She grinned when he wrapped his arms around her. "I agree. It's important to make sure the new comforter works."

"Exactly." His lips found hers and he kissed her with the want that had been building in him all morning. The want that had never left him in the weeks since their snowboarding trip. Three weeks when they'd spent every day and night together.

They'd even had Thanksgiving with both of their families together. He'd been sous-chef for Mandy's delicious feast. And he'd spent the entire meal bathed in delirious gratitude for Mandy, for family, for the way his new life was unfolding.

The kiss undid her just the way he intended. Her breathing hitched and she clung to him when he turned her around, walking her backward until they hit the mattress. He lowered her to the bed and lay down next to her. Teasing her mouth with his, he slid his hand under her T-shirt, relishing her small gasp when his fingertips found the clasp of her bra. He'd never get used to this. Never stop wondering how he'd been lucky enough to be chosen by her.

She draped her arms around his neck and kissed him fiercely, as if goading him to lose control. He answered her fervor with his own, pinning her wrists over her head on the quilt, filling his free hand with her curves, yanking clothing off to reveal them, relishing the soft whump when their clothes hit his newly refinished wood floor.

"Have I told you how much I love home improvement?" he murmured, slowing down and letting his lips roam over her neck.

"Your room looks so much better," she gasped out. His tongue traced small circles and her body bowed against his.

"*Everything* is so much better," he said against her ear. "Since I met you." He closed his eyes and lost himself in the floral scent of her skin, the sweet and salty taste of her body, the sound of her uneven breath and the feel of himself inside her. It was perfect, it was unbelievable, it was like holding a small piece of heaven in his arms.

A blissful hour later, they finally hung the map on the wall. "It looks great," he told her.

"I hope this room feels more like home now."

"It does. Especially with you in it." He'd just had her, but it wasn't enough. He reached for her again. Pulled her in and kissed her long and slow, savoring every second. She was soft and curvy and he nestled his arm down around her waist and buried his face in her hair. "You know, I didn't really pay enough attention to how the bed felt just now…"

"I think it's important to reevaluate it." She laughed into his shoulder. "It may need to be tested out many times."

It was the permission he needed. He scooped her up—she weighed pretty much nothing—and walked with her back to the just-made bed. Sat down with her on his lap.

And when she shifted to kiss him, when she

stroked her tongue over his, he let himself get lost in her again.

They'd skipped church this morning to finish the bedroom project. But he could worship here, with her. Earlier they'd been famished and fast. Now he wanted to love her with awe and gratitude. To show her the depth of his feelings. So stirring that each breath between them was a prayer.

A loud knocking downstairs had them both freezing like guilty teenagers. "What the…" Arch shifted her off his lap and crossed the room to the window. Leaned on the frame to look down. *Oh, hell.* He didn't want to say the words, but he had no choice. "Mandy, it's the sheriff. There are three cars down there."

She looked at him sharply. "Is there anything I need to know?"

"No." Her instant suspicion stung. "When you're on parole they can do checks anytime. You'll probably want to leave for it. It's never pretty." No way did he want her around while he peed in a cup.

She went to him and threw her arms around his neck. "I love you. Okay? I don't care about this stuff."

He nodded briefly. The knocking started again. "I'd better get down there before they break the door in."

"Let's go," she said.

They straightened their clothes and went down the stairs together. When they reached the door, Mandy glanced at Arch. "Let me get it."

She opened the door to six officers. Two had their guns drawn. She gasped and her hands automatically went up, palms out. The universal *don't shoot* signal.

"Hey!" Arch said, pulling her back behind him. "What the hell?"

An older man stepped up. "Arch Hoffman?"

"Yes, that's me," Arch said.

"I'm Sheriff Davidson. We need to ask you some questions."

Arch tried to keep the fear out of his voice. "Can you put the guns down? We're unarmed."

"Step forward, please."

Arch knew what that meant. He moved a few steps closer. Ashamed that Mandy was seeing this.

A tall deputy stepped in front of him. "Arms and legs out, please." He ran his hands down Arch's sides to start the pat down.

At least it wasn't Patrick Norris, though he was in the group, eagerly looking on. Probably fingering his handcuffs with longing.

The sheriff turned to Mandy. "I didn't expect to find *you* here."

"Hello, Mike." Mandy sounded like she was at

a cocktail party, and not in front of deputies with raised weapons. "How's Tiger doing?"

Mike smiled, looking grandfatherly now. "He's a great dog. I'm glad you talked me into adopting him."

"He's such a sweet guy." She turned to Arch. "Mike, I mean, Sheriff Davidson, adopted Tiger. He's a Lab mix who was dropped at our ranch."

"Great." His pat down was over, but it was a little hard to focus on the small talk. He glanced at Mike. "I'm happy to comply with whatever you need. But I'd like to show my girlfriend out first, if that's okay?"

The sheriff looked from Arch to Mandy. "I wasn't aware you two knew each other. But, son, I'll need her to stay. We have to ask you both some questions."

He held out a paper to Arch. "It's a warrant to search your property. There were a couple break-ins in town last night. Some folks said they saw a tall man fleeing the scene."

"Arch was with me," Mandy said.

"If you could please wait," the sheriff told her, "we'll be speaking with each of you individually. Mandy, we'll need to pat you down, too. It's just standard procedure when we're working with a parolee."

"But she's not on parole," Arch protested.

"No, but she's here with you, and you're currently a suspect in a robbery."

A female deputy stepped up. "Ma'am, can you please raise your arms and spread your legs apart?"

Mandy's cheeks went bright pink, but she complied. Thankfully, the woman kept the pat down quick, obviously seeing that Mandy would never be a threat. But it still burned like acid in Arch's gut. Mandy shouldn't be here. Should never be a part of something like this.

At least the deputies had put their guns away.

The sheriff turned to Arch. "We'll need to search your property for stolen goods. It's time to do a general parole check anyway, so we'll kill two birds with one stone, okay?"

Arch nodded, focused on Mandy. Who was looking at him with a hell of a lot more love and sympathy than he deserved.

"Normally we'd have you wait outside, but it's still pretty snowy out there. My deputies will search the living room and kitchen. You two can wait in those rooms once they finish."

"We can't wait together?" Mandy asked.

"We'll need to ask you individual questions," Mike said. "I'm sorry you got caught up in this, Mandy."

Not as sorry as Arch. But right now he had bigger things to worry about. "Sir," he said to Mike,

"Deputy Norris and I know each other from high school. He is very angry with me for some things I did back then. A couple weeks ago, he showed up at my brother-in-law's repair shop and cuffed me for no reason."

Mandy gaped at him, eyebrows raised like question marks. He'd never mentioned it to her.

"So I'm respectfully requesting that Deputy Norris not be a part of the search."

"Are you suggesting my deputy would plant something in your house?" Mike's face went red, and for a moment Arch wondered if he'd made a really bad move.

"I have a video of the incident at the repair shop on my phone, sir. If you'd like to see it." He made a mental note to thank Todd again for sending him the video.

"Mike, please listen to him," Mandy added. "I know Arch. He wouldn't ask for this if he wasn't really concerned."

"The rooms are clear, sir," one of the deputies said.

Mike nodded. "Norris, you'll sit with Arch in the living room. Mandy, you'll sit in the kitchen with Deputy Abrams."

The female deputy took Mandy by the arm and the two women left the room.

Arch watched her go, his insides leaden. He'd dragged her into this.

Patrick Norris led him into the living room and sat down in a chair, indicating that Arch should take the chair opposite his. Arch complied, trying to stay calm as he faced the smug deputy. "I assume it was you who suggested I was a suspect?"

Norris flashed a cold blade of a smile. "We always search the homes of low-life parolees when we have a crime. And ninety-nine percent of the time, they're responsible. Because people don't change, Hoffman. Ever. Maybe you didn't commit this particular crime. But at some point you'll slip. And you'll get caught. And you'll head back to jail where you belong."

Arch breathed deep and sat back. Trying to let the scornful words wash over and off him. *No stupid mistakes.* That was exactly why Norris was goading him. Assaulting an officer could get Arch several years.

"So, you and Mandy Allen." Norris leaned forward in his chair and clasped his hands together in a mockery of earnest inquiry. "I have to know. Every guy in town has wanted to tap that for years. But she's cold. Then you come to town and *blam*!" He clapped his meaty hands together with a sound that had Arch jumping. Then he mushed his hands together in some crude simulation of sex. "How the hell did you do it? Is it that jailhouse stank the lady can't resist?"

Arch gripped the arms of his chair. Because if

he was gripping, he wasn't hitting. But the pieces of truth wrapped in Norris's crude words blew shrapnel holes in his heart. Bits of poison tunneling in to fester there.

He'd done this to her. Because of him, she was sitting in the other room, watched over by a deputy like a criminal. Because of him, she was exposed to the speculation and ridicule of lowlifes like Patrick Norris. By letting her raise him up, he'd brought her down.

"I'd sure as hell like to fuck Mandy Allen," Patrick was saying in an eerily conversational tone. "I figure it'll happen pretty soon. You'll do something stupid and get yourself locked up again, and she'll be in need of some consolation from an upstanding young deputy like myself. So thanks, Arch, for paving the way. I'm gonna enjoy getting some of that pretty blonde…"

Arch was halfway out of his chair when Norris drew his gun. A smile of evil delight twisted the deputy's dough-boy features. "Gotcha," he hissed. Then he radioed for backup.

The sheriff was there in an instant. Icy cuffs clamped down on Arch's wrists. Hard hands marched him to the patrol car. The dim interior of the backseat opened like a throat, ready to gulp him back into the guts of the justice system. He hesitated, and a hand on his shoulder forced him in.

CLAIRE McEWEN   331

Arch glanced back at the house as the door slammed shut between him and all he'd had. And saw Mandy's face, pale and stricken, at his kitchen window.

A FEW HOURS LATER, Arch faced Sheriff Davidson across an old metal table in a pale green room.

"What the hell happened back there?" The sheriff set down his foam coffee cup and leaned in. "We found nothing on your property. Your alibi is solid. You didn't commit the crime. So why the hell did you go after Norris?"

Arch's age-old instinct was to say nothing. Because when other kids were learning their fairy tales, he'd been schooled in not cooperating with the law. But prison loomed. And whether the sheriff believed him or not, he couldn't just roll over and let Norris insult Mandy.

"Deputy Norris tried to provoke me, sir. He told me I'd be going back to jail and that when I did he was going to…" He stopped. Even after ten years in prison, surrounded by the worst possible language, he had trouble getting the words out. "Sleep with Mandy. But he didn't use those words. He used extremely disturbing, disrespectful language."

The sheriff sat back and pursed his lips. "I'm surprised. Norris is a little hotheaded, but overall he's a good deputy. I'll speak with him."

The truth of how things went for an ex-convict had never been so starkly laid out. "You'll *speak* with him. Meanwhile, I'll get locked up for attempting to assault an officer."

"Mandy's a special lady. Everyone in town knows it. But you can't let one man's ill-chosen words get you heated like that. You'll never make it if you do."

"And if it was your wife, Sheriff? And someone was talking about wanting to *tap* her? And worse?"

He saw the anger behind the sheriff's attempt at a bland mask. "I'll speak to him, Arch."

The room seemed to dim. "And it will be his word against mine. At least watch that video on my phone. The one my brother-in-law took at his shop. You'll see that Norris has a grudge."

Mike nodded. "I'll look at it. And I'll ask you to write down exactly what he said today in a report. After that, it's a personnel issue. That's all I can tell you." He sat back, arms crossed. One more frustrated bureaucrat.

"So what happens to me now?" Arch asked.

"We call your parole officer and let him know what happened. He'll take it from there."

Steve was a fair guy. Arch felt a thread of hope meander through the darkness engulfing him inside. He'd lost a lot today, but there was a chance he wouldn't lose his freedom. He watched while the sheriff picked up the phone, praying for reprieve.

MANDY HAD THE Marker Ranch kitchen gleaming in the noon sunlight. The scents of coffee and baking filled the run-down house. Fresh bread, an apple pie, Arch's favorite blueberry muffins. She'd been here since they took Arch away yesterday afternoon.

When she'd called the sheriff's office, they'd told her not to come. That his parole officer had ordered him to spend the night in the cell as a warning. When she'd called again this morning, there'd been great news. Today he'd go free. No charges.

Relief and gratitude had her baking. So did worry. Arch in a jail cell. She'd seen how he relished every moment of his freedom. Every breath of fresh air and every chance to do something new. It was only one night, but she was sure it had been a rough one.

She'd give him the best welcome home she could.

Glancing at her phone, she saw Arch still hadn't called. Maybe she should just drive to the sheriff's office and pick him up?

But they'd told her he'd call when he was ready. Mandy poured herself a cup of coffee and glanced out the window. And saw Arch walking toward the front porch.

She was out the door and into his arms in an instant. "You're here!" She went on tiptoe to kiss him. He turned away and her lips brushed his cheek. "You're home."

Grabbing his hand, she led him inside and into the kitchen. "I'm sure you'll want a shower. But afterward, there's muffins, and here—" She grabbed a clean mug and filled it. "Coffee."

He looked dazed. His eyes cupped by dark shadows. The stubble thick on his cheek. She added milk to his cup, just how he liked it. He took it and held the mug in two hands, as if needing its warmth. "Thanks."

"You're welcome." There was a distance about him. A remote look that had her moving to the other side of the table. Of course he was upset. He needed his space. "How did you get here? I was waiting for your call. I would have picked you up."

"I walked. I needed the air."

"That's a really long walk." She wanted to reach him somehow. "I'm so sorry. About what happened."

His eyes darkened. Shuttered. Like he'd gone inward, away from her. "I lost my temper. That deputy, Patrick Norris, we hated each other growing up. He just kept talking, provoking me. He started in on you and I lost it."

She could tell from the disgust etched into the exhausted lines of his face that she didn't want to know what the deputy had said about her.

"Well, it's over now. Why don't you go shower? Then come eat. Let's just put it behind us. Can you rest today?"

"I'll head out to see Dalton soon." He took a gulp of his coffee. Closed his eyes once. And when he opened them she saw a fierce resolve there. "To tell him goodbye. And now I'm telling you the same."

Mandy's mind went leaden. "Excuse me?" She stared, stunned. "What?"

"It's time for me to move on."

She reached for the back of a chair, fumbled to pull it out and sank into it. "It's not time to move on. You just got started. With me."

"And that was a mistake." He set his mug down and knelt beside her chair. "You must see that now. After yesterday? You can't be with me. That will happen again. Every time a crime goes down around here, I will be a suspect. You will be, too, just because we're together."

"That's not true. It might be like that for a year or two, but you'll get off parole."

"I'll always be at the top of their list when something happens. Parole or not." He took both of her hands in his. "Mandy, listen to me. I was up all night thinking about this. You and me, we met at a certain time, for a reason. I needed you to lift me up. To get me seeing what's possible. You needed me to help you find your strength and courage again. We did that for each other. Can't we just accept that it was all we were meant to be? Can we go on with our lives grateful that we had time with each other?"

"That's what you thought about as you sat in your jail cell? How to say goodbye to me in the most stupid, convoluted way possible?" She pulled her hands away, standing up so suddenly that her chair went over behind her. "If you want to end this, just say so, straight-out."

He rose and turned away stiffly, shuffling to retrieve his coffee cup, moving as if he had an extra burden pushing him down.

"You promised me honesty." Her voice had an edge to it, a hysteria she couldn't control. "If you don't love me, tell me."

"Don't ask me to say that," he said.

"See?" Tears spilled down her cheeks. Her heart fragmented in her chest. "You do love me. And I love you. So don't leave."

He raised his hands in a helpless gesture. "You came into my life like this angel, and you showed me everything I wanted. Everything good. I wanted to rise to your level, not drag you down in the dirt with me. Yet that's exactly what's happened."

"It was *one* day. *One* bad thing that happened. Does it wipe out all the great things we've done?" She was begging. But he was turning their love into shrapnel, and when he walked away she'd be left digging out the pieces.

"My brother was right. Your sister, too. I don't deserve you, Mandy. And you…" He paused, swallowed hard, and she saw despair glittering in his eyes. "You deserve a man who can give you the best life. Who has a career and a home and the respect of other people. Not a homeless ex-convict on the top of the usual suspects list."

"Don't do this." Her voice came out a tortured whisper. It was all she had left.

"I swear, one day you'll thank me for ending this. For setting you free."

She turned to him then, fury and heartache wrapping her in a suffocating grip. "Don't you dare act like you're doing me a favor. Or that you know what's best for me. If you're a coward, if real life and a real relationship scare you *that* much, just admit it and go. But stop talking like you're helping me. Because you're not."

She was suddenly tired. Yesterday's stress, the night of worrying, *this*. This shredding of her love into tiny discarded bits. "Just stay," she whispered.

He shook his head. "I won't ruin your life."

"You *saved* my life. I was stuck. Frozen in time when you showed up. You've changed everything for me. Let me help change things for you?"

He came to her then. Threw his arms around her and pulled her close, and all the tears she'd been holding back came pouring out. She leaned on his chest and sobbed. He stroked her hair in that way she loved, with his big palm running over her scalp. Trying to soothe, but his words offered no comfort.

"I attacked an officer yesterday. He pulled a gun on me. I could have been shot. What if you'd been there? What if I'd gotten *you* shot? You've shown me the man I can be, but I'm not him yet. And I won't drag you through the dirt, or put you in danger, while I find him."

He set her away and she brought her hands to her face in a useless attempt to wipe off the tears. "I'm going to go pack my bag. And then I'm leaving." His voice shook. Broken. "I love you, Mandy. I'll always love you. Please believe me."

She covered her face in her hands and turned away from him. Went out the back door and into the snow-covered yard of Marker Ranch. Kept walking until she hit the fence where Wade's horses were stabled. And sat down in the cold and cried.

Later on, when she had no tears left, she stumbled on numb limbs back into the house. Wandered through the thick silence and up the stairs into the room they'd been decorating just the day before. It was still so perfect looking. But it was missing the only thing that mattered. Arch.

CHAPTER TWENTY-ONE

ARCH STARED UP at the ornate metal sign over the doorway of San Diego Metalworks. Once again, he had reason to thank Dalton Carter. The artist had been angry at Arch for leaving. But once he'd finished calling him names and telling him what a fool he was for losing Mandy, he'd promised references. "I believe in you, though the way you're acting right now, I don't know why."

Then he'd made Arch a list of metal artists he knew and respected. Told Arch to hit the road and work for them all. That he'd provide an email introduction and a reference.

Arch had spent two weeks working on the installation of a huge outdoor sculpture in downtown Los Angeles. Another three weeks helping that same artist install a piece in a park in Denver, Colorado. He'd spent the last four months working on mobiles and other wind-powered sculptures for an elderly Santa Barbara artist who could no longer do the heavy lifting. And now he was here. To learn about ornate gates and signs and how to work with iron.

He silently practiced the speech he'd prepared. And opened the door. A big bearded man was firing up an old-fashioned fireplace in the middle of the workshop. He had a bellows and an anvil, and Arch felt like maybe he'd stepped back in time. "My name's Arch Hoffman," he told the man. "I think my former employer, Dalton Carter, spoke with you?"

"Yes, Dalton's protégé. Come on in. I'm Shane Turner."

Arch dropped his duffel bag by the door and held out his hand. "Nice to meet you, Shane. I'm hoping to work for you. And learn." Because the harder he worked, and the more he kept learning, the easier it was to survive without Mandy.

But the truth was, all he was doing was surviving. He might know a whole lot more about working with metal than he had five months ago. But his heart hadn't healed one damn bit.

IT WAS SO good to feel the sun after the longest, coldest winter Mandy could remember. May had always been one of her favorite months. Spring. Wildflowers starting in the meadow. Baby chicks in her henhouse. New life. But this year everything felt tarnished.

She was planting marigolds in the flower beds near the porch, hoping that some of their spring-time hope would rub off on her.

"Hey, Mandy!" Lori was hurrying up the lane to the house, Snack trotting along next to her. In her hand was a big envelope. "Jim grabbed the mail on his way in from town. This was in it."

Mandy stood and pulled off her garden gloves. Lori put the envelope in her hand like she was presenting a trophy. "The San Francisco Culinary Institute. Did you order a brochure?"

"Um…sort of." That night, months ago, when Arch was out with Kit… "I actually applied. This might be their answer."

"You applied to culinary school?" Lori gaped at her. "I didn't even know you wanted to go away."

Mandy smiled at that. "I don't know if I did want to go away back then. I just figured I'd fill out the application and see what happened."

Lori clasped her hands together. "I had no idea! I'm so proud of you! This is exciting!"

Mandy stared at the envelope, her heart bang-ing around in her chest.

Lori shifted impatiently. "Well, open it!"

It was easier said than done. Mandy's fingers weren't working right. She fumbled with the paper. "What if it's a no?"

Her sister gave Mandy's shoulders a bracing

squeeze. "You've been through a big heartbreak already. This couldn't be worse than what happened with Arch."

"No, but it might add another layer of awful onto it."

"Or it just might be the news you need."

"You do it." Mandy gave up and handed the envelope to her sister. "Please?"

"Okay." Lori ripped open the envelope. The papers she pulled out trembled. "It's a brochure," she said and disappointment squeezed down on Mandy's lungs, the pressure so familiar now.

"Oh, wait! There's something else." Lori unfolded a cream-colored paper. Her eyes scanned briefly down the page, and her voice took on a wondering note. "You're in."

She looked at Mandy, a huge smile illuminating her face. "You're *in*!" She handed her the letter.

The words were blurry through the tears that stung Mandy's eyes. But she caught the most important part. *We are excited to welcome you to our program.*

It was the reprieve she needed after so many months of missing Arch. She could go to school. In a big city. New people, new skills and, most important, new sights and sounds to distract her from the way her heart hurt all the time. From the way she wished so badly that Arch was here to share her good news.

But he was living in San Diego now. That was what Wade had said the other day. Just dropping it casually, so Mandy would know. And she did want to know. Not too many details. Just that he was okay.

"When do you go?" Lori was bouncing around Mandy, wringing her hands, and Snack was bounding around their feet in his own doggy celebration. "Oh, Mandy, this is huge. This is a big, big step. I can't believe it! My sister, the chef. Do you want to come back here and open a restaurant afterward? Or a bakery? I'll start putting money aside, just in case."

Mandy couldn't even begin to answer Lori's questions. Anxiety kicked in. She hadn't thought this through. Could she even afford it? She'd never lived anywhere but the ranch. What if she hated San Francisco? What if she got to the school and she was terrible compared to the other students?

Her heart sped up as adrenaline poured through her system. She staggered over to the porch steps and sat down, putting her head between her knees. From a distance she heard Lori's frantic voice. "Mandy? Are you okay? Mandy, what's happening?"

"Panic attack," she gasped out, fighting for her

breath, fighting to stay on the ground and not spin off into that airless place of chaos inside her mind.

"Breathe," Lori commanded, and Mandy heard her footsteps thud across the porch and the bang of the door as her sister ran into the house.

And then she remembered Arch. His words when he wanted her to feed the animals. *You can choose your feelings. It's natural to choose the negative stuff.* She was choosing the negative. She was choosing the fear. She needed to make a different choice.

Lori was back, shoving a glass of water at her. "Drink this."

Her breath was returning, her heart slowing from its adrenaline-fueled patter. She took a sip of water. She was choosing to panic. Because panic was familiar. What if instead she focused on the excitement of being accepted to such a prestigious school? Or on how desperately she needed this change?

Her sister plopped down next to her. "Have you had panic attacks before?"

Mandy nodded, still trying to take deep, calming breaths. "Lots of times."

Lori's voice was tentative. "Why didn't you ever tell me?"

"I don't know. You just always seem so strong, I guess. Like you wouldn't understand."

"I'm married to a guy with PTSD. And I

have my own issues with worry. Believe me, I would've understood. I *do* understand."

"It got better when Arch was here," Mandy said. "I don't think I realize, sometimes, how much it's affecting me. When you're anxious all the time, it just starts to feel normal after a while."

"It's the decision, isn't it?" Lori's voice was unusually gentle. "Decisions can be so hard. Especially if you made some in your past that didn't work out so well."

Mandy nodded, not able to push words past the lump in her throat. She leaned on Lori's shoulder and stared down at the letter. She was accepted to culinary school. It was the chance of a lifetime, right here in her hands.

"If Mom were here now, what do you think she'd say?" Lori asked.

Mandy smiled. "That's easy. She'd be pulling my suitcase out of storage and packing it for me. Remember how much she loved to cook? I bet she'd have loved a chance to study it."

"Is that your answer?" Lori put her arm around Mandy's shoulders and tugged her even closer. "Would *you* love the chance to study it? Because if you would, I'll help you every step of the way. With money, with moving, with all of it. I want you to be happy."

"I want to go." As soon as Mandy said it out

loud, she was sure it was true. A new start. A chance to become what she'd only dreamed of becoming.

"Really? You're going?" Her sister hugged her tight. "I'm so excited for you!"

"Thanks." Mandy hugged her back.

"San Francisco," Lori murmured, picking up the brochure and leafing through it. "You're going to have such a blast."

Mandy looked out over the yard toward the barn. She listened to the wind in the pines and the sound of her chickens over in their coops. Missing it already. But knowing it was time to finally reach for her future. It was bittersweet. But a whole lot of life was like that. And losing Arch had taught her that the only way to have more of the sweet part was to make it herself.

ARCH'S CELL PHONE rang while he was on his lunch break. He set down his notebook and pencil, reluctant to leave the sketch he was working on. He didn't recognize the phone number, but he was still on parole. It could be the local police checking in. He had to answer.

The voice on the other end oozed out of the past. "Hello, son."

The sandwich Arch had just finished rose sour in his throat. "What the hell are you doing calling me?" He glanced around the quiet courtyard of

San Diego Metalworks. Shane had just gone out for a lunch meeting, but Antonio and Tom were both here somewhere. He walked to a corner near a splashing wall fountain. "Do not call me. Ever."

His father's laugh had always been a menacing sound. "Ten years. I haven't talked to my boy in over ten years and he tells me not to call? Come on, son. Where's your respect for your elders? Don't you at least want to know how we're doing?"

"No." He thought about just hanging up. But if he didn't hear him out, his father would call back. Once the old man got an idea in his head, he gripped it like a pit bull, jaws locked down.

"Well, I'll tell you anyway. We're doing great. Business is booming. We've got ourselves a villa down along the Sea of Cortez. It's like something from a goddamn magazine."

"I'm not interested." Arch tried to sound calm. To breathe normally. His dad would latch on to any sign of weakness.

"Well, speaking of magazines, Blake and I saw your photo in that San Diego society rag. Look at you, the fancy artist, schmoozing with the elites."

"It was a few pieces in an exhibit, Dad. Not a big deal. I'm just starting out. And I'm broke, if you're calling to ask for money."

The spewing laughter made Arch want to clean his phone.

"Need money? Oh, no. I'm calling about a moneymaking proposition for *you*. You're the golden boy now. That article talked all about it. How you went to jail and did your time and you're starting your life again."

Arch silently cursed his stupidity. He'd said too much in that interview. But the young woman who was writing the story had told him it was her first big article. And she'd had long blond curls like Mandy. Naturally he'd answered all her questions. "So?"

"Art-buying idiots will buy a lot more than art from you. Those stressed-out businessmen and their Barbie doll wives love their party favors."

"You want me to sell drugs?" He was going to puke. He leaned an arm on the courtyard wall and rested his head against it.

"I've got men building a tunnel as we speak. It's gonna come up in a nice-looking furniture warehouse outside Otay. That's not far from San Diego."

"Stop there." The fury was so electric, it took away the sick. "I don't want to know *one* thing more. I won't work for you, Dad. Ever. And I'll let my parole officer know you contacted me today. And if you call me again, I promise you I'll go directly to the police."

Arch ended the call, breathing hard like he'd just run fast. He sank down on the edge of the fountain and put his head in his hands. His father's toxic voice still polluting the air around him.

But that voice wasn't really here. It was in Mexico, and he'd just told it to go to hell. Arch sat up, looked around the courtyard, which suddenly looked more inviting. The geraniums were brighter, the noise of the fountain soothing.

He'd told his father no. There was not one part of him that had been interested in his dad's scheme. Not one part of his brain that had perked up at the idea of quick money and an easy life down in Mexico. All he'd felt was revulsion. Which meant he was free of his father. Free of his past. Really, truly free.

He'd never thought revulsion could feel so good.

Arch scrolled through his contacts and pressed on Steve's. When his parole officer answered, he told him everything. And when the call was over he walked around the courtyard, suddenly restless.

Because there was one person he really wanted to share this moment with. One person who would understand what it meant to know for sure, deep down inside, that he wasn't that messed-up guy he used to be. He wanted Mandy. But he'd pushed her away.

His lunch break was over. Arch headed back

inside, still reeling. Because maybe he was more than an ex-convict. Maybe he was more than a parolee. Maybe he could finally look into Mandy's eyes and know he was worthy of the sweetness she offered. Maybe, when his time working here was up, it would be time to go home.

CHAPTER TWENTY-TWO

"THE PRODIGAL SON RETURNS." Dalton's voice was full of gruff sarcasm. But Arch knew him, and could see a smile hidden in his deep-set eyes.

He slammed the truck door behind him and crossed the few yards of dusty gravel to shake hands with his mentor. "And I'm not on a bicycle, thanks to you."

Dalton eyed the nearly new pickup truck. "Did well for yourself down south, did you?"

"I was supposed to work for room and board, but all your buddies kept paying me. And I sold a few pieces in that show you talked Shane into letting me join. And that led to a couple commissions. I don't have much, but at least I have transportation that takes me a lot farther than that bicycle."

"Well, I kind of miss that fancy blue helmet." Dalton gave a wheezy chuckle. "I wish I'd snapped a photo of you that first day, pleading your cause with that neon mushroom on your head."

"Glad you didn't have a camera." Though now

that it was over, Arch kind of wished he did have a picture of himself on Todd's bike. It was a part of how he'd gotten this far. And it sure would keep him humble to look at it now and again. "But seriously, Dalton, thank you for getting me all those jobs. I didn't know it was possible to learn so much in just a few months."

"You've got promise." Arch thought he detected a flash of affection in the sculptor's eye, but then the humor was back. "I'm just glad you didn't make me look like a fool for recommending a jailbird like you."

Arch grinned. "Because you care so much about what people think about you, you old hermit."

Dalton's guffaw echoed out into the empty sky. "Hey, the more I keep to myself, the more of my art people buy." He raised a gnome's eyebrow. "It adds to the mystery."

Arch shook his head. "You've got a good gig going, Dalton. But I think it's the art they're buying. Not the mystery." He pointed to a new piece he could see through the barn door. A fantastical creation of steel scrolls and circles. With a single metal gong hanging down that looked like it came from a Buddhist temple. "Going abstract, I see."

"Just trying out something new. Which reminds me…" Dalton pulled a piece of paper from his pocket. "I've got one more guy I want you to meet."

Guilt, at disappointing the man who'd opened up so many doors, clogged Arch's throat. "I'm not going back to Southern California," he blurted out. "Not right now. Maybe never."

"This job is in San Francisco." Dalton waved the paper at him. "And this artist does it all. He's got a big company doing installations for some of the richest computer nerds on this earth. But he also does some smaller pieces and creates sculptures on the side. You'll love it."

It was perfect for him. But as much as Arch wanted to keep learning, he wanted Mandy more. "This is great, really, but I was thinking I'd stick around here for a while."

"Fall in San Francisco is pretty nice," Dalton said.

"I'm planning to stay out on Marker Ranch. I was hoping you'd let me work with you again." Arch paused because Dalton looked like he was about to giggle. Which was crazy, because he would *never* giggle.

"You fool." Dalton shook with glee. "*Mandy's* in San Francisco. You think she'd sit around here waiting for you to get your head on straight? She's smart enough to know that may never happen."

"San Francisco?" Arch repeated stupidly. "What's she doing there?"

"Went to some fancy cooking school. Came by here to say goodbye and left me with a freezer full of her blueberry muffins."

"That sounds like her." Disappointment weighed on him. He'd hoped to see her today. Missed her more with each mile he'd closed between them. Then Dalton's words sank in. Culinary school. She'd done it. She'd gone after her dream.

It took Arch about ten more seconds to connect the dots. He reached for the paper Dalton still held out to him. "San Francisco sounds just about perfect. I truly appreciate the reference."

"The guy's name is Liam. He's expecting you within the week. He said to just give him a call when you get into town. He'll help you find a place to stay."

Hope was putting down roots in Arch's heart. He looked at Dalton, knowing this was the chance to ask what he'd been wondering. "Why me?" he asked. "Why do you do so much for me?"

A faint flush crossed Dalton's Santa Claus cheeks. "I don't have anyone else coming out here to bug me," he said. "And I don't joke around about talent. You have it and it's rare. I don't want you to waste it just trying to get by."

Arch nodded. "That's not everything, though. Right?"

His mentor looked away, out beyond the truck

to where the sagebrush rolled east forever. "Tehachapi prison," he said. "Six years for robbery."

"I thought maybe so." Arch swallowed hard. "I truly am grateful for your faith in me."

Dalton met his eyes briefly. "Just pass it on. Once you get set up in San Francisco, find some kid who's just gotten out of juvie and give him a chance to learn. So he doesn't end up where we did."

"Sounds like a good plan." Arch felt something click into place inside him. It was a great idea. He'd make sure it happened.

"Drop me an email and let me know how it's going out there. And send me photos of your work so I can tell you all the stuff that's wrong with it."

This was the Dalton he knew best. "Will do," Arch promised. He shook the sculptor's outstretched hand and got into his truck. He could see his mentor in his rearview mirror as he drove away, a solitary speck under the high desert sky. If it were anyone else it would have seemed lonely, but he knew Dalton liked it that way.

But not Arch. He'd had enough lonely to last him a lifetime. He'd found his dream woman once. Now he needed to track her down again. And beg her to take him back.

But first he had one more thing to do, and it wasn't going to be pleasant. He needed to tell

Nora and Wade about that phone call from their father. Maybe they wouldn't care. But they had a right to know that their dad was still alive and as crooked as ever.

ARCH WATCHED WADE'S truck as it pulled up to the porch. He'd called Nora from the road and she and Wade had agreed to bring pizza out to Marker Ranch for dinner. A family night on the family ranch.

Who would have thought something this casual would ever be possible between them?

The pizza Nora balanced as she stepped out of the truck smelled like grease and heaven, and Arch took the porch steps quickly, relieving her of the boxes. "Thanks for coming," he told her. "And for letting me stay here tonight."

"You can stay longer," she said. "No one's lived here since you left."

"Which is something we wanted to talk to you about." Wade grabbed a six-pack of soda out of the back of the truck. "If you don't mind this being kind of a business dinner."

"Any kind of dinner is fine with me," Arch said, leading the way inside. "And I've got something to tell you, too."

He'd already set the table, so it was just a question of loading their plates with pizza slices and pouring drinks before they were all seated. Nora and Wade sat on one side of the table, facing him expectantly.

"I need to tell you something that might upset you," he told them. "Which is why I waited to tell you in person. Dad got in touch with me a few months ago, when I was down in San Diego. Guess he saw that magazine article I emailed to you? Somehow he found me after that."

Wade froze with his pizza halfway to his mouth. Silence flattened everything. After a sharp look of horror, Nora was studying her fork.

"I hate to ruin our dinner," Arch said quietly. "But I think it's best you know."

"What did he want?" Nora asked.

Wade made a snorting sound. "Sorry," he explained when they stared at him. "But that's the right question to ask about our dad. He'd never call unless there was something he was after."

"I wish I could tell you he'd changed," Arch said. "But you're right. He wanted me to meet him at the other end of a smuggling tunnel and sell drugs for him here in the States."

"He is such a...a..." Nora stabbed the air with her fork, as if she could spear the right word.

"Horrible person?" Arch offered. "Yes."

"I hope you told him where to shove his offer," Wade said through clenched teeth.

"I kept it as short as possible. Just told him not to call again and that I was going to tell the police I'd heard from him. I reported the call to my parole officer, also."

"You did the right thing," Nora assured him.

"And he hasn't called back?" Wade whistled low. "You're lucky. Used to be he wouldn't settle for no. He'd just keep pushing until he got what he wanted."

"I was pretty clear with him," Arch said. "Which is partly why I'm here. I finished my apprenticeship in San Diego. And…" Arch braced himself for their anger. "I want to see Mandy."

"You dumped her." Wade glared at him. "You hurt her."

"I hurt both of us," Arch said quietly. "Because I didn't believe I was good enough for her." He forced himself to meet their disapproving eyes. "All this time I was worried that I still had a piece of Dad inside me. A part of me that might be tempted to do something wrong. But when Dad called, I felt completely disgusted by his proposition. When I told him no, I knew for certain that I'd really changed."

"So what does that have to do with Mandy?" Nora asked. "Don't you think you've caused her enough heartache?"

"Of course. I feel awful that I hurt her." Awful didn't even begin to describe how he felt.

"So why did you?" Wade asked.

Arch fished for the right words, ones that would

make them see. "That whole situation—being accused of a crime, spending a night in jail—it was like I was forced back into my old world. And I felt like I'd dragged Mandy right back there with me. I hated myself for involving her."

Wade nodded. "I get it."

"But with everything that's happened since then, my work, my art, that call from Dad—well, it's different now. I *know* I won't be pulled back into my old ways. I *know* that I can have this new life."

"Well, that's good," Nora said. "But your timing is messed up. Mandy's not here."

"Dalton told me. He also gave me a contact for some work in San Francisco. I'm heading there tomorrow morning."

"Don't push Mandy," Wade said. "She has a whole new life now. She's worked hard for it. She's worked hard to get over you."

"I won't." Arch ached for the grief he'd caused her. "But I have to ask if she'll take me back. You get that, right?"

"He does," Nora answered for their little brother. "Because he had to do the same thing with Lori. He dumped her, even though he'd loved her all his life. It took Lori falling off a cliff and almost dying to get him to see reason."

Arch stared at his siblings. "Seriously?"

Wade suddenly took a great interest in his

pizza. "Maybe," he muttered and took an enormous bite.

"Yes," Nora said. "But I almost lost Todd, as well. Or maybe he almost lost me. It's hard to say, really. Anyways, the bottom line is that even though I'm upset that you hurt Mandy, I understand why you left. And Wade does, too, though he won't admit it. So go get the girl. But first we have to talk about the fate of this ranch."

There was something about having his sister's blessing that gave Arch hope. "I think the ranch is your decision, Nora. And Wade's. You're the ones who worked so hard to get it going."

"It's your land, too." Wade gestured with his pizza for emphasis. "So tell us what you think. This house sits just about in the middle of the property. We're thinking of taking the northern pastures and combining them with Lori and Mandy's land to make one big ranch. The properties already share a well up at that end, anyway."

"Sounds reasonable," Arch assured him.

"And we're thinking of taking the southeastern part that has the more scrubby pastures, and making that part of the wild mustang sanctuary," Nora added.

It was perfect. One side of the land for practical cattle ranching. The other side to preserve a dream of wild horses, running free. "It's a great idea."

"You don't mind?" Wade asked. "It doesn't leave much for you."

"I don't want to ranch," Arch said. "I guess if I'd ask for anything, it might be that this house be available, in case I want to come back here and set up a workshop someday. But I know it's a lot to ask. It's already falling down. Maybe we should just let gravity and time finish the job."

"I had a different idea," Wade said.

They both turned to look at him.

"What if we set up a bank account for this house? And we all put a little money into it every month. Pretty soon we'd have enough to renovate it. And then we could rent it out to tourists. People from LA and San Francisco who want some peace and quiet. Maybe they could even help out on the ranch or visit the wild horses if they wanted."

"It's a great idea," Nora said. "And then the house would be kept up if you wanted to move back here, Arch."

"If you can convince Mandy that you're not a total loser, you could even raise a family here one day." Wade punctuated his gibe with a brotherly kick under the table.

"Ha-ha." Arch kicked Wade back. "You're getting ahead of yourself. I have to convince her to talk to me first." But he liked the idea. Loved it.

Him doing his metalwork out in one of the old barns while Mandy ran some kind of catering business. "Can we put in a big kitchen for Mandy, just in case I can pull this off?"

"Sure." Nora smiled. "You've already pulled off a few miracles. You served your time. You found your gift and became an artist. And you broke free of our dad—for good. I'm sure you'll figure out a way to get Mandy back."

"Thanks," Arch said. "I hope so."

"And speaking of miracles..." Nora flushed a little. "I'm pregnant."

"No way!" Wade threw his arms around his sister.

Arch had no words. Him sitting here, being part of this moment, was a miracle on top of all the others. He stood, leaned, put an awkward hand on his sister's shoulder. "I'm so happy for you."

"I'm gonna be an uncle," Wade said. Then looked at Arch, the excitement lifting the serious lines of his face. "We're gonna be uncles!"

Arch sat back in his chair, trying to let the news sink in. "I never thought I'd get to be an uncle" was all he could come up with, and even that came out gruff. "I'm glad I get the chance."

"Me, too," Nora said.

WHEN NO ONE could stomach any more pizza, they cleared their plates and Arch walked them to the porch. And spotted some unfinished business there. "Can you guys stay an extra few minutes?"

"Yeah," Wade answered. "What's up?"

Arch pointed to their dad's old chair. Forever tainted by bad memories. "Wanna burn it?"

"Yes!" Nora said.

Wade just crossed the porch in two strides and grabbed it. "The footstool, too," Nora called, and Arch picked it up, the weathered wicker crumbling in his hands.

"There's a fire pit around the side of the house. Lori and I made it last year." Wade led the way around to the gravel area.

They threw the furniture into the center of the stone ring and Nora ran to the kitchen, returning with a big box of matches. "Let's each strike a match and light it together."

The flame caught fast and consumed the wicker quickly until it was just the three of them and the skeleton of the old chair, a black outline in the flames.

"I wish I'd protected you from him," Arch said. "I wish I'd packed you both up and moved somewhere else. I could have saved you from so much of his abuse."

"You were a victim, too." Wade's voice shook a little. "You only knew what you'd been taught."

"And we made it. We're okay now," Nora reminded him. "Somehow we all came out okay."

The frame of the chair collapsed in a heap, the flames leaping higher to consume it completely.

"To new beginnings," Wade said quietly.

Arch felt something nudge his hand. It was Nora, slipping her chilled palm to his. He grasped it and glanced over to see that her other hand was in Wade's. They were together. They were a family. Watching the demons of their past rise in the smoke and disappear into the night.

CHAPTER TWENTY-THREE

AUTUMN IN SAN FRANCISCO was the secret summer that only locals knew about. The fog skipped town with the tourists, just before Labor Day, and left luminous skies and eighty-degree weather. After her last class, Mandy changed from her chef's uniform into a summer dress she thought she'd never have the chance to wear in the city.

It was a relief to step out of the institute doors. She'd been inside since seven this morning, attending a workshop on French sauces. Now it was six in the evening and she could relax, taking comfort in the praise of the visiting chef, who'd tested her rémoulade just now, and pronounced it *magnifique*.

Normally she'd take the Muni bus out to the tiny studio apartment she rented near Golden Gate Park. But the evening was so warm, maybe she'd walk along the bay for a while. Decompress. Tomorrow was her first day off in ten. She might as well start enjoying it now, even if she was nearly asleep on her feet.

A man was leaning on a lamppost near the

school exit. He was tall. Dressed in jeans and a tight black T-shirt. Such a familiar look that it had her glancing his way again. A cotton sweatshirt was tied around his waist. He was reading something on his phone. Just a typical San Franciscan. But then he glanced up and answered the question that had been jelling in her mind.

"Arch?" She was blocking the busy sidewalk but she couldn't seem to move. "What are you doing here?"

"I was hoping I'd catch you. I asked inside but they said you were in class."

"Why? Is everything okay? Are Wade and Lori all right?"

"They're fine. I'm here because I wanted to see you. I went to Benson to find you and learned that you'd moved here. That you're in culinary school. Which is awesome, by the way." He gave that wide smile she'd missed so much. "I'm proud of you."

"Thank you." She couldn't think of what else to say. It had been almost a year and she still wanted to yell at him for shattering her heart. For leaving. She'd been so sure she never wanted to see him again. But here he was, and she couldn't stop looking.

"You look absolutely beautiful," he said, shoving his phone in his pocket.

"Ugh. Don't start." No compliments. Nothing

to chip away at the walls she'd built around the pain he'd caused. "I'm greasy from cooking all day."

"Well, it seems to suit you. How do you like living in San Francisco?"

"It's fun. I like it more than I thought I would." Making small talk wasn't her strength at the best of times. Making it with Arch felt totally bizarre. Especially standing on Market Street, in danger of being mowed down by all the people trying to get to their evening trains. "I was heading down to the bay to take a walk. Do you want to come?"

"I'd like that."

She told him about her classes as they made their way toward the Embarcadero, the busy promenade bordering San Francisco Bay. She babbled about her job working a few nights a week for a catering company. Arch was all enthusiasm and kindness and she wanted to kick him. He'd hurt her, shredded her, and now he'd shown up here.

He was as handsome as ever. All kinds of people walking by shot a look his way. How could they not stare? He was a few inches taller than everyone, and eye-catching in all his ways, from his hair waving to his shoulders to the intensity of his craggy face as he listened to her talk about work. Why couldn't he have gotten a bad haircut in the past year? Or shrunk?

"So what brings you to San Francisco?" She

veered to the right of the Ferry Building and onto the wide sidewalk that ran along the blue-green water. The Bay Bridge rose in front of them. A real-life postcard. She loved coming here.

"Work is part of it." Arch walked at an easy amble, hands in his pockets. She'd never seen him so relaxed. "I've been down in Southern California all this time. Apprenticing myself to different metal artists and craftsmen that Dalton connected me to. Now I have a chance to work for a guy up here. He does a lot of modern stuff. Custom railings and staircases. Big practical things that are also works of art."

"So you're going to live in San Francisco?" She'd come here, in part, to escape him. The thought of running into him around the city, or worrying that she might, clenched her stomach into a fist.

He was oblivious. "I've just rented the world's smallest studio apartment, over on Potrero Hill. It's near this guy's workshop."

"You *are* living here." She tried, not very successfully, to keep the dismay out of her voice. "For how long?"

"I'm not sure." He pointed to an old wooden pier reaching out into the water. "Can we pull over for a moment?"

She followed him across the deck to the railing and looked over the edge. Murky green bay water sloshed. A discarded paper cup floated, bumping into the pier. She tried to think of something to say. Something to fill this space between them that she didn't understand. He'd ended it. Now he'd shown up. She felt like that old cup. Adrift. Smacking into the same wall over and over.

"For the last few months, I worked for this guy Shane, down in San Diego. He knows a lot of gallery owners and he got one of them to exhibit a few of my pieces."

"That's great." She was happy for him, of course. It was selfish, that tug of unease, because he'd done so well without her.

"Well, the gallery was in a magazine. There were photos and a story about me and my artwork. One day my dad called me. Said he'd seen the article online. He asked me to sell drugs for him."

She whirled to face him. "Seriously?" She wanted to touch him, to reach out. But that wasn't her role anymore.

"Yeah. It was bizarre. Awful. But it made me realize something. All this time, since I got out of prison, I suspected, deep down inside, that I was still bad. That the same flaws that got me working with my dad in the first place were still inside, just waiting for the chance to come out."

She nodded, remembering his words when he'd left her. That he'd never be good enough.

"But my reaction, when my dad called, proved

me wrong. Made me realize that I'm not bad or weak. That I'd *never* go back to my old life. It's been a huge relief."

She could see it. The lightness in him. The ease. "I'm happy for you."

He took a step closer. Put a hand to her shoulder that warmed her with memories she didn't want. She directed a pointed glance at his hand, and he dropped it to his side. "Mandy…"

"Don't." She stepped back to replace the distance between them. "Don't come here starting something you can't finish."

He nodded. "I get it. You have every reason to distrust me. But here's the thing. After that call from my dad, all I wanted was to talk with *you* about it. It's been like that with everything. Each job. Each success. That gallery show and that magazine write-up, they would have meant so much more if you'd been with me. I knew, already, that I had to see you again. But my dad's phone call showed me that I might actually be someone who deserved to see you."

It was overwhelming, hearing all this. She'd worked so long and hard to be okay on her own. "You say you want to deserve me. You say I'm this special person you want to be worthy of. But actions speak louder than words. You *left*. You never called or texted or anything. You were just gone."

"I hurt you. I know it. And I'm grateful you're even listening to me right now." He looked away, out over the water. Mandy turned, too, and leaned on the railing again. Waiting for him. Waiting for something inside her to give her guidance.

When he spoke again, his voice broke over the words. "I wish I'd been more whole when we met. I wish I'd already learned the things I've come to know about myself during the past months."

She wished he hadn't shown up tonight. She didn't want to know that this new Arch Hoffman was out there, full of self-knowledge and success. It was easier to accept their ending when she could think of him as troubled and lost. "Look, it's good to see you. It really is. But I need to get home."

He straightened off the railing. "Of course." They walked in silence back to the promenade.

"I'll catch the Muni over there." Mandy pointed across the busy Embarcadero traffic.

"Mandy, before you go…" Arch shoved a hand through his hair, which the evening breeze was blowing in every direction. "I was wondering if you would go out with me sometime. On a date. Or, hopefully…on a bunch of dates."

She opened her mouth to say no. Her life was okay and it was moving forward. Why risk such hard-won equilibrium?

"I know it's a lot to ask. When I left you, I

needed time to figure myself out. But through all of it you were the one I wanted. That never changed. And there was never anyone else."

He stood, palms open in appeal. He was magnetic. He was larger than life. When he'd been hers, the whole world had seemed brighter.

He was asking her to trust him. He was asking her for courage. Months ago on her ranch he'd done the same, and it had changed everything. Healed her, made her strong, set her free and gotten her here.

She'd missed him every day. A sharp ache she'd learned to live with. Maybe part of loving Arch was knowing that she could be strong without him if she had to. She took a deep breath, summoning the words that could change everything. "I have tomorrow off. I was thinking of walking across the Golden Gate Bridge since the weather is so nice. Want to come with me?"

"Yes." He looked like he'd just won something. He looked like hope.

Seeing that hope helped shush the whispers of anxiety. Because she knew loss and she knew heartache. But she also knew Arch. Like so many things, he came with risks. But he'd helped teach her that some risks were okay. That sometimes they were worth it. "I still have your number," she said. "I'll call you in the morning."

"I'll look forward to it. See you tomorrow, Mandy."

The light changed. She gave him a quick wave and stepped into the sea of people crossing the road. On the other side she turned and saw him still standing there, watching her. He raised a hand in goodbye. He couldn't possibly hear her, but she said it anyway. "See you tomorrow, Arch." Such mundane words. So full of possibilities.

EPILOGUE

"Do you remember the day we walked here for the first time?" Arch looked out over the white-capped bay. A ferryboat was making its way through the choppy water to Alcatraz Island. "It was two years ago. The first official date of our second attempt at dating."

Mandy was struggling to subdue her swirling curls with a hairband. "Two years ago today? I didn't realize it was our anniversary." She finished making her ponytail. "It wasn't nearly so windy that day!"

"That day was a fluke. Isn't this the real Golden Gate Bridge experience? Wind howling? Oh, and look up. The fog is starting to blow in over the towers."

Mandy arched her neck to see. "It's beautiful," she said. "I don't know if I'll ever get used to how pretty it is here."

He loved watching her like this. Out and about in her adopted city. So fearless now. So different than she'd been when they met. Back then, if he'd suggested a walk on this noisy, windy bridge with cars rushing by and just a railing separating her from the deadly drop, he had no doubt she would have said no. But these days she had life by the horns and was wrestling it to the ground.

He smiled at the image. Two years living in the city, and he was still a country kid at heart.

Two miraculous years. Mandy worked as a pastry chef in one of the city's top hotels now. And he was the second in command at Metal Magic, the company he'd joined when he first moved here. It was fun creating and installing custom railings and staircases in the fancy homes of Silicon Valley executives. His sculptures were selling well at local galleries and were scheduled for shows in Santa Fe and New York. It was going to be a busy year. An amazing year.

Especially if the woman he loved gave him the answer he wanted. Though he'd better ask the question soon, before they froze, or blew away, or both.

She was at the railing. Pointing at the city skyline still lit up by afternoon sun. The fog hadn't reached it yet. "I can see the top of the hotel from here!"

"No thinking about work. Not today." He came up behind her and wrapped his arms around her shoulders. Rested his chin on her head. She fit right into him. Fit him so perfectly in every way. He kissed her hair. "Hey," he murmured in her ear.

"Hey what?" She tilted her head to look at him out of the corner of her eye. "You okay up there?"

She'd given him the perfect opening. But his heart was speeding up, and his voice felt thick. She wasn't the only one who'd changed. When he'd met her, he hadn't known one emotion from another. Now emotions came hard and fast. Love. Hope. Wonder. Gratitude. And fear. Because they'd never talked much about marriage. They were happy together, but she might say no.

"I'm okay," he lied. "But there's something that would make me even better."

She turned wide eyes on him. "We can't do that *here*!"

And there was the laughter. She healed him with it daily. "I'm not actually thinking about *that*," he told her and turned her gently to face him. And went down on one knee.

"Oh, my gosh!" Her hands flew to cover her mouth.

A streak of sunlight made it through the incoming fog and lit her hair. A halo for his angel. "I love you," he said.

"I love you, too, Arch." She had tears on her cheeks. Come to think of it, so did he.

"Two years ago, after I'd messed up everything between us, you took a chance on me again. And I knew, when we first walked together on this bridge, that I'd do everything in my power to make you happy. And that if I succeeded, I'd be a good enough man to ask you this question." He was losing it, tears streaming, his voice raw. "Mandy Allen, will you marry me?"

She nodded, swiping at her face with the sleeve of her coat.

"Say yes!" someone shouted. They were surrounded by people now. Joggers, tourists, cyclists had all stopped to cheer them on.

Mandy was smiling and trying to shove back the wisps of hair that had escaped her ponytail and were sticking to her wet cheeks. She knelt down on the pavement with him, threw her arms around his neck and said for only him to hear, "I'll always love you. I'd be so honored to marry you."

Arch closed his eyes and breathed her in. His own miracle. When he looked up, the circle of people were still waiting expectantly.

"She said yes!" He raised a fist in triumph. The applause cut through the traffic and wind, and he held Mandy tight, letting tears come, letting the reality sink in. She wanted him. Forever.

He stood, pulling her with him. Tucking her under his arm and kissing her soft hair. People stopped to shake their hands, to clap him on the back. Strangers wishing them well.

He remembered how, on the day he'd met Mandy, he'd wished that he could be a normal guy, an accepted guy, with a job and a home and a life. He felt like that guy now. And he'd never stop being grateful for it.

Their onlookers moved on, and he and Mandy became just another couple again, standing side by side at the railing, looking at the view. The wind gusted just as he pulled the ring box out of his pocket. "I'm not sure how to do this next part. What if the ring blows away?"

"Here." She took his hand and led him several yards to the nearest tower. Tucked them against it on the bay side, so the steel wall blocked the wind. When he pulled the ring out, she gasped.

"The diamonds remind me of the snow on the day we first went snowboarding. The pink sapphires are for your spirit. For the quiet way you glow. And the blue sapphires are for your eyes."

She touched the stones with a delicate finger. "They look like flower petals."

"Chicory. When I met you, I thought your eyes were the color of chicory. It's a weed that grew outside the prison walls."

Her chicory eyes were teary again. "No more prison," she whispered. "No more walls."

"Amen." He slid the ring on her finger. And pulled her close against his heart. And held her there, between sea and sky, sheltered from the wind.

* * * * *

LARGER-PRINT BOOKS!
GET 2 FREE LARGER-PRINT NOVELS PLUS
2 FREE GIFTS!

⊕HARLEQUIN® *Romance*

From the Heart, For the Heart

YES! Please send me 2 FREE LARGER-PRINT Harlequin® Romance novels and my 2 FREE gifts (gifts are worth about $10). After receiving them, if I don't wish to receive any more books, I can return the shipping statement marked "cancel." If I don't cancel, I will receive 4 brand-new novels every month and be billed just $5.09 per book in the U.S. or $5.49 per book in Canada. That's a savings of at least 15% off the cover price! It's quite a bargain! Shipping and handling is just 50¢ per book in the U.S. and 75¢ per book in Canada.* I understand that accepting the 2 free books and gifts places me under no obligation to buy anything. I can always return a shipment and cancel at any time. Even if I never buy another book, the two free books and gifts are mine to keep forever.

119/319 HDN GHWC

Name	(PLEASE PRINT)	
Address		Apt. #
City	State/Prov.	Zip/Postal Code

Signature (if under 18, a parent or guardian must sign)

Mail to the **Reader Service:**
IN U.S.A.: P.O. Box 1867, Buffalo, NY 14240-1867
IN CANADA: P.O. Box 609, Fort Erie, Ontario L2A 5X3
Want to try two free books from another line?
Call 1-800-873-8635 or visit www.ReaderService.com.

* Terms and prices subject to change without notice. Prices do not include applicable taxes. Sales tax applicable in N.Y. Canadian residents will be charged applicable taxes. Offer not valid in Quebec. This offer is limited to one order per household. Not valid for current subscribers to Harlequin Romance Larger-Print books. All orders subject to credit approval. Credit or debit balances in a customer's account(s) may be offset by any other outstanding balance owed by or to the customer. Please allow 4 to 6 weeks for delivery. Offer available while quantities last.

Your Privacy—The Reader Service is committed to protecting your privacy. Our Privacy Policy is available online at www.ReaderService.com or upon request from the Reader Service.

We make a portion of our mailing list available to reputable third parties that offer products we believe may interest you. If you prefer that we not exchange your name with third parties, or if you wish to clarify or modify your communication preferences, please visit us at www.ReaderService.com/consumerschoice or write to us at Reader Service Preference Service, P.O. Box 9062, Buffalo, NY 14240-9062. Include your complete name and address.

HRLP15

LARGER-PRINT BOOKS!

HARLEQUIN

Presents®

GET 2 FREE LARGER-PRINT NOVELS PLUS 2 FREE GIFTS!

YES! Please send me 2 FREE LARGER-PRINT Harlequin Presents® novels and my 2 FREE gifts (gifts are worth about $10). After receiving them, if I don't wish to receive any more books, I can return the shipping statement marked "cancel." If I don't cancel, I will receive 6 brand-new novels every month and be billed just $5.30 per book in the U.S. or $5.74 per book in Canada. That's a saving of at least 12% off the cover price! It's quite a bargain! Shipping and handling is just 50¢ per book in the U.S. and 75¢ per book in Canada.* I understand that accepting the 2 free books and gifts places me under no obligation to buy anything. I can always return a shipment and cancel at any time. Even if I never buy another book, the two free books and gifts are mine to keep forever.

176/376 HDN GHVY

Name	(PLEASE PRINT)	

Address		Apt. #

City	State/Prov.	Zip/Postal Code

Signature (if under 18, a parent or guardian must sign)

Mail to the **Reader Service:**
IN U.S.A.: P.O. Box 1867, Buffalo, NY 14240-1867
IN CANADA: P.O. Box 609, Fort Erie, Ontario L2A 5X3

**Are you a subscriber to Harlequin Presents® books
and want to receive the larger-print edition?
Call 1-800-873-8635 today or visit us at www.ReaderService.com.**

* Terms and prices subject to change without notice. Prices do not include applicable taxes. Sales tax applicable in N.Y. Canadian residents will be charged applicable taxes. Offer not valid in Quebec. This offer is limited to one order per household. Not valid for current subscribers to Harlequin Presents Larger-Print books. All orders subject to credit approval. Credit or debit balances in a customer's account(s) may be offset by any other outstanding balance owed by or to the customer. Please allow 4 to 6 weeks for delivery. Offer available while quantities last.

Your Privacy—The Reader Service is committed to protecting your privacy. Our Privacy Policy is available online at www.ReaderService.com or upon request from the Reader Service.

We make a portion of our mailing list available to reputable third parties that offer products we believe may interest you. If you prefer that we not exchange your name with third parties, or if you wish to clarify or modify your communication preferences, please visit us at www.ReaderService.com/consumerchoice or write to us at Reader Service Preference Service, P.O. Box 9062, Buffalo, NY 14240-9062. Include your complete name and address.

HPLP15